Elizabeth's Secrets

Paul D. Alexander

First Edition: February 2012

Elizabeth's Secrets

Cover Art by Joshua Medling

ISBN-13: 978-1470135553 (paperback)

For information: www.pauldalexanderbooks.com

EPIGRAPH

Missouri Ozarks – July 1881

COILED BENEATH the parched, sun-drenched grass, a thick wagon-length rattlesnake drew back its head and hissed. A deadly rattle echoed across the hills and hollows.

Dine stumbled; a blood-caked hoof freed a jagged rock and sent it bouncing wildly down the steep incline. It slammed against the battered underside of the over-laden wagon and barely missed the weary settlers that shuffled behind.

Beck snorted in loud protest, leaned outward against the wooden yoke, and with a giant's strength, broke his brother's fall a knee width shy of the razor sharp flint that littered the un-trodden terrain.

The thunderous crack of a whip sliced through sweltering air and great globules of sweat erupted from Dine's grimy white hide beneath the sharp impact of the weathered latigo.

Emaciated from ravenous months on the desolate trail, the massive oxen, Dine, once a beautiful snow-white, and Beck, now a scarred and filthy jet-black, no longer attempted to raise their heads. Their only focus was the path ahead and the sting of the whip.

The immigrant family, one of seventeen, struggled to keep stride with the relentless beasts that pulled their tattered covered wagon packed with worldly reminders from a once prosperous plantation.

They made their way through a thick stand of red oaks and volunteer blackberries across a broad ridge, which two generations hence would yield hardscrabble crops and be called the *airplane field.*

Near the center, they stopped and wished each other well. Sixteen families turned north-northwest bound for a settlement called *Forest Hill.* For the first time in two months, the expedition left one family behind.

The stooped patriarch pored over a plat until the 16 were nearly out of sight. He stuffed the map in its leather case beneath the wagon seat. With a single snap of the whip, Beck and Dine plunged through thick briars. At the bottom of a steep hollow, sweet water boiled to the surface between two rocks.

The family crowded shoulder-to-shoulder with the oxen and greedily drank their fill. "We must be close," an apprehensive whisper floated up from the rippled surface of the shallow pool.

Two fox squirrels leaped from tree-to-tree trying to escape an unknown threat. Dying shards of yellow light from a rapidly falling sun danced across the hollow's steep western slope. The crack of the whip shattered the silence. Mother, father, and six children slowly climbed out of the *Waterin' Hole Holler.* Their steps quickened. They passed the giant *Hoot Owl Tree* and entered a small clearing at the apex of three ridges.

George Washington McKenna, Sr. excitedly dropped the reins, drove a broken shovel into the hard ground, and reached toward heaven. "Mother, this is our homestead!" he declared.

The McKennas escaped war-impoverished North Carolina the same way in which their ancestors fled Ireland. For generations, the family carried a burden of betrayal, death, and disappointment.

Six grueling days of every week, they broke their backs to clear the land, grow and hunt food, and build a home. By the flickering light of a crackling campfire, they shared jugs of corn whiskey and family history.

Sunday afternoons, they joined the remainder of the original seventeen in fellowship. Between a country church and an ever-growing garden of granite, they played their fiddles and sang the songs of Ireland and Appalachia.

Frailly leaned against his bent sassafras cane, George Sr. sat in the shade with the other old men. Between spats of tobacco, he retold stories of his Confederate Army days and the family curse. Almost to a person, they died too soon of hardship, illness, and whiskey.

Throughout the generations, the family's unwavering faith in God was a refuge and at times a comfort. For the McKenna's, it was never a cure.

PROLOGUE

St. Louis to Fort Myers, Saturday Morning, April 1, 2000

I WAS 43 when the love of my life died at my hand.
The beginning of the end was a muggy Saturday night, August 14, 1999. It was late, an hour before midnight. Every thick breath lay upon my tongue like an invisible waft of crude salt.

It had all the earmarks of an accident. Everyone said it was, but in my heart, I know better. When I close my eyes, even if only for a second, I relive every morbid detail as vividly as if it was all happening again. It was murder.

His name was Ted. I hope by writing it here, I will one day again be able to get it past my lips—Ted, Ted, Ted.

I was sitting on his right. The Cessna's engine exploded and caught fire 6,500 feet above the choppy black surface of the Gulf of Mexico. I grabbed the controls and declared myself Pilot in Command. He was a new pilot. We had agreed that if anything ever went wrong, we would depend upon my experience to save us. From the *moment of the explosion until the nose of our single-engine airplane was upside down in the sand, everything that happened was on me.*

I have no way of knowing how much Ted suffered in the crash or during the final month of his life. He never opened his eyes or made any intelligible sound. When he took his final breath, I believed with all my heart it was my fault.

My father tried to comfort me. He said no one could have prevented the crash. He theorized that there had been unseen forces at work, a series of unfortunate circumstances beyond my control.

My mother agreed. "You were in God's hands. Ted is with Him now. You can't blame yourself, Bette. It's all part of His plan."

I respect my mother too much to disagree, so I kept my mouth shut. However, like my father, I believe there was something else at work, something evil that had nothing to do with God and everything to do with my secrets.

I think myself a writer. I've made my living writing commercial copy and always prided myself upon a sparse, effective use of the English language. Nonetheless, on these pages, I have no thought of sparing anything. I plan to pour out my heart and purge my soul of guilt. I desperately need this, but I'm fearful it's an elusive dream. When I am free of the guilt, even for a moment, it feels like a parlor trick, a product of smoke and mirrors.

AMETHYST INK spilled from the golden nib of my pen as it scratched cotton parchment in measured strokes saturating the page with meandering thoughts. In the place of ink, I saw only the red of my lover's blood. It stained every cathartic memory as I struggled to find redemption. Not an ounce of joy existed in my life. Awake or asleep, I found no relief from my nightmarish reality.

Like all of my family, I was without question, cursed.

My existence became a lingering march to death. It was not the kind of agony I always feared, it was something much worse.

THIS IS MY FIRST ATTEMPT at an entry in this journal— a diary, which is at the same time old and new. It was a Christmas gift from Ted.

A rich intoxicating smell of new leather still clings to the dark brown buffalo hide cover. The hand-debossed images of enchanted mushroom shaped trees and a longhaired mystical being magically float across its surface. To their right, an ornate nickel button protrudes. A single binding cord hangs loosely against my leg. Near the spine, a spreading stain from the natural oils in my skin reminds me I have carried this book with me constantly since the funeral. Until today, the binding remained wound around the button.

We were like small children our first Christmas together. Unable to sleep, we were up before daylight. I ground the beans and made a pot of coffee. Ted kindled a fire in the fireplace. The week before, I tried to imagine the look on Ted's face when he opened his gift. Mexico and Mexican culture fascinated him. When I found a two-peso gold coin, I was convinced every detail would be perfect. A jeweler fashioned a setting, and I hung it from a long gold chain. I put the coin and chain in a velvet box and wrapped it in tightly patterned gold paper with a matching ribbon.

He tore off the paper and opened the box. When he saw the chain, he stopped. My first thought was that he thought it too feminine. He hugged me, then went straight to the Christmas tree, and came back with a small crudely wrapped box. He must have hidden it there while I was in the kitchen. I had searched for some hint of a gift every day during the weeks before and found nothing. Roughly folded corners and too much tape convinced me he had wrapped it himself. Relishing the moment, I carefully cut away the gaudy paper.

Inside the box, I found this journal professionally wrapped in crisp white tissue sealed with the McKenna coat-of-arms in crimson wax poured and stamped on the triangular flap. I was careful to remove the seal intact. When I first touched it, it was as though the book was trying to communicate with me. Moreover, the idea of preserving my thoughts enchanted me. I have always wanted to discipline myself to record everything important and meaningful in my life. I must have told Ted my dream, and he remembered as he remembered everything that was important to me.

We were good together. Unlike O. Henry's short story, "The Gift of the Magi," that first Christmas we fulfilled each other's dreams without sacrifice.

Several times that day, I told Ted how I would fill my journal's pages with my thoughts. Like so many other hollow resolutions in my life, my good intentions lacked true determination. It took his dying to get this book out of the original box. Until today, not so much as a dot of ink has marked its pages.

AFTER A FULL WEEK in the hospital, the gut wrenching sights and sounds of the crash still played in a continuous slow-motion loop in my head. I sat helplessly by Ted's bedside, physically and emotionally fractured, trapped in a hospital wheelchair, watching in agony as his life dripped away. Every muscle in my broken body ached. With my only unbroken limb, my right arm, I stretched to touch his bandaged face; my atrophied muscles throbbed. Ignoring the pain, I took his cold hand in mine.

"It was my fault," I whispered. "The crash was my fault." He didn't react in any way to my words or touch. "I was Pilot in Command. I should have done a better job.

"Elizabeth McKenna," I scolded myself, "it should be

you lying in this bed, not this man."

I squeezed my eyes tightly shut and tried to convince myself it was all a dream. The petrifying sound of ripping aluminum as our airplane flipped tail-over-nose on the rocky beach and burrowed into the coarse sand at the water's edge destroyed my intended calm.

MY MOTHER named me Elizabeth after her grandmother. She invented my middle name, EraStella. When I was in high school, she told me she did it because from the first moment she laid eyes upon me she knew I was exceptional and of my own time. I have yet to see the truth in her premonition.

On the first day of first grade, halfway through an alphabetical roll call, the teacher read my full name aloud. I smiled proudly until I realized that the snickers, which fell like a cold rain, were at my expense. Tiny droplets of humiliation sharply stung my thin skin, and I buried my face in my desktop. At recess, I rode the merry-go-round. With each pass, the boys taunted me until I cried. After that, they spared no effort in discovering what else about me was laughable. Since then, I have believed that if anything was personal, private, or a secret for me, it was a joke to everyone else. Throughout my life, people have continually proven me right.

Ted Wilson was one of four people who I believed I could trust with my secrets; he never betrayed me. Of the other three, two are my parents. The fourth is my best friend, David.

All that has passed has brought me to an important time and place in my life. What others have done to me, and said about me, hurt. In the end, they made me stronger. They helped me to find myself, to see me for who I am.

THE WORDS I write in this journal are my promise to myself and to God. I will be strong and unwavering,

persistent and resilient. Somehow, I will find my way. I will not rest until I know the truth about how Ted died.
The question is simple. Am I responsible?

ONE

I T WAS NOTHING MORE than an unfortunate series of intertwined, unrelated events—an innocent two-day business trip to Tampa, Florida, no big deal. I wasn't even scheduled to go. However, a coworker had a conflict. It fell to me to fill in.

Since the day he earned his pilot's license, Ted had talked about a celebratory weekend fishing trip with two of his friends. Almost every night for weeks, they drank beer and organized their gear in the garage. They planned to fly our Skylane down to the Arkansas border and fish the White River, a guy thing.

Wednesday morning, the two-year old son of one of the trio caught the flu. He cancelled. That same afternoon, my boss asked me to fill in at the meeting in Florida. Suddenly, I needed the airplane. Ted did not.

Ted insisted he accompany me. "My weekend is wide open," he pleaded. "I can chauffeur you for a change. You can relax while I log some hours. This is a win-win." He smiled sheepishly. It was obvious he didn't want to stay home alone. "Besides, you've been hoggin' the plane."

We were airborne by 5:30 Thursday morning and immediately climbed through a thick overcast. I flew left seat, the pilot's side. The weather demanded we follow Instrument Flight Rules, something that was beyond Ted's capability and license. With only 33 hours on the Hobbs meter, which recorded elapsed time since the aircraft's engine was overhauled, the Skylane performed like new.

I was delighted with my textbook perfect Instrument Landing System approach to Birmingham, Alabama. By the time I returned from the ladies room, a cute blonde attendant in a red tank top and skimpy white shorts with an enviable tan had finished the refueling

A brief radio exchange with Birmingham tower reopened our IFR flight plan. We quickly climbed through billowy cumulus clouds into smooth air above. The mid-August sun illuminated the bright white cloudscape of delicate mountains and ever-shifting valleys. I relaxed and tuned the FM radio to an oldies station. Ted slid his hand in mine and squeezed.

Tampa tower accurately reported a left quartering 15-knot headwind and light rain. At 500 feet, we broke through the ceiling, and the wide runway ahead dwarfed our airplane.

POUNDING THUNDER and crashing waves shook me awake. Ted sat on the edge of the bed holding a steaming cup. Even his presence and the intoxicating aroma of black coffee couldn't prevent a frown from creeping across my face. "Is it Saturday already?" I asked disappointed because I already knew the answer.

"'Fraid so." Ted stroked my arm and handed me the cup. "From the looks of the weather, I'm not sure we're leavin'." He pointed to the window and shook his head. "Least not this mornin'."

I pulled myself up and leaned against the headboard. Unlike the sunny day before, now our lavish ocean-view suite at the pink Don Cesar hotel felt more like an unwelcome rain shelter.

Hourly, throughout the morning, I checked the weather by telephone. The broad storm cell was intense and slow moving from the southwest. We checked out of the hotel before noon and spent a restless afternoon reading in the lobby. I prayed for a break in the weather. With every passing minute, I became more disconcerted.

In a deserted 24-hour cafe near the airport, I picked at my late dinner. The clock on the wall struggled to count the minutes as the hands slowly passed through 9:30 P.M. Ted devoured his hamburger as if it was his last meal.

Ignorance is bliss, I told myself, thinking that Ted's limited experience kept him from completely understanding our plight. Once with my dad, similarly weathered in for three days at a small country airport, we slept on the floor, ate stale cupcakes, and drank weak coffee from a pair of stingy vending machines.

Across the table, Ted dragged a french fry through a puddle of catsup. A premonition of vertigo washed over me. I tensed and steadied myself on the arm of my chair. Nothing felt right. I had logged more than 7,000 hours in a dozen varieties of single-engine airplanes. There was nothing special about this night, except how I felt. I was awash in an inexplicable sense of impending doom.

In my twenties, I rented a 1940 Stearman military trainer, an open cockpit biplane piloted from the back seat. I wanted to surprise my dad and take him up in a plane he had never flown.

The first take-off of my checkout flight felt good. I was relaxed with an instructor in the front seat. One smooth circle around the grass field at 800 feet, I lined up for final approach. At 200 feet above the ground, I realized I was too low and slow in an approach that would have been perfect for nearly any aircraft, but not the Stearman.

The seasoned pilot never moved. "Flyin' rock," he

calmly called out over the wind. The intercom crackled with his words. Heeding his warning, I dropped the nose in the last possible instant and greased the antique bird onto the grass in a perfect wheel landing.

Airplanes and flying have never frightened me. However, on this Saturday night in Florida, waiting for the weather to clear, plagued by a sense of disaster, I was afraid.

The minute hand dragged past ten o'clock. The sky grew lighter. I called weather again. The bored voice on the other end of the line told me the storm had pushed off to the east. Minimums were above the required ceiling of 1,000 feet with 3 miles visibility for Visual Flight Rules. Ted smiled; he would get his chance at the controls after all.

His words crisp and clear in my headset, a man somewhere behind the dark glass of the Tampa tower cleared us for departure and directed us out over the edge of the Gulf of Mexico. Ted made a smooth, climbing right turn to the northeast. He tuned both navigation radios and pushed a series of buttons on the long-range navigation device that established our direct track to Birmingham, Alabama. He filled me with pride as he skillfully handled every cockpit task. I folded my hands in my lap and wished my father could see the efficiency of his student.

Everything was perfect, yet the nagging fear stamped its feet in the back of my mind, and demanded I take note. Our route would keep us just west of the coast, a few miles out over the still unsettled water of the Gulf, and direct to our only necessary fuel stop. The engine ran flawlessly. I nervously checked my watch; it was straight-up eleven o'clock eastern time. *One hour 'till midnight,* I told myself. *Thank God, this day is almost over.*

Ted eased the nose down, leveled the Cessna at 6,500 feet, and in a professional voice, reported our altitude and heading. The yellow transponder light on the instrument panel blinked reassuringly with a code assigned by Jacksonville Center. I envisioned a man on the other side of the state hovered over a screen in a darkened room watching a dot and number that represented our two souls. Other assigned numbers also moved across the screen at varying speeds, altitudes, and headings. The vigilant controller would help keep us safe.

Through the red half-light of the cockpit, Ted looked over and smiled with pride-brightened eyes. I had seen this look once before, six months earlier on an overcast day in February when he slid from the cockpit of my father's weary Cessna 172 having just finished his first solo flight. My dad congratulated his student, and told him he would make a great pilot.

Ted nodded as if he knew what I was thinking and then returned his attention to a thorough scan of the instrument panel. He twisted his head slightly to the left, pulled his headset away from one ear, and listened intently to the throaty hum of the Continental engine.

The unstable air bubbled in the aftermath of the storm. An almost imperceptible, undulating vibration seeped through the airframe surfing bumps hidden in the wind. I had felt something similar, thousands of times before, but this vibration wrapped its icy fingers around my lungs and squeezed until I gasped.

Unaware of what I was experiencing, Ted leaned forward and put his right hand between the seats. With one easy tug on the lever, he moved the cowl doors the last two notches to fully closed. The 20-year old airplane was sealed up and as aerodynamic as its design allowed.

With the final element of drag minimized, it was like letting go of a kite in a strong wind, a momentary burst of un-tethered freedom. Fear loosed its grip on my lungs. I sighed with relief. *All in your imagina*—

WHAM, as though thunder and lightning simultaneously struck the cockpit, the engine exploded and severed my thought. A ball of fire, 11 quarts of oil, and mangled engine parts ripped through the top of the aluminum cowling. In slow motion, the airplane rolled onto its right side, threw its nose straight down, and plummeted seaward. Blinded by the yellow-blue blast, I blinked. A black shroud of engine oil covered the expansive windshield.

Instinctively, I grabbed the yoke and wrested control from Ted. He jerked his hands away. I was the experienced pilot. We both knew it was up to me to fly the plane.

I pulled the yoke to my chest and with all my strength twisted it to the left. Nothing happened. For a moment, we floated weightlessly through space, and my actions yielded no results. A millisecond dragged by. The controls fought my efforts to correct our attitude. The Cessna seemed to want to die.

Finally, it acquiesced. I was able to begin a reluctant uncoordinated roll to the left and lift the nose. With a sharp mechanical bang and a shockwave that penetrated my soul, the propeller freed itself and began to spin. I thrust the red fuel/air mixture control all the way in, forcing gasoline into the carburetor. I double-checked the ignition and frantically pumped the throttle.

A glimpse of the altimeter showed the needles passing through 5,000 feet. Uncertainty clouded my judgment. We raced toward certain death.

Only able to see out of the unobstructed window on my right, moonlight danced gaily on the surface of our watery grave. Less than 30 seconds had passed since the explosion. We had already lost 1,500 feet. *This won't take long,* my mind screamed in a macabre, experienced voice.

A second, smaller fireball belched from the torn cowling and rocketed out of sight. A hoarse combusted cough followed. A small surge of power telegraphed through the throttle and carried a wave of hope. I checked the fuel valve and moved it from right-tank-only to both. The engine restarted.

"Bette, you okay?" Ted's frightened voice crackled in my ears.

I dared not face him. He would have seen the truth in my face. "Yeah, you?" I tried to sound calm, grateful that the continuous explosions and accompanying fireballs cloaked my fear.

"What can we do?" He shouted. "Will the engine run like this?"

"Odds are, no." I answered, unable to hide the truth, still avoiding his gaze. "We're 20 miles from the coast. There's no oil left in the engine. It's beatin' itself to death. We're feedin' a gas fire, but without it, we can't stay in the air.

"Call Jax center," I commanded, "declare an emergency and ask for help. Tell 'em we need a place to land." Ted didn't answer. "Do it now!"

The sole push-to-talk switch was mounted on the pilot's yoke, opening only the pilot's microphone, which meant I couldn't speak directly to the tower. Ted was our voice to the outside world. With that exception, I had total control of the airplane.

"Jax Center, this is Skylane 9er5-4-5-5 declaring an emergency. We need a place to land."

"Skylane 4-5-5, Jax Center, acknowledge, say your emergency."

"We have limited power. We're on fire."

My headset crackled. *He's probably too shocked to answer*, I thought.

"We have you on radar." The controller said in a strained voice. "Crystal River airport is 2-0 miles; turn right to 3-2-0 degrees."

I pressed my cheek against the oil-streaked Plexiglas side window and searched for the lights of Crystal River. The coastline was far off, definitely on our right. The town should have been just beyond. We were flying northeast. A heading change to 320 degrees would take us out to sea.

I questioned my reasoning and wondered if vertigo had clouded my judgment. I distrusted my senses. *"Believe your instruments,"* my father's voice resounded. Uncertain white letters danced in the liquid bath of the magnetic compass while the directional gyro spun out of control.

"Ted, that heading can't be right." I commenced a shallow right turn without waiting to find out if I was correct. "The airport's gotta be east. Tell 'im—tell 'im now!"

"Jax Center, 4-5-5, 3-2-0 degrees can't be right." Ted spit the words into his headset's boom mic. "Check heading, over?"

I held my breath. The static in my headset was deafening. I maintained the turn, waiting.

The nervous voice came back, "4-5-5, sorry—uhh—my error." White noise blasted my inner ear. "Turn to 0-8-0 degrees. Airport is 1-9er miles. G-luck, stayin' with you."

The engine, a sledge pounding a steel plate, relentlessly thrashed the airframe. I pumped the throttle nonstop. Every few seconds, it rewarded me with a fresh fireball rocketing past the oily funeral shroud on our windscreen.

"Can we make the airport?" Ted asked. His ghostly face glowed in the dim red light.

I checked the counterclockwise swing of the altimeter's white hands. "We're losin' altitude, but should be 'nough," I answered with a quick calculation. "Need to keep the engine runnin' and hope fire doesn't get wor—"

"Four-five-five, Jax Center," the familiar voice cut me off, "you're one-four miles from airport. It's closed. TWA captain has—uhh—activated runway lights. Emergency equipment's standin' by, over."

Nearly 2,000 feet below, rocks protruded from the moonlit surface of the Gulf of Mexico. Options raced through my mind. *Turnin' the fuel off will put out the fire,*

I reasoned, *but we'll lose all power. Dad says there's always more than one alternative. Can't survive a landing in the rocks. With the engine, we might make the airport. I've gotta keep this thing in the air; I've gotta keep the engine runnin'.* I visually swept the surface for another place to put her down.

I BLINKED. In the momentary blackness of my mind's eye, I found myself in the pilot's seat of my dad's old Skylane staring at outdated Narco hand-tuned navcoms. He sat calmly in the right seat, his glowing pipe clinched tightly between his teeth. *"Worry about what you control. Fly the airplane. Don't second-guess your instincts. Feel your machine; don't fight it."* I blinked again.

FIREBALLS, in short, irregular Roman candle bursts, continually lit the night sky. I ignored them. They were outside my control.

A soulless metal-on-metal screech resonated through the cockpit. Fear's icy fingers plucked my heart from my chest. The propeller slammed to a stop—no fire, no banging, and no hope.

"TED, WE CAN'T MAKE IT!" I screamed. "TELL 'IM, TELL 'IM NOW!"

"Jax, 4-5-5, engine's gone," Ted shouted. "I repeat, we're dead stick. Gonna try for the beach, over."

I threw my headset over my shoulder. Ted did the same. "Sorry, hon," I said. Calm came over me. The only sound was the rush of the wind as the needles of the altimeter spiraled down. "I'll do my best."

I lowered the nose, steadied our glide, and applied a slight backpressure to slow our descent. Following a mental checklist, I closed the fuel valve and set the flaps to 10 degrees for lift.

The radio popped. Something like a sinister laugh came from the cockpit's external speakers, "ha-ha-ha," a soul-shattering chill bore through me. "Ha-ha-bitch, ha—"

"...lane 4-5-5, Jax 'enter." The controller's voice severed the laugh. The broken voice was panicked. "Wind's from 3...0 at 1... Goo' luck, God spee... "

I didn't understand the wind speed or direction, but it no longer mattered. I only had one choice. I snapped off the master switch and steeled my nerve.

"Fly the airplane." My dad's voice steadied my hand on the yoke. I banked slightly to the right. A mile ahead, bathed in eerie moonlight, the rocky beach waited. *Just a runway,* I told myself, trying unemotionally to envision an approach. A slight forward pressure on the sluggish yoke dropped the elevators and increased our glide speed to a solid 80 miles per hour. *Standard approach, keep the landing gear out of the sand as long as possible.*

Ted sat stiffly with his palms buried beneath his thighs like a man on death row.

"Sorry, hon." I felt compelled to apologize again.

He turned and smiled.

"Tighten your shoulder harness," I ordered in a terse voice. "Beach's our only hope—looks rough."

Blindly, I gauged my final turn, took a shallow breath, and guessed at our height above the ground. I counted 90 degrees on the erratic magnetic compass and rolled out on final.

The invisible ground cushion cradled the airplane for an instant. I pulled back on the yoke and discovered too late that ground effect had fooled me; we were too high. We lost our lift, stalled, and fell nearly straight down. Frantically, I dropped the nose and salvaged too little lift, too late. In the span of a single heartbeat, our landing gear collided with the sand at 50 miles per hour.

The screech of ripping aluminum filled the air. We plowed through sand and rocks. Our momentum and the crush of our weight flipped us tail-over-nose. Nearly full fuel tanks spewed high-octane gasoline across the beach.

Toxic fumes choked my final prayer. "God, save u—" My world went black.

TWO

A NEEDLE OF CRIMSON LIGHT pierced my pain-filled eyes. I struggled to focus. From the shadows, in the subconscious hollows of my concussion-swollen brain, a stocky man in dirty blue coveralls stepped out. He lifted his right arm and made a menacing fist. A malicious smile swept across his pocked face. A gloating laugh billowed up. I knew the fist. I knew the laugh. Fear pinned me to the bed.

"You got what you deserve." Acidic words spewed from snarled lips. "You and your fancy schoolteacher got taught a lesson. 'Bout fuckin' time!"

I must be dead, I thought. *I'm dead, and this is hell.*

"I'm talkin' to you," he continued. Dark gray eyes glared at me. "I've been waitin' a long time for this day—patiently waitin' for you to get what's been comin' to ya. You ruined my life; now it's my turn. I know you hear me." He leaned in. "You ain't dead, but you're gonna wish you were.

"At the end, you said my idea of foreplay was two shots of Wild Turkey and a joint." He laughed, even more sinister than before. "You don't know shit 'bout me. You think yer so sweet that sugar don't melt in your mouth. I'm here to show ya otherwise. Fuckin' up your precious airplane, now that's my idea of foreplay. Get ready bitch, 'cause the dance is about to star—"

"Ms. McKenna, can you hear me?" A feminine voice cut him off. Small, overly warm hands caressed my arm.

I willed one eye fully open, then the other. A round face smiled. Short blond hair hung haphazardly above a hideous pink flowered top. "Elizabeth, do you understand me?"

"Where am I?" I asked with cotton muffled speech. "Where's Ted?"

"I don't know how that man got in here." The nurse shook her head.

I ignored her comment. "Where am I?" I demanded, forcing the image of my ex-husband out of my mind. "Where's Ted?"

"You're in the hospital in Tampa," she said soothingly. "You were airlifted in last night. You've been unconscious for 12 hours."

"Where's Ted?" I insisted. I didn't care about me. I remembered the crash. *Obviously, I'm in a hospital*, I thought. *Where else would people dress like you?*

"Mr. Wilson's in another room," she reluctantly answered.

"Is he okay? I wanna see him," I demanded. "Right now!" I tried to move, but couldn't. The sheet that covered me looked like an overstuffed mattress. An air cast of some sort encased my exposed left arm. My right hand was free, but it hurt when I moved my fingers. "Please, take me to Ted?" I pleaded.

"I'm—I'm sorry, I can't do that, miss." She gently touched my forehead with the back of her hand. "Doctor wants you to stay right here and get a little better first. Your parents called. They should arrive soon. Your mother was so sweet on the phone. She'll be relieved to see you're awake." She continued without taking a breath. "The Doctor'll stop by shortly. He asked me to call him when you woke up. He'll answer all your questions."

The Doctor pulled a wheeled stool to my bedside. Snow-white hair framed his deeply tanned face. At my insistence, in kind consoling tones, he gave me a technical explanation of Ted's condition and then mine. I heard very little of what he said and understood even less. It sounded like convoluted subterfuge as though he didn't want to tell me the truth, but couldn't lie. The only thing I understood was Ted was alive and in a coma.

Soon after, my parents arrived. Although she made an obvious effort to be strong, my mother lost her composure. A nurse led her from the room. My dad stood alone at my bedside holding my hand.

Uncountable hours passed. My parents seemed to find new strength. My mom's tears disappeared. I was relieved. One stayed with me, the other with Ted. They switched at irregular intervals, each time bringing me news of his condition.

After two agonizing days in intensive care, they wheeled me down the hall and pushed my bed alongside Ted's. I was unprepared for what I saw. A broken and bruised man lay almost entirely hidden beneath a stiff white sheet.

Ted was a man's man. At six feet two, he towered over me by a solid six inches. Barefoot, standing together, my head fit perfectly beneath his strong chin. I loved his muscular frame and taut stomach that he called his *four-pack*. The distorted creature who lay before me was none of those things.

I gingerly touched his chest. The beat of his heart was uncoordinated and weak. Bandages swathed much of his head and face. I saw enough to know that his thick head of hair was shaved. Shallow recesses in the bloated face took the place of mischievous brown eyes, which had always brimmed with joy. His mouth was a mere slit in a heavy bandage wrapped tightly around the lower portion of his face and his neck. A clear plastic oxygen mask moved slightly with each labored breath. A machine connected by a transparent tube clicked rhythmically as it forced air into his lungs.

Only the strong hands looked like Ted. I traced the oddly shaped tan line on the ring finger of his left hand where my Great-Grandfather George Jr.'s Irish Claddagh ring should have been. He had never taken it off since the day I gave it to him as a token of my love when we exchanged our non-official vows by the river.

I squeezed my eyes shut as I often did during our stay in the hospital. My memories were much more palatable than my reality. I remembered the perfect proportion of his hands to his masculine frame and artfully chiseled features. I thought about the moment on campus, years before, when I saw him for the first time. It was love at first sight.

I opened my eyes and found myself still lying in the stark, surreal place with plastic tubes connecting Ted to plastic bags filled with fluids. Colored wires linked him to noisy machines with flashing LED displays. Anchored to my bed, I struggled to get as close as possible.

I closed my eyes and counted, *one-two-three, wakeup.* I opened them to find no change in the disfigured being that everyone said was Ted Wilson.

"He'll regain consciousness soon." I assured my mother, even though I was unconvinced. "When he does, I don't want him to be alone." I pleaded for her help in a tone that sounded like a command. "One of us needs to be here when he wakes."

A uniformed contingent of bleary-eyed doctors and nurses frequently read the charts, touched their patient, and checked the machines. When they talked to each other, they always turned away from me and spoke in hushed tones.

Three days after the accident, I pitched a fit. The nurses acquiesced and helped me from my bed to a wheelchair. After another day, a few close friends and family began to arrive along with an inundation of flowers and cards.

The sparse flow of well-wishers, with their looks of shock and dismay, brought me more stress. They stumbled over their words searching for some ill-planned note of encouragement. I made an effort to listen, but I could not be consoled. On the fifth day, they began to leave. By Sunday, eight days after the accident, only my parents and I remained.

Gradually, I noticed that I didn't understand much of what was said in the room. People's muffled words ran together. I blamed it on selective hearing. It occurred to me that it might be some sort of delayed reaction to my head injury. For the first several days, I saw crimson spots when I closed my eyes. After a time, the spots went away. The hearing impediment didn't.

I told no one about my condition. I was afraid they would take me away from Ted. On the few occasions when he and I were completely alone, I noticed a painful ringing in my ears.

As the days dragged by, the ringing worsened. *It's sinus or a change in barometric pressure. Maybe a storm's comin'.* I tried to convince myself it was no big deal. Still, I told no one. Ted was my focus.

The doctor formally released me at the end of the second week. I refused to leave the hospital. I knew all of the nurses by their first names along with those of their children and the things they hated about their husbands. They put a bed in Ted's room for me, fed me, and treated me as if I was still a patient. The doctors and nursing supervisors pretended not to notice that I lived there.

Another week passed in a series of excruciating

individual minutes, each far overstaying its welcome. Ted's condition remained unchanged. Resolute, I spoke to him as though he was conscious. After a fashion, I began to answer for him as my mother did when she asked her dog a question and then in a different voice answered. *He can hear me,* I told myself.

One morning, early in our fourth week in the hospital, my mother began pacing the floor. Every second time across the room she glanced at the clock.

"Mother, what is your problem?" I demanded to know after 10 nerve-wracking minutes.

"The doctor wants to see you," she blurted out. "He asked me to bring you to his office at eleven."

I looked at the clock on the wall. The minute hand had already begun its final saunter toward the hour. "Cutting it a little close, aren't you?" I asked with trepidation. My mom hates delivering bad news and has always procrastinated until the last second.

She wheeled me down the hall. At my insistence, she pushed me into the small office and waited quietly just inside the door.

"Elizabeth, I know what a difficult time this is for you." The doctor began without looking up from the open file on his desk. "The nurses seem to think you're having difficulty hearing."

Nosey bitches, popped into my mind. I temporarily forgot their kindness. "Yes," I answered. *This is about me, not Ted,* I thought, with a heavy sigh of relief.

"Describe what you're experiencing." He came around the desk and shined a bright light in my ear.

"One day, I noticed a loud ringing in my ears," I explained. "As near as I can remember, I was fine before the accident. Now, there are certain things I can't hear at all. I can't understand anything when several people are in the room talking."

From the pocket of his knee-length lab coat, he

produced a tuning fork. He struck it against the desk and then held it at varied distances from each ear and asked me to describe what I heard. He made a few notes on a lined pad. Finished, he put his notebook down, leaned against the front of his glass desk, and crossed his arms. His face was stern.

"It's most likely Tinnitus," he stated matter-of-factly. "The good news is the tests, we did when you were first admitted, confirm you don't have an aneurysm or tumor. Either of those would be a worst-case scenario and rarely occur in these circumstances. Tinnitus is usually the result of a high noise lifestyle. Airplanes, motorcycles, guns, and loud music, if you like that sort of thing, are the typical culprits. Unfortunately, there's no cure. We'll most likely find you have permanent hearing loss in the 4,000 and higher decibel range."

"The ringing is driving me crazy," I said, finally giving voice to a frequent thought. "There must be something I can do to make it stop?"

"I'm sorry. There's nothing. Something like 36 million Americans suffer from Tinnitus. Most people condition themselves to forget about the sound and make adjustments for the deficiency. Many say that within six months of a diagnosis, they're able to completely ignore the noise and function normally."

The doctor placed his hands palms down on his desk as though he needed the support. His eyes narrowed. His expression tightened.

"Uh-hmm." My mother nervously cleared her throat.

"What is it?" I demanded. "What else?" I braced for the meeting's true intent.

"Well…"

I remember only some of what followed. Later, in the hallway outside Ted's room, while a nurse sponged him clean, my mother helped me to understand. They had done everything possible for Ted. There was no evidence of brain activity. It was only a matter of time. Then she dropped the *D* bomb.

This part, I remembered word-for-word. "Ms. McKenna, Elizabeth, the *decision* is yours. Perhaps, you should consider removing the life suppo—"

"No," I blurted out before he could finish. "As God is my witness, he will recover. If it is his time, that's God's decision, not mine and certainly not yours!"

Friday morning, the last day of the fourth week since the accident, I awoke gasping for air beneath soul crushing despair. A palpable sense of doom pervaded my consciousness. Afraid of what I would see, unwilling to accept what might be true, I peeked over my bed rail. Ted's condition seemed unchanged. Relieved, I dropped my head on my pillow. *It must've been a bad dream,* I rationalized. *Stop paying attention to other people's negative vibes.* I reprimanded myself ignoring my own mental image of unavoidable truth.

Infant sunlight crawled in beneath the window shade. The doctor slipped quietly through the partially open door and closed it. I pretended to sleep while he checked the chart, pressed his stethoscope to Ted's chest, and gently held his wrist.

He faced me. It was obvious. He knew I was awake. He pulled a chair to my bedside and sat uncomfortably on the edge. With a cold hand, he checked my pulse.

"I'm very sorry, Elizabeth." He broke the silence. "We've done everything within our power." He looked into my eyes. "Ted's vitals are rapidly weakening. He's in God's hands now."

"He's always been in God's hands." I reminded the doctor and myself in a voice so small I barely heard my own words. "How much ti—?" I choked.

"One, maybe two days at most, it's difficult to judge. His organs are already shutting down."

Ted and I were alone in the abhorrent room. I stared out

the window and fought back a tear. Balancing my breakfast tray on one hand, a nurse pushed through the door. One look at me and she backed out without a word.

In a coarse whisper, I began a speech I'd mentally rehearsed a thousand times. I had hoped never to deliver it.

"Where do you think you're going, Ted Wilson?" I leaned over his bed. "How can you do this without me? How can you leave me? Why'd you insist on coming with me to Tampa? I should've been alone in the plane. I should've done a better job of getting us down. If I had, we'd be home. We'd be safe.

"Dear God," I lifted my face and closed my eyes, "please let me trade places with this man. Don't make me live the rest of my life alone. I've waited too long. I can't lose him, not now, not Ted."

THREE

Within 24 hours, the greatly expanded woeful horde returned.

Their ebb and flow, in and out of the cramped room, brought an unpredictable tide of disconcerting conversation. Without comment, the hospital staff adjusted for our number. Everyone seemed to accept the inevitable, everyone except me.

I refused to leave Ted's side. From time-to-time, when she caught me squirming, my mother insisted I go to the bathroom. She forced me to eat by threatening a hunger strike of her own.

There were never less than a half-dozen visitors packed like sardines in the antiseptic room. If I wasn't napping on my bed, someone else usually was. We took turns holding Ted's hand. I watched everyone of importance in our lives silently press their good-byes against his cool skin.

Ministers, like coyotes, roamed the halls searching for carcasses and intermittently stopped by. Each seemed to think he knew the answer to everlasting life. They read from their Bibles and said their prayers. One, obviously excited about our home with God, read from second Corinthians. Another closed his eyes and recited the Twenty-Third Psalm, "Yeah though I walk through the valley of the shadow of death..."

I listened respectfully to them all. However, when any member of the clergy asked that we bow our heads, I resisted. Instead, I scolded God for his decision. Everyone prayed for a painless end to Ted's suffering while I begged for a new beginning.

I sensed a change in Ted before it was obvious to anyone else, even the nurses. His hands were too warm, his forced breathing imperceptibly different.

I wrapped my fingers around his hand, squeezed, and closed my eyes. On something like a movie screen inside my mind, I watched him walk excitedly across the tarmac and climb into the Cessna for the last time.

With my hearing impaired, I was acutely aware of my other senses. I hated the sterile hospital smell. I despised the tubes and wires that hung from the support machines. I abhorred the scratchy sheets. Most of all, I loathed my existence.

With my face pressed against Ted's chest, I struggled to conjure up happy memories. I imagined I heard someone humming. *You're losing your mind,* I told myself as I tried to sort the sound from the noise in the room and my mental images. Then I realized the humming had been there all day like music in an elevator. One-by-one, I searched the faces in the crowded room for the source. In my mother's sad countenance, I found movements that matched the sound.

"Ma, what are you humming?" I whispered.

"Oh," she answered, bewildered. "Was I humming?"

"What is it?" I asked, taking her hand. "What's the song?"

"Uh, I guess I don't know." She tilted her head to one side and began again to hum, appearing to listen as though she was the audience and not the performer. At first, the notes were broken and varied. She closed her eyes, clasped her hands, and started over. Her face lit up. She opened her eyes and smiled a smile, which is an indelible part of my childhood memories. She started humming again; this time the notes were even and sweet.

She stopped. "*God Will Take Care of You*," she pronounced with certainty. "It's from our hymnal." She squeezed my hand. "Do you remember it, Bette?"

I searched my memory. "No, it's not familiar, but I like the name. Ma, you sound like an angel. Do you know the words?"

"Oh, Bette." My heavenly comparison caused her to glance nervously at the ceiling. "I'm not sure." She hummed a few more bars and then began to sing.

"Be not dismayed what–e'er be–tide, God will take care of you;

Beneath his wings of love a–bide, God will take care of you.

God will take care of you, through ev–ery day, o'er all the way;"

A second voice joined in and then a third. Their soft mix of pitch and balance grew more precise with each verse. Every new voice helped fill the air and overpower the harsh mechanical sounds of life support. Every eye was closed, every word perfect, and to a chord every note on key. They grew in confidence and vigor until they sang the hymn perfectly.

"He will take care of you, God will take care of you.

"No mat–ter what may be the test, God will take care of you;

Lean, wea–ry one, up–on his breast, God will take care of you."

Syllable-by-syllable the words slowly died away in gentle regression, replaced by low humming.

I screwed my eyes shut until my face stretched tight.

Please, God, forgive me my sins. My prayer was loud and clear in my mind as though spoken aloud. *If it be your will, spare Ted's life.*

The humming died away, devoured by a deathly quiet that fell upon a room holding its collective breath. *The silence is too much!* my mind screamed.

"Again." A whispered voice raised up a single word. Every head turned to face me. I realized the voice was my own. Song again filled the air. *Amazing Grace* reverberated through the room and touched my heart.

Angry thunder set upon the gray and gloomy mid-afternoon. Each consecutive clap, more developed than the last, pounded the windows and violently shook the plate glass. Out of boiling clouds, a vicious sword of light struck the ground. Sheets of horizontal rain thrashed the building in opposing rhythm to the thunder, nature's chaotic backdrop to the unbearable veil of sorrow, which smothered us all.

Ted's blood pressure fell to fifty over zero. The clock's hands stopped. Tensely, we waited. He rallied to sixty over thirty. "Kick its ass, Ted," a voice whispered. Nervous laughter skittered across the room.

Genuine night swallowed the remaining shadows of storm-darkened pseudo night. A strong sea breeze roared in sweeping clean the clouded sky. Sequestered stars escaped and sparkled brightly around the full moon like a spit-shined military complement. The attending nurse checked Ted's pressure again. Velcro tore free of Velcro as she removed the cuff. Acutely aware of the harshness of the noise, she leaned in to capture my downcast eyes and shook her head sadly.

Tears of dread clouded my gaze as I studied Ted's softening features. Obstinately, he clung to the few remaining vitals of a shattered life. In silent desperation, I cheered him on. Familiar faces surrounded us. All wore a singular look. I understood how not alone I was in my grief. Every eye filled with tears—only Ted's were dry. *Perhaps*, I thought, *due to a lack of cognizance, or maybe*, as I preferred to believe, *he's found inner peace. When one so special stands at Heaven's Gates, there is no room for sadness.*

The nurse threaded her way through the standing mass and slipped out of the room. In what felt like the blink of an eye, she was again at my side. She wrapped her fingers around my forearm and squeezed. "Strong hear—"she attempted to whisper. Her voice cracked and betrayed her words. She pressed her cheek against mine as though we were sisters.

Pride welled up in my chest. "Big heart," I answered, smiling through my sorrow.

One-by-one, the minute hand stretched for and finally reached each consecutive number on the wall clock's big face. More than 60 times, it completed the agonizing process. Ted's irregular, ever-softening breaths continually miscounted the seconds as though he was on a different plane of existence from the clock.

Onlookers whispered meaningless words. Faces glided in and out of the room in a natural order of change and balance that existed in the similarities of a multifaceted organism comprised of separate personalities, which in that particular moment, shared one heart. That communal heart lay incognizant at the center of a hospital bed about which the individual parts of the whole ebbed and flowed.

Draped uncomfortably over the edge of the hard bed, its rail, and my wheelchair's arm, cut into my flesh. I was a distinct part of those who filled every corner of the stifling room. Yet, I was very alone.

Dead and dying flowers drooped from cheap colored glass vases. The offensive odor of early organic decay interlaced with antiseptic offended my heightened sense of smell.

From the closet door, a loosely knotted dark blue

ribbon weakly anchored a mostly deflated Mylar balloon, emblazoned with a ludicrous *Get Well Soon*. It hung more than it floated as though waiting to fall. Blown about by the continual shifting of the visitors in the room, it wistfully drifted matching my own emotional response. Both helplessly anchored in the confines of a stagnant space, we bobbed and swayed neither one able to control our destiny. Together, we waited.

Surreptitiously, without labor or any outward sign of pain or discomfort, Ted's breathing slowed. I counted the seconds in the interval between his last breath and the next. With each consecutive one, the span of time increased. "Pop," my father's weathered countenance brightened with my call, "lift me up. Please, help me. Put me on the bed."

My dad scooped me from the chair with one fluid motion and cradled me in strong arms. "Bette-girl, you're wastin' away," he whispered. Every eye turned to me. Embarrassed by my broken body and ashamed of my wounded spirit, I buried my face in his chest. "You can't weigh more than a buck twenty, including casts."

"Daddy," a three-day stubble scratched my lips as I kissed his cheek, "you're sweet, but I weigh a buck twenty-five without the plaster."

My mother helped guide me to Ted's bed.

I squirmed uncomfortably and pulled my face up against Ted's. "I love you," I whispered. "We will see each other again, if not in this life, then the next." No larger than the head of a pin, a lone tear emerged from the corner of his left eye and crept slowly down his cheek. His breathing stopped. On the other side of the room, something shiny moved. The balloon fell the last few inches to the end of its tether and hung lifelessly from the closet door. It was precisely 8:10 P.M. Eastern time.

A sorrowful cacophony of hobbled sobs filled the room. My mother's face reflected a rare distortion of anger. The color drained from her face. She pursed her lips. "Ted." One word escaped. Her knees buckled; she collapsed like a rag doll. My father caught her just before she reached the cold tile floor.

I held my cheek tightly against Ted's still warm face. *How can a creature so thinking and vibrant be struck down so easily?* I demanded to know. *If God has a plan, how can it include the loss of one so special? Why must bad things happen to good people? In this time of miraculous technology, why couldn't you be saved? God, why him and not me? Why today instead of 50 years from now? Can't someone push a few buttons, turn some knobs, or connect a new IV, and fix this? How can everyone stand idly by and let you die?*

After a time, the room began to thin. I stubbornly refused to abandon my love. My eyes were open wounds. My legs and arms throbbed. My muscles cramped. My shattered heart labored to beat. Two whispering nurses appeared with a death package. I glared and pointed at the door.

I looked at my own broken body next to Ted's lifeless shell. A red filament bound us in an unbreakable coil like a delicate cocoon, an umbilical of our history that encompassed our memories and experiences and connected our past to our present. Beyond the coil, outside my reach in the place where I imagined our future should have been, there was nothing. Near the end of the delicate band were distinct markings from the past five weeks. They were representations of joy that quickly descended into disbelief, dismay, and non-acceptance. The final symbol at the end of the Yuan was overtly clear; it was my permanently shattered will.

I blinked. The image was gone. I was alone in a bed of despair alongside the love of my life's remains.

FOUR

MAC McKENNA COCKED his good ear toward the northwest, squinted, and appeared to hone in on some sound. I tried to force the debilitating static out of my mind. A minute later, I heard the high-pitched whine of a single-engine Cessna Centurion. My dad smiled. The red and white high-wing airplane came into view.

In the Tampa sun, we waited as the Cessna wound its way down from cruise altitude, executed a perfect landing, and taxied across the sizzling tarmac. My dad stood on one side of my wheelchair and my mom on the other. I found no joy in the friendly face from home. My only thought was of the idling hearse just beyond the chain-link fence.

"Good flight?" My dad grinned as his friend slid down from the pilot's seat. Behind him, the interior of the airplane was barren. The right front and rear seats were missing.

"Hey, Mac, good ta see ya." Gerald flashed a tentative smile and avoided looking my way.

"Smooth as silk," he answered the last of my dad's questions and reluctantly faced me. "Sorry, Bette—sorry for your loss," he said solemnly.

"Thanks for comin'," I said with a forced smile. "It means a lot to us." I nodded toward the hearse. "He needs to go home."

Gerald grimaced. "I stopped by the funeral home, and Harrison gave me the board." He pointed to a man-sized piece of plywood with oval hand holes down both sides and criss-crossed with three sets of black vinyl straps. A folded white sheet lay neatly in the center of the board secured by one of the straps.

"Yeah, Harrison told me," my father answered as he walked slowly around the rear of the plane. He dragged the fingers of his left hand down the fuselage and across the control surfaces in the fashion of a preflight check. Arriving at the passenger's door, he popped it open. Neither man spoke as they pulled the board from the plane and started toward the hearse in single file with the lightweight plywood between them. I watched in amazement as two powerful men seemed to struggle with their burden.

"Ma, I—"

"We'll wait here." She squeezed my shoulder. "Let the men take care of this."

Using aircraft-style hand signals, my dad directed the driver as he maneuvered the rear of the hearse to the Centurion's open passenger door.

"Pop, I wanna fly home with Ted." I declared loudly across the 20-odd feet that separated us. My mom started to turn my chair away from the hearse. I locked the brakes and shook my head.

"It won't work, Bette. There's no room," he said in normal tones, walking nearer. "Gerald took the seats out to get the boar—"

"I know that. I can sit on the floor behind Gerald's seat."

"Girl, don't fight me on this, please." He squatted at

my knees; we were eye-to-eye. "You're gonna need the whole back seat of the old Skylane. Even then, you won't be comfortable."

"I don't give a shit about comfort," I pleaded. "I just wanna be with Ted."

He searched my mother's face for help. She dropped her eyes signaling he was on his own. He slowly shook his head.

The thin sheet did little to hide the contour of Ted's emaciated frame. The two funeral home attendants had secured him to the board. The straps looked like they could cut him in fourths.

With my father and the two men outside, and Gerald inside the cabin, they carefully negotiated the corpse through the Cessna's doorway. My mother again tried to block my view. She stopped when I gripped her wrist so hard my fingers turned white.

Halfway in, diagonal to the fuselage, and turned nearly on its side, the body board hung precariously from straining fingers. I sensed the wind before I felt it. The gust hit, and the Cessna's high wings rocked substantially. The burst tugged at an unsecured corner of the sheet uncovering an alabaster foot. "Mac!" my mother gasped.

Like a human-sized ragdoll, with one arm and two leg casts propped helter-skelter wherever they would fit, I watched from the backseat of my Dad's Skylane. Gerald's red and white airplane broke free of Tampa's runway and quickly faded into the clear northern sky. My dad taxied into position, smoothly turned into the wind, and began our takeoff roll. A feeling of dread settled upon me as I replayed a memory of *the worst thing that can happen.*

Sullen and dejected, I picked at my food. It didn't taste any better in Birmingham than it had in Tampa.

Gerald had fueled his plane and gulped down his lunch by the time we arrived.

My father had refused to let me see Ted and carried me

directly from his airplane to the airport restaurant in spite of my protests.

Gerald drummed a nonsensical tune on the tabletop with his fingertips and glanced at the entrance at least once every couple of minutes.

"Take your time, honey." My mom smiled, ignoring my mood. "We're goin' to rest here a spell. You're exhausted."

My Dad gave Gerald an off-sided, *let's go see a man about a dog,* glance. I knew the look well. He and his favorite brother had used the same nonverbal signal on many New Year's Eves just before they disappeared on a liquor run.

Outside on the tarmac, the two men seemed intent on some subject that was obviously not for me to know. Twice, my dad threw a furtive glance in my direction. After the second time, he pointed to the north. Gerald nodded and without looking back, headed for his airplane.

"Dad, he's not leaving without us, is he?" I demanded, before he was through the door. "I want to go with Ted."

"No, Bette." He touched my good arm. "Makin' yourself sick isn't gonna do anybody any good, and it's too hot to leave the bod—Ted out there. Besides, the Centurion's a lot faster. Gerald would beat us by an hour even if we left first. You know he'll take good care of Ted." His face grew stern. "Bette, let it go. We need to—to—I wanna ask you somethin'."

My heart thrashed the inner walls of my chest. In my experience, anytime someone told me we needed to talk, it was always bad. My mother's chair scraped the tile floor like fingernails on a chalkboard as she scooted in close and took my hand. "What now?" I forced the dreaded words into the light of day.

"A nurse told your mom there was someone with you the day after the accident, just before we arrived. The description matched your ex." He grimaced. "Was he in

Tampa? Did you see him?"

Exhausted and miserable, this was the last memory I wanted to relive. "No," I answered sharply. "I'm sure it was a nightmare. Dad, I don't wanna talk about this. Mom's right. I'm tired. I wanna forget about the hospital and everything that happened there."

My mother stepped behind my chair, laid her hands on my shoulders, and whispered directly into my ear. "Sorry, Bette, I was worried, that's all."

"Okay," I gathered my strength, "let's get this over with. I was beginning to regain consciousness. I had a nightmare, and it was Leon. That's all. It didn't seem real then, and it still doesn't." My parents looked at me as if I had just told them I had cancer. "There was a voice, and it sounded like his. It was threatening, but I can't remember his voice ever not sounding like that. It was my imagination. I thought I'd died and gone to hell, and of course, he was there. He always said he'd see me in hell."

"The nurse seemed to think there really was someone there," he persisted. "Doesn't sound like a dream ta me."

"Yeah, she did say somethin' about a man, but it didn't make any sense." I paused and tried to remember exactly what the girl said. "Somethin' about she didn't know how the man got in my room."

My dad frowned. My mom squeezed my hand. "Normally, I would agree," he said. "The problem is I talked to the nurse."

"What'd she say?" I asked, terrified of the answer.

"She saw a short pudgy man with thin hair and greasy coveralls. Bette, she said he was carryin' a wrench."

FIVE

THE UNWELCOME RING of the telephone shattered the silence and catapulted my mind out of the pages of the novel where I was hiding.

"Bette, it's for you. It's David," my mom called from the kitchen.

"Tell 'im I'm busy. I'll call him back."

She spoke in low tones, and then laid the receiver on the desk. I ignored her as she quickly walked the length of the narrow living room wiping her hands on a sunflower apron with each step. She stopped in front of my overstuffed leather chair, and with motherly influence, pried my eyes from the book in my lap. Sifted flour clownishly streaked her cheeks.

"He said he's not hangin' up. He's waitin' on the line. Honey, you're gonna have to speak to him sometime." She reached for my hand.

I shrugged and didn't take her hand. *If I give up too easily on this, she'll probably want me to go outside tomorrow,* I thought.

She shook her head and looked dismayed, which under

different circumstances could have made me stand on my head. She circled the Christmas tree and plugged in the lights. "Why won't you leave the lights on?" she asked, seeming to forget about David and the telephone.

"I don't like their color, and the glare makes it hard to read. I'm perfectly happy with the glow from the fireplace." I motioned toward the crackling blaze that served as my source of comfort. "You know I have no interest in the tree or Christmas for that matter."

"Honey, you always loved Christmas," she proclaimed as though telling me what I used to like would somehow make it true again. "Now, young lady, pick up the phone and speak to your friend. He keeps callin' and you need ta talk to someone other than your dad and me. It'll do ya good."

"Hello?" I answered as if someone had shoved a spoon of castor oil in my mouth.

"Elizabeth, you alright?" David blurted out with a tense voice.

"I'm fine. Haven't wanted to talk, that's all," I answered flatly. "I need to be alone."

"Ah, sweetie, it's been almost four months. You can't hide forever. I've been worried 'bout ya. Let's get out and have dinner. We can talk about whatever you want, or nothin'. Just the two of us, okay? I won't take no for an answer."

"Alright, I'll call you tomorrow." I agreed, knowing he wouldn't believe me. "I promise." I dropped the handset on its hook.

TREE BRANCHES for fingers, the wind defiantly scratched my bedroom window and slowly drew me out of a blissful sleep. *Saturday,* I remembered, stretching my toes against crisp sheets—*no school.* It was early March. We had already begun the countdown to the end of second grade. I didn't typically like change, but I wasn't crazy about school either. The promise of summer was high on my emotional radar.

After school the Tuesday before, I stood in front of the fireplace and watched with dismay through our front window as the moving trucks arrived at the faded blue and white house across the street. I didn't see the family, but there was a boy's bike. *Crap,* I thought looking around for my mother and her notorious bar of Ivory soap. *The last thing I need is another cruel kid in my life, especially a boy.*

It didn't matter to me that I didn't have any close friends. I liked it that way. I preferred being alone.

I was eight, but not stupid. Friends ask personal questions and expect answers. Maybe I was too young to understand the concept of letting down your guard and baring your soul, however, I understood perfectly how it felt when people betrayed my confidence and talked about me behind my back. Some things of importance to me were jokes to the other kids. I knew thoughts and feelings once voiced were no longer mine. I couldn't take them back, not ever.

Anyway, it was late Saturday morning, and I was alone and happy with my kite in the vacant lot next door to our house. The temperature was mild. A biting wind stirred the sleeping grass with peak gusts and filled the air with brown, orphaned leaves long forgotten by their rooted mothers.

Kites were an extravagance around our house, so I usually made mine from tree limbs, newspaper, and homemade flour paste. My mom must have thought me melancholy this particular Saturday morning. Right after breakfast, she slid two dimes across the kitchen table and offered to drive me to the *Westend Store*.

She parked in front on the quiet street in an otherwise residential neighborhood and waited while I went inside. She trusted me to choose my own kite and string. It made me feel grown-up.

I swung open the creaky wood-framed glass door. A wonderful smell of fresh produce greeted me. Long shelves were stacked high with cans and boxes, which wore a thin veil of dust.

The floor was heavily worn tongue and groove pine. Asymmetrical paths from decades of footfalls led me down the aisles of the weathered clapboard building.

The floorboards sang to me in an ethereal language as I rushed breathlessly through the store. In a back corner, a rainbow of brilliantly colored kites protruded from a scarred wooden nail keg like giant paper wrapped toothpicks.

Twenty cents was exactly enough for one kite and a tightly wound one hundred-yard ball of twine. A flashy red one caught my eye and convinced me it would be easy to see against a blue sky.

I confidently laid my choices on the counter next to a tarnished brass cash register and held out my open hand. A man in a white apron towered over me. Without looking up, he stuffed my kite and string into a brown paper bag. "Twenty-one cents with tax, missy," he growled.

"What?" I asked startled, thinking I had misunderstood. I looked slowly from my open hand to his stern face. "Huh," I muttered.

"Gotta take care of Uncle Sam, young lady."

"Be right back," I said, then rushed out the door. The brass bell dinged a dozen clumsy notes and the huge plate glass window rattled discordantly behind me. I cleared the three concrete steps in a giant leap. My mom's window was open by the time I reached the idling car.

"What's the matter, hon?" she asked, above the howl of the wind.

"Need tax, Ma, a penny more," I answered, almost out of breath.

She nodded and pulled a copper savior from her

tattered brown purse.

I tied knotted rags to the bottom of my kite, let out some string, and attempted to hoist it into the air by dragging it through the long dry grass, which snagged the tail. I was getting nowhere fast.

Completely focused on my struggle, oblivious to everything around me, something in my consciousness suddenly changed. It was as though I had entered a comfortable room. A bundled stranger appeared on the porch of the blue and white house and ran across the street. When he reached me, his cheeks were already reddening from the sting of the wind.

"Hi," the boy, who looked to be about my age, timidly greeted me. "My grandpa saw you tryin' to get your kite in the air. He sent me ta help."

"Thanks." I forced a polite response. I didn't want company, and I was embarrassed because I needed help.

He took the ball of twine from my hand and immediately began backing into the wind feeding out line as he went.

My kite in one hand and the tail in the other, I pulled the rags free of the grass and put tension on the line. A strong gust jerked the kite out of my hand. It skyrocketed upward in a semi-controlled arc. "My name is Elizabeth!" I happily shouted over the wind.

"I'm David," he called back as he let out the string.

"BETTE, cut the shit," David said firmly. He lowered his face to the table and peered up into my downcast eyes with a stern gaze.

"I'm suffering, David." I returned his look. "I don't know what else to say."

"I know," he said. "I understand perfectly how you feel." Cradling his face in his palms, he struggled to finish. "When my sister died, you were there for me. You've been there for every challenge in my life since we were eight, since the day we first flew your red kite together. Now, I'm here for you. Like it or not, I'm here for you. Fight me if it makes you feel better, but I'm not goin' away. You've gotta talk about it—so talk to me."

"Okay, I'll try…"

By last call, the Town Tavern was a blur. David drove me home and helped me to my room.

I awoke the next morning, fully clothed, my head pounded. *At least I'm in my own bed.* I rationalized.

My intuitive mother hummed *Danny Boy* as she placed a plate of sausage and eggs on the edge of my bed. "Your dad's favorite cure." She chuckled.

"Why're you so happy?" I pulled the sheet over my head.

"'Cause you got out. You did something besides mope around here. I'll nurse your hangovers everyday if this is what it takes to get you well."

Days and weeks slowly passed. I got better, however, I never really got well. I relived the accident and Ted's final days nearly every night. Like the ringing in my ears, little-by-little, I learned to live with the memories.

"Bette, I hate to bring this up, but since it seems to be all you think about." From his end of my parent's sofa, David faced me. "Tell me again why you think the crash wasn't an accident." Nearby, the sawmill-slab fire in the limestone fireplace roared. The Christmas tree was finally gone. Even though I was a visitor in my parent's home, I treated the living room as my private sanctum.

"It's bad enough I can't stop thinkin' about it," I protested. "Talkin' makes it worse."

"I know, but if the dam's leakin', you've gotta plug the hole," he reasoned. "Without resolution, you'll never get it outta your head."

"Whatever," I acquiesced, hoping my disgust was obvious. "The engine had 39 hours on a fresh overhaul. Damn thing ran like a top. The mechanic's a friend of my dad's, and he's been rebuildin' engines his whole life." My retort was at least two octaves too high. "What're the odds?" I finished with a slightly calmer tone.

"I'm certainly not a conspiracy theorist," I added. "It's all wrong even though I feel it more than I know it."

"We've gotta find a way to settle this," David pronounced with authority. "We'll have to make our own investigation. I think we need to bring the Cessna home." He looked straight at me. "Bette, you're gonna have to face your fears."

"The Federal Aviation Administration interviewed me and examined the wreckage." I squirmed. "They ruled it was an accident as a result of a mechanical malfunction. What are we gonna find that the FAA couldn't? They didn't even think it warranted calling in the National Transportation Safety Board."

David frowned and slowly massaged his temples with his fingertips in a circular motion. "I'm sure the FAA is plenty competent. I'm equally sure an airliner crash gets a lot more attention than a single engine Cessna."

"You mean because only one soul was lost," I said indignantly.

He slid over and put his arm around me. "I'm sorry, Bette." His touch was comforting. "I didn't mean Ted's life was less important. It's how they work. It's how all government agencies and the news people work. Big tragedies are big news."

David pulled a neatly folded handkerchief from his pocket and handed it to me. "Nobody can take their eyes off a train wreck."

"I know. I don't need your handkerchief." I pushed it away. "I'm not going to spend my time cryin' about things I can't change. It's just so personal for me. Knowing Ted's death wasn't newsworthy, doesn't make me hurt any less. He may have been only one person, but he was everything to me."

I borrowed a never used easel with a flipchart from a closet at church. Using my office calendar, the Aircraft Maintenance Log, and my Pilot's Log for reference, David and I created a timeline, which accounted for every relevant hour of the 15 weeks leading up to the moment when I buried the Skylane's nose in the sand.

SIX

OUR FIRST ENTRY in the makeshift timeline was from 15 weeks before the accident. I was returning from a business trip in Detroit and felt an unusual vibration in the Skylane's engine. I landed at a midsized airport in central Illinois and had it checked. Compression varied considerably from cylinder-to-cylinder. More than half of the six were below acceptable limits.

The mechanic agreed it was flyable. "Be extra careful," he added.

Flying above 10,000 feet gave me plenty of altitude for a long glide. Following the interstate was like lining up on an incredibly long runway for the two hours it took to get home. Still, I sat on the edge of my seat the whole way. I arrived safely and didn't fly again for three weeks while my dad helped me schedule the repairs.

Saturday morning, May 22, 1999, I banked the Skylane to final and landed on a remote runway 40 miles west of Stanville. I stopped in front of the lone rusty hangar in time to see my dad smoothly follow the doglegged runway and grease his 32-year-old Cessna onto the grass strip.

A tall aging mechanic appeared in the narrow opening between massive sliding doors and hurried across the earthen apron. His blemished coveralls reminded me of someone else. I cringed. He grinned broadly through a week's growth of whiskers. "Good ta see ya, Bette." My hand disappeared between grease-stained fingers. "Been awhile, ain't it?"

Unsurprisingly, Bill and my dad spent the first hour swapping war stories. From my elevated perch on an old military aircraft seat, the only clean spot I could find in the cluttered one-man shop, I listened respectfully as the two men sat face-to-face on twin five-gallon oilcans and indulged in the veteran pilot ritual. A greasy gray cat sneered as though I had taken its bed and curled up between two yellow Labs, sleeping beneath a canopy of cobwebs in the corner. A caustic odor of used oil and fabric dope hung in the air like a mist before a rainstorm. My dad, an old time Texas crop duster and natural-born flyer, looked happier than a pig in slop.

Eventually, the stories petered out. Bill unfolded the paper I'd brought and checked the compression readings made by the mechanic in Illinois. "Yep." He nodded after marking each number on the page with a greasy fingerprint. "Hours, wear, all adds up. I kin pull the cylinders and call ya, but the answer'll be the same, Mac." Bill was looking at me and talking to my dad. "There ain't a snowball's chance in hell she don't need a major."

"Figured such," my dad answered while looking at me. "Two kinds a planes," he chuckled, "those that's broke and those that's fixin' to break." Bill slapped him on the back. Both men laughed.

Men, I thought.

"Okay," I said, stepping back so I could look them both in the eye. *I'll teach them how to get to the point.* "How long and how much?"

"Hmm." Bill scratched his chin and looked at my dad. "I reckon I can get 'er done in six weeks or so." He looked at the ceiling and wrote something in the air with the index finger of his right hand. "Labor'n parts—hmm—we're prob'ly talkin' somethin' 'round 15 thou. Just a rough guess, mind ya. I'll have ta split'er open 'fore I know fer sure."

I wasn't surprised. I had been around aircraft my whole life. "Okay," I agreed. "It is what it is. Here's my number just in case."

"You got it. Old bird'll be better'n new when I'm finished." He started toward the tail of my dad's Skylane. "Mac, I'll help ya turn the Cessna 'round."

We rotated off the ground and quickly climbed to 2,500 feet. At my dad's insistence, I flew his old airplane from the right seat. "Ted's 'bout ready to take his check ride and get his ticket," he rationalized. "You'll wanna be on your toes until he learns. Anything that can go wrong—will. There're only two kinds a plane—"

"Yes, Pop, I know. Those that are broke and those that are fixin' to."

He laughed as though he had delivered the punch line. Without looking, he positioned his worn barrel lighter over the bowl of his meerschaum pipe and struck the flint. Whoosh, a miniature ball of fire ignited and disappeared into the pipe.

"Dad, one of these days you're gonna blow yourself up. I wish I had a dime for every time I've told you this, drainin' avgas out of the fuel tank for your lighter is dangerous."

He took a satisfying drag on his pipe, exhaled smoke through his nostrils, and smiled. "Whatever you say, girl."

The next entry on the timeline was Saturday, July 3, the day my dad and I picked up the freshly overhauled Skylane.

"Be nice to have your plane home for the holiday

weekend." My dad casually commented. He observed me from the right seat of his Cessna as I lifted us off the runway at Stanville. "You have Monday off?"

Twice that morning, during the 25-minute ride from Stanville to Bill's grass strip, my dad pulled the throttle to an idle and simulated a dead engine. "You have an emergency," he announced each time. "Find a place ta set it down."

"Pop," I said, a little disgusted when he did it the second time. All the while, I was establishing a glide, searching for a suitable field, and setting up an approach. "I have more than 7,000 hours. Do you really think I need to practice an emergency every—single—time? When was the last time somebody pulled an emergency on you?"

"I do it to myself all the time." He looked away. It was an obvious exaggeration. It didn't matter. My dad could land an airplane anywhere, anytime, under any conditions, without even thinking. He and any flying machine were two halves of the same whole.

"Bette-girl, years ago, I believed a backwater Texas farmer when he told me his field was clear. I nearly got myself killed." His brow furrowed. His pipe went out. "I promised myself right then and there, my kids would be ready for anything. An hour from now, you're gonna haul your Skylane off a short, crooked runway with 10 degrees of flaps and an engine that's had every nut and bolt out on somebody's workbench and pawed by a mangy cat.

"Bill's good. That don't mean the damn thing'll run. Now, girl, tell me how you're gonna get this airplane safely on the ground."

Sitting alone in the cockpit of my newly overhauled Skylane, my dad's admonitions replayed in my mind. I edged the throttle forward. The gutsy engine turned reluctant tires in thick grass. Three inches closer to the end of the too-short, crooked runway and my left tire would have dropped into the ditch. His precise teaching voice was clear. *The runway behind will do you no good.* I glanced at the entrance to the rusty hangar. My dad appeared to be engrossed in conversation with Bill. I knew he was intently watching and listening.

I broke ground just before the dogleg, and followed the runway in a shallow climbing turn. The Cessna easily cleared the treetops at the far end.

In a steep counterclockwise upward spiral around the grass strip, the Continental engine gulped air, swilled fuel, and rapidly climbed to a safe altitude. At 5,000 feet, I leveled off, trimmed the elevators, and circled the field for an hour. On the surface far below, looking like ants, my dad and Bill never left their spot between the hanger and my dad's Skylane.

As always happens with summer's precious warm days, the six weeks after the Fourth of July weekend raced by. I had planned to log plenty of hours on the Skylane's engine. However, with only one quick business trip to Traverse City, Michigan, and too many stay-at-home conflicts, I clocked only 20 hours.

"I can help you out with that, Bette-girl." My dad offered without attempting to hide the fact, he really wanted to fly my airplane. With his joy rides and Ted's lessons, they only succeeded in adding another 19 hours.

"Okay, Bette," David turned from the flipchart, which stood in a corner of my mother's kitchen, "makin' this timeline is like watchin' paint dry. We haven't found anything odd. The airplane had 39 hours the day you left for Tampa. You said so yourself; it ran perfectly the entire way down."

"I know all that." I shook my head discouraged. "I agree. What we're doin' is shit. On paper, it all seems fine. Yet, there's somethin' not right. I told you I feel it more than I know it."

"We're never gonna figure it out like this." David fixated on the ceiling. "I was right the first time. We're gonna have to examine the damn plane." He looked at me. "Can you handle it?" he asked. "I know a guy with a truck. I can call 'im?"

I buried my face in my hands. "Okay, but I don't wanna see it. I just can't."

"I know." He stepped behind my chair and gently rubbed my neck. "I'll take care of it. I'll get it up here. Your dad wants ta help. He already told me. We'll get to the bottom of this. If it was more than an accident, we'll find out. I promise."

"There's somethin' else." I slowly began. "I think I'm emotionally out of balance. I need time to figure out how I feel. I can't do it here."

He stopped rubbing my neck and came around to the front of my chair. "What ya thinkin'?" he asked with a quizzical look.

"Remember my dad's old Aeronca 7AC? It was a green and white fabric covered tail dragger that I soloed on my sixteenth birthday."

"I remember a green and white airplane, but it's been gone a long time."

"Well, anyway, I called the FAA and tracked it down," I said proudly. "It's been restored, and the guy who owns it has agreed to sell it to me."

David plopped down on a chair and shook his head. "You never wanna talk to anyone, but you found this plane and arranged to buy it— then what?"

"Well, that's the *finding my balance* part. It's in Florida. I wanna pick it up and fly it from there to California. It'll give me time to figure this out." I gulped. "I've gotta find some kind of redemption for all I've done."

I squirmed. "David, I can't breathe. I've gotta get my head on straight. I'm like an empty shell. Every day, I go through the motions, but no one's really home. I need this. I'd like you ta understand."

"I'm here for you," he agreed, without the fight I had anticipated. "Take your trip. Take as much time as ya need. I'll stay here and help figure out what really happened with the plane. You can count on me."

I hugged him. "I knew I could," I whispered. "There's one more thing."

"Now, what?" he asked apprehensively.

"Remember what I said about an unseen force causin' the crash?"

"Yeah, I've been hopin' it was a figure of speech." He held me at arm's length. "I keep thinkin' we're lookin' for a human error, some overlooked detail in the overhaul that caused the malfunction."

"I know that's what you think." I went to the doorway to the living room and checked to make sure we were alone. "I don't want you to say anything to anyone, especially not my folks. I think it was sabotage. I don't know how or why, but I think my ex had somethin' to do with it."

David dropped to one knee in the seat of a chair and steadied himself against the high wooden back. "Wow, somehow I'm not surprised," he said thoughtfully. "I've wanted to tell you some stuff for a while now, since way back when you first told me you were gonna marry that guy. I didn't because I knew you wouldn't hear me. You were infatuated with the idea of love and some storybook version of marriage. It was like someone had replaced my friend with a *Stepford wife*."

"I always knew you didn't like L. I'm sorry to say he never liked you either. He was prob'ly jealous of our friendship. Who knows what was in his head."

"Bette, it was a lot more than dislikin' each other. To me, he was a weak, morally bankrupt, intellectually challenged parasite. In some way, he knew what I thought. His interpretation of my perceptions would've prob'ly been better described in fluent Neanderthal. All the same, he understood."

I affectionately touched David's shoulders. His big green eyes were full of sadness. "It must have been hard to hold all this in for so long. I'm sorry I put you through it. You're right, I couldn't have heard you then. I want to now."

"Thank goodness." He exhaled deeply. "I've really needed to get his off my chest, but I didn't wanna hurt ya. He was mean. I felt like I had to stand helplessly by and watch it happen. I heard about some of the things he said. I know he betrayed your trust and tried to make you sound like a degenerate. I think he saw you as his property, which meant he could treat you anyway he liked. Don't take this the wrong way, but I don't think he ever loved you. He loved what you were able to do for him—nothin' more."

"Gee," I pulled up a chair and dropped my full weight hard on the seat. "If L despises me enough, he really could be behind what happened. David, if he killed Ted, I could be next. I've never told you this. A week or so after the divorce, he ran me off the road, smashed my windshield with a tire tool, and threatened to kill me."

"Bette," David's voice cracked, "do you really think he was in the hospital in Tampa?"

SEVEN

"**B**ETTE, BETTE," David's insistent voice jerked me out of a daze, "Bette, you listenin' to me?"

"I hear you," I replied, my face pressed against the car window. I counted Interstate highway mile markers; they flashed past at a little more than one per minute.

"I didn't ask if you could hear me," he continued, frustrated. "I asked if you're listenin' to me."

I pried my eyes from the glass and glanced across the car. "What's the difference?" David had one eye on the road and one on me.

"The difference is I'm tired of listenin' to myself. Can we at least have a normal conversation before you get on the plane?"

"Whatever." I twisted stiffly in the seat. "What'd ya wanna talk about?" I pulled my left leg up under my right and faced him. I was trying not to be rude. However, I was tired of unanswerable questions. The early morning rush hour traffic on Interstate 70 in St. Louis rapidly thickened as we sped across the last few miles to Lambert airport.

He exhaled deeply. "Tell me one more time that this is the right thing to do. Reassure me. I need to know it's the only way for you to be better. I've gotta tell ya. It still feels a little nuts, you out there alone in an antique airplane you haven't seen for 26 years."

"We've talked about this a thousand times," I answered defensively. "I've played it over in my head a hundred thousand times more. Mr. Reed assures me the plane is perfe—"

"Like your dad's mechanic friend said the Skylane was like new?"

"I've triple checked everything," I said, ignoring the interruption and the insinuation. "My dad checked the logbooks, and we both talked to Mr. Reed." I switched from indignant to pleading. "David, it'll be okay. Besides, this is the only way. I'm drowning in self-pity here. I've got to get away—gotta work this out on my own."

"Alright." He took the Lambert exit. Both lanes were bumper to bumper at the light. "I just want you safe. If this is what it takes to get my Bette back, then so be it."

"Thanks," I said relieved. "It'll be daylight soon. It looks as if it's gonna be a gorgeous day." The light turned green. We barely made it through before it turned red again.

"Why'd we have to arrive at the airport three hours before your flight if it's gonna be such a beautiful day?"

"I can't sleep, and I don't wanna be late." I paused. "Besides, I like the airport. I like watchin' people who don't know me. It's like bein' invisible. It's how I'd like to lead my life."

Is this the beginning of the end or the end of the beginning? I asked myself. The First Class check-in line was unbearably long and excruciatingly slow. I scanned the calm, expectant faces patiently exchanging smiles, pleasantries, and travel plans. Their nonspecific joy angered me.

DON'T YOU PEOPLE UNDERSTAND? My mind screamed indignantly. *IT DOESN'T MATTER WHAT YOU DO OR WHERE YOU GO. IN THE END, IT'S THE SAME, DARK AND LONELY. LIFE'S FULL OF LONG LINES,   PHYSICAL   LIMITATIONS,   AND DISAPPOINTMENTS—AND THEN YOU FRIGGIN' DIE. WHY DO WE GO THROUGH THE MOTIONS LIKE WE THINK IT'LL BE DIFFERENT—LIKE SOMEHOW— WE'RE THE SPECIAL ONE?*

My frustrated mental voice gasped. The people around me leaned casually against bulging luggage, completely unaware of my plight and theirs. I was desperate to be anywhere but here, and then I realized the horrible truth. There was no place where I could find relief.

I was waiting for someone to do something, a change to occur. I used to say my greatest trait was persistence. Now, I think my only positive is my ability to breathe, and I just don't see the point.

If it weren't for my mom, dad, and David, I reminded myself, *I wouldn't have made it this far. Plenty of people told me I would get better with time. They said I would learn to live with loss, like the Doc said I'd learn to live with the stinkin' ringin' in my ears. Not a single person who said so, has left the love of their life alone in a cold grave. Only I know how I feel. Too much in my life reminds me of my biggest mistake. I have to find a way to make it stop.*

SATURDAY MORNINGS used to feel special. It was as though the spirit of all things natural granted me permission to marinate in my own thoughts.

During my mid-twenties, waking to the sound of rain against the windowpanes of my cozy 1950's style bungalow in a quiet Kirkwood neighborhood was a true joy.

Soon after my twenty-fifth birthday, the second year in

my first real job, I won the coveted Creative Contributor of the Year award for copywriting. In a much-too-bright spotlight, the company President handed me a glass and walnut trophy and told the audience that my copy pops off the page. It was the pinnacle of what I best remember as the decade of my quarter-life crises.

I was good at my work and bad at virtually everything personal. I failed miserably at relationships and quickly realized that there were things much worse than being alone. In some, *if you can't beat 'em join 'em* sort of way, I was relatively content in my solitude.

One Saturday, during the summer of the year I won the award. Behind Spencer's Grill in Kirkwood, I parked in the last spot in the postage stamp size lot. A fine mist dotted my windshield. A plate of basted eggs and sausage patties hung in my mind's eye like meat in a butcher shop. I hurried around the corner of the building with the Saturday Post-Dispatch covering my hair.

"Eggs and sausage this week, right?" The counter server with yellow hair and porcelain skin asked in a familiar tone as she poured a steaming cup of coffee.

"You got it." I nodded and smiled. "I've been dreamin' about your eggs."

"Honey, you need a man." She flashed a toothy grin and held up a shiny new engagement ring with a diamond so small I had to squint to see it. "The last thing on my mind in the mornin' is eggs." She winked and hurried away.

You don't know the half of it, sister, I thought, looking at my reflection in the brimming cup.

The door behind me rattled. A stocky, not handsome man with prematurely thinning hair blew in with a gust of damp air. I looked up. He smiled. Reflexively, I smiled back. He threw his leg over the only other empty stool two places away from my corner spot. Once settled in, he looked past the two university professors that separated us and tried to catch my eye. Thereafter, every time I looked up, he was looking at me.

I did my best to ignore him as he noisily wolfed down a tall stack of pancakes. Finished long before me, he paid his check. To my chagrin, he made a production out of asking for another cup of coffee.

The yellow-haired china doll pushed my change across the counter and discretely winked. "Thanks," I said with an *I'm not interested* look. I rolled up my paper and threw my purse over my shoulder. Ignoring my signals, she winked again.

Something like a striking snake, he popped up from his stool and beat me to the door. "Really comin' down," he commented in a guttural voice. Nodding toward the crashing rain, he swung open the glass outer door.

"Sure is," I answered, thinking that the spirit of all things natural was no doubt enjoying the joke. "I prefer a steady soakin' rain," I finished, careful to exclude emotion from my tone.

"Yeah, we could use a good soaker," he agreed. "You parked in back?"

"Yes," I grimaced. The truth was impossible to avoid.

"Me too. Come on, let's run for it." Before I could object, he peeled off his jacket and held it over my head. An inch shorter than me, he stretched to hold the coat high enough to shelter us both from the rain.

"Thanks," I said with a forced smile. *Not my type*, I thought.

"You're welcome," he shouted through the glass. "I'm Leon."

A TALL MAN in a dark blue suit sauntered past my chair with a full cup of coffee rocking on a china saucer. Still two hours until my flight to Ft. Myers, the recently opened First Class lounge was otherwise empty. Sunlight was finally beginning to fill the room. *David was right,* I admitted to myself. *It's early.*

On the tarmac below the plate glass wall, a uniformed lineman drove by on an aircraft mover. The memory of my broken airplane crept into my mind. *I wonder how they got my Cessna off the truck and into the hangar.*

FROM THE OTHER SIDE of the kitchen table, my father suspiciously nursed his fifth cup of coffee. A strong March wind roared outside. My mother scurried over with the pot. "Have another cup," she said nervously, already in mid-pour.

"What's up with you two? Is the Skylane arrivin' today?" My mom turned and slipped away. My dad stared at his ashtray. "Pop!"

"Mac," my mom said over her shoulder in a pleading voice.

He meticulously packed the bowl of his pipe with a special blend of tobacco from his worn leather pouch, lit it, and took a drag. He rolled his head all the way around once and exhaled smoke from his nose. "Yes."

"I wan—"

"No, you aren't goin' out there. We've talked about this. You don't need to see that thing, not now."

I bit my tongue. I had already had this argument with my dad and David a dozen times.

That night, when the house grew quiet, and I was convinced my parents were asleep, I slipped out and drove to the airport. I fumbled with my key in the lock. It went in, but wouldn't turn. I leaned against the cold steel door. *Why does this shit always happen to me?* I asked myself, sliding to the ground.

"Bette-girl," my dad whispered, "I was afraid I'd find you here." He stepped out of the shadows and helped me to my feet. "This is exactly why we don't want you to see her, girl." He hugged me. "You don't need a reminder of what happened."

"STILL DRY I SEE." An unremarkable raspy voice broke my concentration.

I looked up from the hardware bin where I was searching for a new power cord for a lamp.

"Leon," he said, reminding me of his name, "from last Saturday at Spencer's."

"Oh sure, I remember," I answered politely. "How are you?" I turned back to the assortment of plugs.

"Fine, how 'bout you?" he persisted. "Never did catch your name."

"Sorry," I reluctantly looked up. "I'm Elizabeth." His nearly black eyes seemed dull under the hardware store's harsh fluorescent lights. Barely visible traces of acne scars dotted his pale cheeks.

He shoved his hand into mine; stubby fingers stretched three-quarters of the way across my palm. I cringed at his touch. He shook my hand. Traces of ground-in grease outlined gnawed fingernails.

"Elizabeth." He rolled my name around his tongue. I winced. "Hmm, pretty name. Is that what people call ya?"

"No." *No way out of this*, I told myself. "My friends call me, Bette," I reluctantly answered. "Sounds like *bet* on the horses. I spell it with two "t's" and an "e" at the end," I prattled, hoping to avoid more questions.

"Look, Bette, we don't really know each other, but would you like to have lunch today?"

"I appreciate the offer, but I really have a full day," I lied. "My parents are expecting me for lunch."

I CHECKED my watch for the umpteenth time. It was still an hour until my flight. A polite server arrived with a spicy *Bloody Mary* in a tall glass and a leafy celery stalk twice its height. The First Class lounge was finally filling with business travelers. *I don't want to think about L anymore,* I chastised myself. As always, I avoided saying or thinking his name. *After too many miserable years both during and after our marriage, he still worms his way into my thoughts. Of all the people I could think about, he's the worst. He hurt me more than anyone.*

A vodka buzz kept the edge off. The gathered crowd at gate C-10 jostled for line position to board flight 270 to Ft. Myers. With gritted teeth, I wormed my way through standing bodies to the First Class pre-board queue.

My duffel slid easily into the overhead bin. With my flight case under the seat in from of me, I settled into 5C. I took three Ibuprofen and washed them down with a plastic cup of champagne. My weary muscles relaxed. I fought to stay awake until we were underway. *Sleepless nights and booze,* I thought, *a lethal combo.*

Night, for me during the previous six months, had come to be nothing more than overly long interludes between sunset and sunrise. I passed the time performing snowless, inverted angels on a single-bed in the room where I spent my childhood.

Will this trip really fix me? I posed the recurrent question. *Am I doing the right thing or just running away?*

My dad was pleased when I told him I was buying back his old Aeronca. However, neither he nor my mom understood my need to fly it coast-to-coast. "We can go down together and fly it home." He suggested almost every time the topic came up.

Am I the only person who understands, I asked myself, remembering that at times even I was unconvinced. *How does anyone know what's the right thing to do? If Ted were here, what would he say?*

My face felt strange. Maybe a little numb from the liquor, but odd even for that. I touched my lips. I was smiling. I shook my head in disbelief. *Ted always made me smile.* It felt good, exceptionally good. I closed my eyes and pictured his face. *"Carpe diem,"* he whispered. *"Seize the day. Do what you think is right. After all,*

*what's the worst thing that could happen? We can't
control the future, so let's enjoy the present. Like Robert
Frost intended, whatever path you choose is the right
one."*

Between us, Ted was never crippled by emotion or the
opinions and cruel words of others. He didn't regret
sharing his thoughts with the people in his life. He hadn't
made so many poor choices, that was my burden, mine
alone.

A bell dinged. The *Fasten Seatbelt* sign illuminated.
The Boeing 727 vibrated. We were airborne.

I dragged my fork slowly across the plate and
attempted to eat. I tossed back two glasses of red wine and
tried unsuccessfully to hide within my own consciousness.
Except for 5A, the window seat next to mine, First Class
was full. The aroma of coffee brewing filled the air and
lent flavor to muffled conversations of surrounding
passengers.

I opened a novel, a revenge thriller about a young man
drowning in his own misery, which I had started to read
the August before. I had liked the book then. Now, I
finished one page, and realized I remembered nothing of
what I had just read.

Two rows forward in an aisle seat across from me, the
animated movements of a man with two open books on his
tray table caught my eye. Transfixed, I studied him as he
highlighted sentences and whole paragraphs in the book on
his left using broad strokes. Intermittently, he stopped and
studied the book on the right. Oddly, he made no marks in
the much thicker book.

The lavatory door popped open. The *Occupied* light
extinguished. Blinding eastern sunlight flooded the cabin
through the cockpit door as the captain returned to his
station. I loosened my seatbelt and headed for the front.
One discreet glimpse as I passed the man revealed the title
of his paperback book, *How To Listen To God*. It wasn't

necessary to read the title of the familiar book on the right. It was the Bible.

Grandma Damon always said, "God is everywhere. We have to be open to what he has to say. We have to learn to listen and read the signs."

The tiny stainless steel and plastic room reeked of strong disinfectant and raw sewage. I pressed my face against the polished metal mirror. One palm on the countertop supported my weight. "I wish I had a code book," I whispered. "Why can't someone show me how to translate my life into something I can understand?" I leaned back and studied the smudge my face had made on the mirror. It was a troll's caricature with a McKenna nose and a pointy chin. It looked how I felt, *an urchin who should live alone beneath a bridge.*

Even before the familiar click of the intercom and the Captain's garbled voice rattling from worn speakers announcing our descent to Florida, a searing pain stabbed my inner ear.

"Ladies and Gentlemen, we have crossed the Florida state line. If you would like to visit the lavatory before we land, now is a good time."

From inside my flight case, I retrieved my buffalo hide journal and a fountain pen. With my index finger, I traced the raised ethereal scene on the cover and slowly unwound the rawhide-binding strap from the ornate button and flipped to the first page. Virgin paper swallowed purplish blue ink.

St. Louis to Fort Myers, Saturday Morning, April 1, 2000

I WAS 43 when the love of my life died at my hand...

The words came to me one-at-a-time. A single tear diluted random letters on the page. Disappointed, I looked at the mess and scolded myself for being too human.

My memories form my life. They are the mold of who I

have become, of who I have always been—idealistic, sometimes proud of something that doesn't exist or doesn't matter—at least not for others.

I can no longer hide behind my memories of Ted, believing that what he was will cleanse me. I have to take ownership of my life, my actions, and my mistakes.

Ted's strong clear voice rang true in my mind as he paraphrased someone's words he had once read and liked, but could never remember the author's name or the book. *"Joy shared is joy doubled, and sorrow shared is sorrow halved."* I always loved it when he said this to me.

The airliner's tires squealed in protest against the tarmac. "Welcome to Ft. Myers." The flight attendant's voice crackled over the intercom.

I pressed the journal against my lips and spoke softly. "Let the adventure begin."

EIGHT

I LAY IN BED, wide-awake as usual, on the second to the last night at my parent's home in Stanville listening to faint voices debate my past and future.

My protagonist perched on my right shoulder and in a soulful whisper occasionally reminded me of something good I had done in my life. Her opposite number, undaunted, kicked my other ear with the sharp toe of her boot and droned on regurgitating every detail of every mistake I ever made.

I futilely tried to push them both away. I wanted Ted to be the last thing on my mind before I slept and the first thing I thought of when I woke, and he was. Only, he wasn't alone.

At some point, I must have slept because I awoke disoriented. I reached out in the dark hoping to find Ted. Instead, the coarse sand-painted wall of my childhood room scratched my knuckles. Lit by a small incandescent bulb, numeric flappers on the pre-digital 25-year-old bedside clock reflected 4:31 A.M. The outside world was black. Diminished fragments of light from a distant streetlight drifted in through uncovered windows.

Friday, I remembered, *one more day until my flight to Fort Myers*. I found my dad at the kitchen table. Surprisingly, he did not greet me. A dim light in the vent hood above the propane range cast muted shadows in the airy room. Already too warm outside, the cast-iron wood cook-stove sat idly against the opposite wall even though my mother preferred it. Bubbles churned as thick black coffee percolated in the glass pot over a dancing blue gas flame.

My dad, who looked like a sinewy bear clad only in a coat of curly gray fur that blanketed his chest and arms, was deep in thought. A steaming cup sat directly in front of him next to a large square glass ashtray overflowing with mostly burnt pipe tobacco. A wispy cloud of white smoke drifted overhead like a veil of bad luck hanging over a cartoon character. I inhaled the calming aroma of coffee infused with the intoxicating burn of my father's hand mixed blend of Half & Half and sweet cherry tobacco.

I filled my own heavy stainless steel mug, which waited at my usual place on the opposite side of the table, and sat down. I took a careful sip and waited for him to look up. "Mac—"

"I hate it when you call me that. It always comes before somethin' I don't like."

"Okay, whatever, Pop. I know you're not wild about me makin' this trip, but I'm leavin' tomorrow."

"I've accepted the fact you're goin'," he said resignedly. "Jim Reed answered all my questions. I'm satisfied the Aeronca is safe." He relit his pipe for the third time since I sat down. "I'm not worried about your flyin'. I just don't understand why you've gotta leave here to do whatever it is you think you're gonna do. One place is as good as another for thinkin'. Go down to the river and stay 'til you know what you want." He paused, drained his cup, knocked the ash out of his pipe on the lip of the ashtray, and refilled both with unconscious precision. "Hell, you can talk to the fish."

I sipped my coffee and waited. Obviously, he wasn't finished.

"I don't know. Maybe you have enough money to never work again, but you loved your job." He looked away. "You shouldn't 've quit. What you do defines you. The words you put on paper have changed people's lives. I'm no expert, but how can you work through your problems without writing? It's the thing that makes you—you."

"We're talkin' about two different things." I sighed heavily. This conversation was one I never wanted to have with my dad. For me, it was something akin to the birds and the bees. "What I wrote for work targeted a specific audience with an unambiguous message. It was never about me." He looked at me with understanding. "I need time alone, away from here, from my routine, so I can focus on my feelin's. I'm hopin' the 7AC will be a connection to the past. It was the first airplane I ever flew without you. In many ways, it's my *Rosebud*." I hoped my dad would recognize my reference to a lost childhood as portrayed in the movie *Citizen Kane*. "I wanna be in a place where I have no reason or expectation ta talk. Pop, I just can't do it here. I don't wanna talk ta the damn fish."

He chuckled. His eyes softened. In a small way, I was relieved.

"You're right. I need to write. Ted gave me a leather journal, you might say a diary, our first Christmas together. I've been carryin' it around since the funeral. Startin' tomorrow on the plane, I'm going to record my thoughts and feelings every day." I rose and quickly retrieved the book from its hiding place beneath my pillow. I laid it on the table in front of my dad.

"Until I've dredged up some old memories and forced

myself to interpret them, I don't think I'll ever find peace. It's about being able to understand and accept myself for who I am. I need to be happy in my own skin."

He dropped his eyes. "It's the family curse," he muttered. "Paranoia, mistrust, restlessness, it's all plagued the McKennas for generations since way back before the family left Ireland. I hoped it would miss you.

"Besides, what about your friends?" He paused awkwardly between questions. "What about your house? Have you even been there this winter?"

"I went once," I answered, relieved we were finished discussing the family curse. "I love that house, but they're too many painful memories inside. I can't bring myself to sell it. I need to wait and see."

He repacked his pipe.

"Pop, tell me everything you know about the crash."

He stared at the ashtray. "Not much to tell really. We had quite a time gettin' the engine out of the plane. It was balled up in the firewall. We used saws more than wrenches and finally got it out without a lot of damage. We've cleaned the case. Now we're takin' it apart one piece at a time and shootin' pictures as we go."

"You have a theory?" I pushed him. "Come on, Pop. I can take it. Tell me."

He padded over to the stove. His bare back was slightly less hairy than his chest. Baggy khakis hung from a rail thin waist. Tense muscles outlined a lithe, powerful frame. I crossed the room and draped my arm over his shoulders. We must have looked quite the pair—me in pajamas, and he in rumpled slacks. Even in bare feet, I stood one inch taller. With morning hair, it probably looked more like three. "It's okay, Pop, really. I can handle it."

He dumped the dregs from the pot into his cup and made a fresh pot by spooning coffee from the can over the used grounds in the combination glass and aluminum basket. "No sense wastin' coffee," he remarked.

"Here's what I think." He turned up the blue flame. "It had to start with the connecting rod bolt in the left front cylinder. Maybe it wasn't properly torqued, or it could've been a flawed bolt. Anyway, when it sheared off and the spark plug fired in the power stroke, it ejected the piston and the rod out into the center of the engine case. The case wall is relatively thin there. When the crankshaft came around, it rammed the entire mess straight up through the aluminum. It made a hole something like 12 inches in diameter from cylinder base to cylinder base. I've never seen anything like it. It would have all happened in seconds."

He looked at me, trying to gauge my reaction to his words, and then returned to the table. "When all that shrapnel ripped through the cowling, it's what you described as an explosion. The prop probably stopped when the piston was wedged between the engine case and the crankshaft." He fidgeted with his pipe and coffee. I waited.

He continued in a much lower voice as though he was afraid someone was listening. "All of the oil, something close to 12 quarts, soaked the inside of the cowling. Enough made it through the hole to cover the windshield. Fuel entering the open cylinder through the intake valve and igniting when the spark plugs fired, caused the fireballs. If you hadn't cut the fuel when you were ready to land, the whole thing would've probably caught fire on impact."

"Man," was all I could muster. The images of those horrible seconds were clear in my mind.

"It's a miracle the engine ran at all." He shook his head. "I've never even heard of anything like this. If you've ever wondered if God protects us, this should remove all doubt. There was no oil to lubricate the engine, on fire, and a huge hole in the case. The thing should've just froze up. With raw fuel continually pumping into a confined space, it could easily have exploded." He lifted his muted blue eyes from the table and fixed them on mine. They were a mirror image of my own.

"Wish I'd been there." He propped his elbows on the table and cradled his face in his palms. "Not because I could've done a better job. I'd just like to know I could've done as well as you." The Mac McKenna who sat before me in this moment was a version of my father I did not know.

"I've been flyin' my whole life," he said pensively. "I've had a few scrapes and always came out fine. Nothin' like this ever happened to me. What you did, the way you kept your cool and flew the plane was nothing less than incredible. Bette-girl, I'm proud of you."

"Thanks, Daddy." I smiled. "You would've done exactly the same or better. I know you would've. I constantly remind myself of how you flew yourself out of the power lines when you were dustin' in Texas. It's why I'm always ready for anything, like you taught me." I touched his hand. "I would've felt safer if you'd been there. I always feel safe with you. Maybe you could've saved Ted.

"It's funny, well, not funny ha-ha, funny strange. It was as though you were with me in the cockpit. A couple of times, you reminded me what to do. I even thought of some situations we'd been in together. The memories were interminable, even though it all happened so fast."

He took my hand. Thick calluses scraped my skin. "You did everything possible. Never blame yourself for what happened to Ted. Your mother's right. It was God's will."

AT THE EPICENTER of the welcoming throng in the Ft. Myers airport terminal, a small piece of cardboard crudely imprinted with *Elizabeth* protruded above an uneven sea of bobbing heads. I pushed through the crowd to the small man holding the sign. A tiny woman hung on his arm.

"Mr. Reed?" He turned to me and smiled.

"Elizabeth?" He reached for my hand. "Call me Jim. Welcome to Ft. Myers."

The frumpy woman wrapped her arms around me and squeezed. "I'm Mabel, honey. We're glad you're here."

Jim Reed was an inch shorter than my dad and wore a bleached-white tee shirt, jeans, and cowboy boots. A faded red DeKalb Seed cap was cocked over closely cropped salt and pepper hair. A well-worn meerschaum pipe hung from his teeth.

Mabel stood no more than five-feet two-inches tall with soft features and thin hair, grayer than her husband's. A blue polka-dot dress hung loosely from her thin frame. The Reeds looked more like brother and sister.

"Call me Bette, everybody does. I really appreciate you pickin' me up. I hope it wasn't too much of an inconvenience."

"None at'll." Muscular hands pulled the green canvas bag off my shoulder. He looked hard at my saddle-brown leather flight case. Seeming to understand its significance to me, he did not attempt to take it. "Mable'd kick my butt if I let a lady carry her own bag." He smiled broadly. "Truck's out front." He held his cold pipe by the bowl. With the chewed stem, he pointed at the glass double doors.

"You remind me a lot of my dad," I remarked as we started across the lobby.

"I thought you'd think so," Mabel remarked offhandedly. She nervously slipped her arm through mine and squeezed.

Why would she think that? I wondered as we crossed the street side-by-side, me in the middle.

Mabel insisted I ride shotgun and climbed into the faded green pickup first. We headed east into Florida's ruralopolis. Over Mabel's shoulder and through the back glass, only a little of my duffel was visible from its place in the grimy truck bed on top of an empty feed sack where Jim had casually tossed it.

Astraddle the floor shift, Mabel was nearly oblivious to everything around her and talked nonstop like an overly embellished Saturday morning cartoon character. Every time Jim pulled the shifter back, it lifted her skirt whereupon she squirmed, uttered a protestant squeal, and pushed her hemline back to her knees.

I bit my tongue to keep from laughing and tuned out their conversation. With my fingertips, I traced the edges of my flight case, which was securely stored behind my legs. Hidden behind dark glasses, I squeezed my eyes tightly shut against the glare of the baking midday sun and blindly massaged the leather. When my index and second finger found the textured spot on the case's surface, where I knew there to be a large heavily scrubbed Rorschach, I held my breath and refused to succumb to sadness.

After the funeral, my father had changed the subject every time I asked about my flight case. He finally returned it more than a week later. The moment I saw it, I knew he had scrubbed away bloodstains.

"…we're 'riginally from Iowa, ya know." Mabel tapped my arm as if she knew I wasn't listening. "We don't get many visitors from up north anymore." She stopped and peered behind my glasses to see if I was paying attention. "I guess the new wore off. There's plenty of snowbirds down here every winter. We don't generally see 'em. They don't have much use for agriculture unless it's cooked and on their plates. We never go to the beach. Always too much ta do 'round the farm. We also have a part time hand, Billy. He likes takin' our produce to the Farmer's Market. Thinks he'll meet a girl there. I told him if'n he does, she'll prob'ly be a good cook." Mabel laughed at her own joke and continued without waiting for a response. "Anyway, he's the one who sees the tourists.

"Bette, I'm sure we're gonna have such a nice visit. You know you're welcome ta stay as long as ya want. Jim's not much for talkin'. You'n me 'll have ourselves a good ole time!"

Jim Reed tossed a sympathetic glance my way, rolled his eyes, and turned his attention back to the narrow two-lane road.

Mabel continued her incessant chatter with only short breaks for the next 30 minutes. I was considering crawling out the window when Jim wheeled into a chat driveway and ground to a halt in a barnyard amidst a ménage of cream-colored tin buildings with green roofs.

The sweet smell of freshly cut grass and newly tilled soil emanated from every corner of the place. A two-story rectangular barn was the largest of the regiment of stoic sentries, which surrounded a much smaller house. Close to the neatly mowed grass strip, massive double doors hung from heavy-duty galvanized hinges at the center of the barn. Two small asymmetrically positioned casement windows, high on intersecting walls, were near the corner of the building and away from the house.

"My office is in the hayloft," Jim noted, following my gaze to the windows.

Crops radiated out from the buildings in long straight rows, as spokes in a wheel. Staked tomatoes comprised the eastern cardinal heading. Watermelons to the south, cucumbers the west, and the already majestic spring corn distinctively pointed toward true north.

In the center of the lush lawn, I stopped and one at a time faced each direction feeling like a Lilliputian standing on the axis of a giant's compass rose.

"Somethin' isn't it?" Jim asked with a sheepish grin. "Sort of pilot meets farmer kinda thing."

"I've never seen anything like it," I answered with genuine awe. "It's an organic compass. Are all of the farms around here like this?"

"Oh, no, most are about the same size. Ours is the only one laid out in a circle. I've even been asked if it's some kind of alien markings." He laughed. "It was kinda fun to create. Sure makes findin' the farm from the air a cinch.

"Folks 'round here usually call operations like this a *truck farm*. They call my place an airplane farm." He pointed first to a lackadaisically drifting faded-orange windsock mounted on the peak of the barn above the office windows, and then to a manicured east-west strip, which bordered tomatoes and cucumbers on the south side. "We sell everything freshly picked to the local supermarkets or the Farmer's Market that Mabel mentioned. It's a whole lot different from the farmin' I did in Iowa, but we like it here. I can fly my plane year-round, and we aren't freezin' our asses off."

"My dad would love this." I smiled.

"Yep, he sure di—" Jim caught himself and turned away. "I'm sure he would."

"Jim Reed," Mabel yelled from a flowerbed a few feet away where she was adjusting an irrigation head. "James Edward," she added in a disgusted tone as she huffed across the lawn and stopped nose-to-nose with her husband. "We promised."

"You promised what?" I demanded as the oblique comments began to add up.

"Honey, I'm sorry." She pushed her husband back and stood between us. "The cat's outta the bag." She gave Jim another dirty look. "Your mom and dad were here a month ago. Your dad came to check the plane himself. They wanted to make sure you'd be okay, that's all. We promised to keep it a secret. Obviously, my husband isn't too good at that."

I looked past her. Jim's eyes were riveted to the grass. He fiddled unconsciously with his pipe. "Sorry," he muttered.

"You should be." Mabel's eyes narrowed. "You gave

them your word."

"That explains a lot," I said, recalling my parents' unprecedented break in routine.

"Out of the blue one Friday last month, they said they were going to fly my dad's Skylane to Indianapolis for the weekend to see a sick friend. It seemed odd because the friend happened to be the same guy my dad sold the Aeronca to." I shook my head in disbelief. "They didn't go to Indy at all."

Jim smiled. "They didn't tell us that part. Was the guy, George Stubbs?"

"How'd you know his name?"

"That's who *I* bought the Champ from." He relaxed and lit his pipe. "Small world."

"What'd they tell you about me?" I pried. In our numerous phone conversations, Jim and I hadn't shared much personal information.

"Not mu—"

"She knows they were here." Mabel interrupted. "Let's not make it any worse, no more secrets."

"I guess they told us everything, honey." She lowered her eyes. "They told us about the accident—about Ted."

"We're real sorry for your loss," Jim added.

"Thanks—it's okay. I would've eventually told you," I said with difficulty. "It's one of my many flaws. I always say what's on my mind."

"Jim," Mabel impatiently stamped her feet, "this girl flew all the way down here to see her little airplane. What are we thinkin'? Take her out there. "

Jim grinned and unlike a man in his late sixties, sprinted toward the barn.

Mabel and I followed. We took no more than two quick steps before I heard the creak of heavily weighted, salt-corroded hinges. Jim swung the first wide door open. By the time we reached the barn, he had the second painted metal door open and propped against the wall.

It had been a lifetime since I last saw the little airplane. Nearly everything about my life had changed, however, not the machine, at least not much. Jim had sent me plenty of photographs both inside and out. I studied every detail of the logbooks. Still, I was unprepared for the bittersweet emotion that washed over me at the sight of the airplane.

She was like an old friend, an anchor from my childhood, a functional work of art. Aeronca Aircraft Corporation manufactured her in 1947, designated her 7AC, and more appropriately labeled her the *Champion*.

I touched her tightly stretched skin; my hand trembled.

"Oh, honey," I felt Mabel's steadying grip on my shoulders, "take your time—we'll leave you alone," she cooed.

Even though I felt foolish, she was right. I wanted to be alone with the Champ. I circled her twice, slowly. Finally, I gingerly touched her slick, tight green and white fabric again and then affectionately flicked her with my index finger. She answered with the rich reverberation of a finely tuned drum. "You don't know how happy I am to see you," I whispered as if I had slipped into church after the bell.

Stooped beneath the wing, on the right side of the aircraft, I hooked two fingers in the handle of the only door and gently tugged. The well-lubricated mechanism popped open. Inside the forward half of the cockpit, I made myself at home on the thinly padded brown leather pilot's seat, which was an ergonomic match for me. The walnut knob atop the black metal control stick between my legs fit my hand perfectly.

In a shallow recess on the left side, opposite the door, I traced the magneto's switch, the throttle, and the fuel valve. The heels of my boots slid easily across the tightly woven brown carpet to the rudder pedals and brakes. Every detail was exactly as I remembered.

"I was only eighteen when I last saw you," I reminded

her. "You didn't look this good then. Your annual inspection came due the day after the last time we flew together. Your fabric was soft and weak. You needed a major overhaul. They took your wings off and hauled you to Indianapolis on a truck."

"You hungry, Bette?" Mabel startled me. "It's gettin' late. Why don't you come in for dinner?"

"Mabel's right," Jim chimed in. They had apparently been waiting just around the corner. "We'll roll 'er outside first thing in the mornin', and I'll get you checked out. Your dad said it won't take much to get you back in the saddle, said you're a natural."

After dinner, Mabel reluctantly agreed to let me help clear the table and wash the dishes. Jim disappeared.

"He's gone to the barn to smoke his pipe. I think he likes it better out there," she said, shaking her head.

I dried the last cast iron pan and handed it over. "Mabel, what else did my mother tell you?"

"I'll swan to Lolly, Bette." She pushed a plate of freshly baked cookies across the kitchen table. "You're as sweet as your momma."

"Thanks. I really wanna know." I took the topmost snickerdoodle from the pile. "Please."

Mabel wiped her hands on her apron. "I guess she told me your whole story."

I swallowed the last half of my cookie and came around the table. "Then she must have told you I'm gettin' a little better every day."

"She did. What happened to you makes me wanna share my story," she said softly with downcast eyes.

"Don't, if it makes you sad," I said sympathetically, trying to mask my curiosity.

"It's okay. It's been a long time. I've made peace with myself. I want to tell you. I think you need to hear it."

For a long time, we sat across the table from one another in silence.

"Jim isn't my first husband." Mabel slowly lifted her gaze until she was looking directly at me. "My ex was a beater—exactly like yours," she explained, demonstrating she really did know my sordid tale.

"I wish my mother hadn't burdened you with my problems," I apologized.

"Oh, honey, it wasn't her idea. We were gettin' along famously, and I decided to confide in her." Mabel leaned in and touched my hand. "She didn't tell me anything about your ex until after I told her 'bout mine."

"And now you want to tell me, too?" I whispered.

"Yes, maybe it'll help if you know you're not alone." She took a cookie from the plate.

"I married my high school sweetheart right after we graduated. I had no clue he wasn't right. Goodness sakes, I didn't even know what a narcissistic sociopath was back then. He was so sweet. Our senior year, he was the star of the basketball team. Everybody loved him. By the end of our first year of marriage, he was beatin' me at least once a week. He always said it was all my fault. He said he could've gone to college, but he didn't 'cause of me. Every day he reminded me that I ruined his life. He blamed me for everything"

Mabel told her story as though it was someone else's. From time-to-time, her eyes moistened. Some of the details were so similar to my own experience they made me cringe.

"I didn't want to leave Iowa. He never asked my opinion. He only said we were moving to Nashville 'cause he'd found a weldin' job there. I was a stranger in a strange place with no family or friends. Every day he treated me more and more like an unwelcome mutt.

"I stuck it out though. After eight years of marriage, we were still in Tennessee. By then, every time he touched me it made me sick. Once, when he was drunk, he tried to kiss me, and I pulled away. He beat me so badly I had to call an ambulance.

"He never even came to the hospital. They released me after two days. I took a taxi home. I was alone in the house and barely able to feed myself. He was nowhere to be found. I was too embarrassed to call *my* family, so I called his sister. I thought she was my friend. She drove down and picked me up. On the way back to Iowa, I told her everything.

"It made her angry, but not at him. She was mad at me. She told me that it's a wife's responsibility to take it. She said her brother was a good guy, and I must've provoked him. When I got home, I told a few close friends. No one believed me." She sighed deeply. "Bette, they thought I was exaggeratin'."

"I know," was all I could say.

"Somehow, he knew when I was well, 'cause he showed up one day, put me in the car, and drove nonstop back to Tennessee without ever sayin' a word. I was terrified the whole way.

"Nothin' changed. When I turned 26, it really got worse. He must've been bored with me, 'cause he was always tryin' new ways to scare me. He bought a gun. After that, every time he drank he'd pin me down on the bed, hold his pistol to my head, and threaten me.

"Six months of that, and I began to pray the gun would fire and put me out of my misery. Twice, he ripped my clothes off and raped me 'cause he didn't like me cryin'. A week after the second time he raped me, I ran away. I got out with only the clothes on my back.

"It was a chore, but I went back to Iowa and finally got a divorce. When I was 30, I met Jim. He was the kindest, gentlest man I had ever known. Even then, every time the phone rang or someone knocked on the door, I hid. Thirty years ago, we moved down here and started fresh. I still lock the doors when Jim's outta the house. Thinking about those days gives me an uneasy feelin'."

I pushed my chair back from the table and crossed my legs. "It's like you're describing my life with L," I said.

She gave me a questioning look. "Your mother never told me his name."

"I'm not surprised. She knows I try never to say it. It's Leon—Leon Berger."

Mabel's serious expression evaporated. She snorted, chortled, and then burst out laughing. Incredulous, I watched as she tried several times to stop.

"I'm sorry, hon!" She dried her tears. "I just couldn't help it."

"What's so funny?"

"You really don't know?"

"I have no idea."

"It's his name, Leon Berger. It's a dog breed." She held her stomach. "I'm really sorry. It just struck me as hilarious. Your abusive ex was a dog." She chuckled.

Her laughter was contagious. Mabel made a face, barked, and repeated his name. Every time she did, we howled a little louder until Jim came running into the kitchen.

"That does it." I struggled to say the words between guffaws. "I don't ever have to say his name again." I made my own version of a bark. "I'll just call him *Dawg*!"

NINE

"**N**OW IT ALL makes sense." I looked across the breakfast table at Jim Reed. "You accepted my offer and agreed to sell me the Champ the Monday after my folks were here."

He stared at his plate.

"Jim, did you sell me the plane because you felt sorry for me?" I asked, embarrassed. "Did my dad talk you into doing something you didn't want to do?"

He looked up abruptly. "Oh, no, Bette, I didn't do it for any of those reasons, although, your dad's pretty convincing." He dropped his fork on his plate and looked straight at me. "Mabel told me about your conversation last night, so I know I can tell you this now. I didn't do it because I felt sorry for you. I did it because of what happened to Mabel and for all of the abused women in the world. Bette, you need the airplane more than I do. Sellin' you the Champ was no sacrifice."

"OFF AND CLOSED WITH BRAKES," I shouted with only a twinge of nervousness. I sat alone in the front seat of the Champ with my back to the barn. It had taken

10 minutes to convince Jim I didn't need to be checked out. I knew I would be fine alone, even though it had been 26 years since the last time.

Jim had installed an aftermarket electrical system and starter. However, I asked if he would hand prop the engine *for old time's sake.*

Wearing a broad smile, he pulled the polished aluminum propeller through twice. With each turn, he swung his right leg in and then pitched it back and out throwing his weight against the prop and stepping safely away.

I pulled my red St. Louis Cardinal's baseball cap down and shielded my eyes from the glare of the low morning sun. A diverse concoction of gas and oil mixed with the sweet smell of a vegetable garden in spring reminded me of an unusual bouquet that Jim described as *farmer meets pilot.* With my heels pressed hard against the brakes, I pulled the stick all the way back into my lap, cracked the throttle, and clicked the magneto lever to both.

"CONTACT—BRAKES," I called through the open door.

The 53-year-old engine sparked on the first hot pull. In seconds, the tachometer showed 1100 Revolutions Per Minute. Jim straddled the landing gear and blocked us from the wind by leaning against the inside of the open door.

"SOUNDS GREAT," I shouted, over the steady beat of the normally aspirated engine.

Jim smiled and nodded. "You sure you wanna do this alone?" he asked again with a tinge of concern. "Been awhile since you flew a tail dragger. By rights, I should prob'ly check you out."

I pulled the throttle back. The engine idled easily at 600 RPM. I squeezed his arm. "I'll be fine."

He nodded, stepped back, and latched the door.

The tattered windsock gently wagged its tail in the

tepid breeze and pointed to the east. I locked the left brake, pushed hard on the left rudder, and advanced the throttle. The nose swung around 90 degrees.

At the western most end of the grass strip, two perpendicular fences converged at one of four corners of the Reed farm. With the brake tightly locked, I pivoted around the stationary left wheel. The tail passed within inches of the fence. Like always, my father's precise instructor voice resounded in my mind. *"Runway behind you will do you no good."*

I inched the throttle forward and stopped the tachometer needle on 1,500 RPM. I turned the rotary switch to each individual magneto, noted an acceptable 75-RPM drop for each, and then set the switch back to both. I relaxed and slowly pulled the carburetor heat knob all the way out. The engine speed again slowed by 75 RPM. I sighed. Savoring the moment, I took an inordinate amount of time for the preflight. I tested the control function of the rudders, elevators, and ailerons. I took a deep breath, turned the plane into the wind, and pushed the throttle lever to its stop.

With the control stick three-quarters forward, in the first 100 feet, the tail began to fly. I eased the stick back, brought the elevators to a neutral position, and leveled the tail with the main gear firmly on the ground. In the next 100 feet, the lightweight airplane reached flying speed. A slight backpressure on the stick lifted us out of the grass. Jim and Mabel waved wildly as we climbed past the barn.

I circled the field in a smooth climbing turn and commanded myself to focus on the flying. I had intended to be alone in the cockpit. Instead, I sat amidst the crowded confines of adamant memories, both good and bad.

My father's stern voice came from the empty back seat. *"Bette, get the pigs out of the cockpit."* A ghostly aroma of burning Half & Half with cherry blend tobacco caused me to glance over my shoulder to be sure, he wasn't really there.

Ted whispered in my right ear, *"I'm proud of you, sweetie."*

My relentless antagonist, a squatter, who lived on my left shoulder, scolded me with a threatening voice. *"Stupid bitch, you can't escape your past."*

I attempted to ignore the cacophony of voices and focused on the Spartan instrument panel. The altimeter needle swept slowly past 3,000 feet.

My antagonist repeated herself. *"Stupid bitch!"*

"ALL OF YOU LEAVE ME ALONE," I shouted. "LEAVE ME BE." I brushed my left shoulder as though I could sweep the little demon away, even though I knew it was going to take a lot more than a simple hand gesture. *After all,* I reasoned, *that's why I'm here.*

The altimeter eventually passed 4,000 feet. A familiar sense of dread ran down my spine. A stench of gun oil and greasy sweat replaced the comforting smell of my dad's pipe. A small imaginary circle of cold steel pressed hard against my temple. *"You think you're so smart—uppity cunt."* My ex-husband's cruel words slashed through my consciousness.

My insufferable antagonist cheered him on. *"Kick 'er ass, boy. She brought it on herself. She shoulda learned to take it!"*

A veil of red fell upon my mind.

"Just so you know, your life's in my hands." The sinister voice laughed. Trapped in Leon's familiar vice, I felt his coarse hand grip my throat as clearly as if he was there. *"I decide if you live or die—just so you know."*

"BETTE," my father shouted.

I shook my head. My mind cleared. Sunlight blinded me. I found myself locked in a spin. Directly below, centered in the windshield, the swirling green roof of the Reed barn was 3,000 feet and closing rapidly. G-force threatened to turn my world black.

"*BETTE,*" my father shouted again. "*FLY THE AIRPLANE!*"

"Not today, Dawg. You won't get me today!" I answered.

I released the controls. The plane immediately rolled out of the spiral. The pressure lifted from my chest.

"GET OUT OF MY AIRPLANE," I screamed. "GET OUT OF MY LIFE, YOU SON-OF-A-BITCH!"

ON THE THIRD consecutive Saturday morning, after I first saw Leon Berger, he nonchalantly walked into Spencer's Grill while I was eating breakfast. He didn't exactly try to sit with me. Instead, he left one stool between us, and made occasional offhanded remarks. I answered when it was unavoidable and kept my distance. I never initiated anything. I knew what I liked in men. He wasn't it. Maybe, it was a beer belly or a hereditary pudge. Whatever the reason, he carried at least an extra 15 unappealing pounds among other undesirable physical traits.

Three Saturdays is enough, I told myself. *If he's followin' me, I'm gonna have to give up breakfast at Spencer's.* The coffee in my cup had cooled, and I blamed him. I had tried being polite. He wouldn't leave me alone. I squirmed on my stool hoping to get the girl's attention and ask for the check.

"What do you do?" he asked.

"I'm a copywriter," I answered flatly, careful not to return his look. The waitress, with her back to me, was engrossed in conversation with the giant cook who was so tall he had to stoop to put his head under the grill's stainless steel exhaust hood. *Turn around*, my mind futilely called to her pleading for a reprieve from the unwanted attention.

"I'm an aircraft mechanic," he volunteered proudly. "I

work at *Spirit of St. Louis Airport*."

I faced him. "I'm sorry, what?" I asked, suddenly curious.

"I'm an A & I. That's a mechanic licensed to work on airplanes and inspect them."

"I know what it is," I said incredulously. "I'm a pilot."

"Really? That's great. Would you like to see our shop sometime? We maintain corporate jets."

"Are you kiddin'—I'd love to." It was too good an opportunity to pass up. "I love airplanes, and I've always wanted to look around one of those big maintenance hangars."

When I think back, I realize, even though I thought his gradual courtship was a series of unplanned events, it was a carefully orchestrated conquest. He understood me perfectly. He knew exactly what to say. Nearly every conversation included something about airplanes. I began to forget about his big ears, acne scars, and pudgy body. I came to see a soft-spoken man who shared my interests, and genuinely cared about what I thought. Most of all, he came into my life when I was lonely.

Once, I mentioned dark chocolate was my favorite. The next time he picked me up, he brought a box of assorted dark chocolates. I said I liked the movies. After that, he always knew what was playing in the local cinemas.

He never missed an opportunity to tell me how wonderful and beautiful I was. He complimented everything I did. I was the focus of our conversations. When we were together, bombarded by all things wonderful, I experienced a feeling of elation. In many ways, it was an extreme emotional high. When we were apart, and too busy to talk by phone, I fell into a shallow depression.

"Leon gets me," I told my mother on the telephone. "For the first time in my life, a man truly understands me. Mom, he cares about what I think."

He represented the end of a series of disappointing relationships. Men seemed to have only one thing on their minds. I was amazed when a seemingly nice man would take me to dinner and later turn into a monster when I refused to reciprocate with a physical reward.

Leon Berger patiently chipped away my protective barriers. I opened up and began to recite the details of my life, my fears, my dreams, and finally—my secrets.

"BETTE," Mabel Reed's soothing voice accompanied the soft knock on my bedroom door and snapped me out of a half-sleep, "telephone, it's your dad."

I staggered stiffly to the kitchen supporting my uneven steps with walls and furniture. Mid-morning sunlight flooded the high-ceilinged room. A complex aroma of from-scratch soup and homemade bread hung in the air. Mabel was busily arranging flat meats and thick irregular slices of hand-kneaded sourdough on a bright red platter. The telephone handset lay near the edge of the variegated-green granite countertop.

"Mornin', Pop, everything okay?" I held my breath half-expecting bad news.

"Everything's fine here, girl." His warm voice bolstered my spirits. He paused and took a deep pull on his pipe. I smiled. "It's your third day away. We wanted to make sure you're okay."

"I'm fine."

Mabel gave me a worried look. It occurred to me, she thought my voice might betray the fact that they had told me about my parent's clandestine visit. I promised her I wouldn't say anything. "It's beautiful here," I said consciously upbeat. "I wish you could see Jim's airport. The Champ's perfect. You'll be pleased. She looks and flies like a dream."

Mabel sighed with relief and returned her attention to stirring thick corn chowder in a deep cast iron pot with a wooden spoon.

"Good," he said.

My mother whispered in the background.

"Your mother wants to know how long you'll stay there?"

"I'm thinkin' 'til Wednesday. Weather shows a high-pressure area movin' in and the flyin' should be perfect. Tomorrow morning, I wanna put a few hours on the Champ and do some aerial sightseein'. I can get 'er washed and ready to go in the afternoon."

"You aren't goin' to Crystal River are ya?" He blurted out apprehensively. "Dwelling on that night isn't good for you."

"No, Dad, I won't go there. I have no desire to ever see that place again." I reassured him and me. "This trip's about healing. I can't continue to relive the accident."

His lighter clicked. Even on the phone, the super small gasoline explosion sounded like a miniature blast furnace. My mother's whispered voice was barely audible over the sound. "Don't bring it up."

"Dad, what's she talkin' about?" A chill ran down my spine. "Don't bring what up?"

"Nothin', really. We found somethin' odd on the Skylane engine."

"What—what'd you find?" My heart pounded.

"Somethin' I've never seen before," he said deliberately. "David and I stripped the engine down to the case, washed all the parts, and laid 'em ou—"

"Mac, get to the point. What'd you find?"

"On the fuel line, an inch from the carburetor, we found a clear plastic membrane like a tube. It looks like some kind of heat shrink. It was mostly intact. I removed it with a razor blade." He stopped.

"And what?" I demanded.

Mabel stopped stirring and stared at me with wide eyes, her skin suddenly ashen. I dragged the long telephone cord behind me as I crossed the room headed for the back porch. I covered the phone with my palm. "I'll tell ya later," I whispered to Mabel as I slipped out the door.

Outside, with the receiver pressed tightly against my ear and my back against the wall, I slid stiffly to the wood floor. "What else—what is it—what does it mean?" My voice cracked.

With the exception of my father's shallow breaths, the line was quiet. Finally, he began. "There was a one-sixty-fourth inch hole drilled in the fuel line."

"Drilled?" My heart constricted.

"I'm positive. There's no tellin' how long it's been there. Maybe it was always there, and we missed it. I talked to Bill. He doesn't know anything either."

"Surely, when Bill did the overhaul, he would have noticed a piece of plastic on a fuel line," I reasoned. "Wasn't it obvious?"

"It was to me," he answered factually, "but I was lookin' for somethin'." He paused again. "On the other hand, by all rights, the plastic should've melted within the first couple of hours of flight and leaked fuel everywhere. It's a miracle it didn't. It must have had exactly the right amount of airflow to keep it cool."

"What are you sayin'?"

"The hole had nothin' to do with the engine failure. It didn't melt enough to release any fuel. It's not what caused the accident, but it was intentional. It was sabotage."

"Bette, Bette, you okay?" Mabel's frightened voice penetrated the heavy red fog that covered my consciousness. "JIM, GET OVER HERE!" she shook me and screamed.

My vision slowly cleared. Mabel's beet red face was close to mine. Her hot gasps filled my nose. "I'm okay," I muttered. "What happened?" I was flat on my back on the porch.

Mabel gently pried the telephone from my hand.

"Mac," she began speaking into the receiver before it was completely free of my grasp, "Bette's alright. It was just a little faint." She pressed the receiver to her ear and softly stroked my cheek with the back of her hand. "Don't worry. I'll call you right back."

"I fainted?" I asked, trying to remember my father's last words.

"If you can call it that," Mabel said as she helped me into a sitting position against the wall. "You were talkin' and all of a sudden I heard a thump. I found you with your eyes wide open. You were out cold. I'll swan, honey. I've never seen anything like it."

Jim arrived at a run and knelt at my side. "What happened?" he demanded of Mabel. "Should I call 911?"

"I'm okay you two. Sorry I gave you a scare. Give me a minute. I'll be fine." Embarrassment blotched my face. "Really, it's okay. It's stress. It's happened before when I was married to—Dawg."

Mabel gave me a look of understanding and pulled me to her bosom.

"YOU'VE BOTH been so kind. Thanks for everything, really. You're wonderful hosts." I smiled across the dinner table. "But I have to leave tomorrow."

"Bette, you sure you're okay to fly?" Mabel asked sweetly. "It's barely more'n a day since you fainted. Maybe you should let the doctor check you out."

"I'm fine. Besides, I have no use for doctors. I watched them sit idly by and let Ted die. I'll go to a doctor when I need a flight physical. Beyond that, the only way I'm goin' to a doc or anywhere near a hospital is if I'm unconscious." I tried to lighten their mood. "If you see me in a hospital, call 911 'cause I've been kidnapped. The weather's exceptional, and it's time I got started."

"Wouldn't mind hearin' more about your route," Jim inserted between puffs on his glowing pipe. The clear night sky appeared to sag beneath the weight of a trillion stars. Crickets chirped. A dog barked in the distance. "Bette, you seem jumpy. Somethin' wrong?"

From the kitchen sink, clanging cast iron pots sounded like muffled bells as Mabel scrubbed them into submission.

"I dunno," I confessed. "I have a strange feeling. It sounds nuts. It's like someone's out there in the dark watchin' us. It started the day I fainted. It's been badgerin' me ever since."

Jim looked sympathetically into my eyes. "Feelin's and intuition are strange bedfellows." He shook his head.

I retrieved my flight case from my bedroom and pulled a matching wicker chair close to Jim's. The brass catches snapped open with profound clicks against the tranquil night. I avoided the oddly shaped scrub spots on the top and one side as I opened the flaps.

DURING THE MONTHS BEFORE, with the frigid Missouri winter raging on the other side of frosted glass, David and I collected current highway maps and matched them to my planned route and my father's antique road maps. We marked reference points and landmarks and estimated fuel usage. The Aeronca was not equipped with navigation radios, so I bought a handheld transceiver with which I could communicate with airports and towers. My plan was to fly in legs, or segments as David insisted upon calling them. I would follow a course plotted for magnetic variation and wind correction. It would be necessary to rely heavily on landmarks for reference. My final route included places I remembered from childhood vacations along with anything else that intrigued me.

"If you get lost, it'll give you extra time to get your head on straight." David joked about the complexity of my plan, which depended upon flight charts and road maps from two very different eras.

I included a brief layover in Stanville so my dad could see his old airplane. Since that cat was already well out of the bag, my stop would give my mother a chance to pinch my checks and assure herself I was still real. Secretly, I intended to steal a look at the Skylane and her broken engine while there.

MABEL CAME THROUGH the screen door backwards carrying a small painted tray with cups of hot black tea. The door bounced hard three times against its frame. "Sounds like a good plan, Bette," she said with an encouraging smile. She placed the tray on the table and served me first. "I envy you. Out there, all by yourself in total control of your life and everything around you. I know you'll find what you're lookin' for."

Heat from the cup soaked into my hands. I took a cautious sip. "I hope you're right, Mabel. I spent too many hours trying to tell my best friend, David, how I feel. He never seemed to get it. You must've gone through somethin' like this after your divorce. How'd you cope?"

"I met Jim," she answered simply with a wavering voice. "He saved my life." She touched his cheek. "Up until I found him in a church pew one Sunday mornin', I was alone in the dark and desperate. I was drownin' in sadness. Jim rescued me. He scooped me up like a droopy-eared stray pup and took me out for coffee. I've never looked back." She kissed his cheek. "Never had to."

On the wide porch, silence surrounded three thoughtful souls with a perfect, impenetrable circle. No one dared be the first to speak. Jim's pipe glowed against the night sky, a crimson dot among a horde of twinkling stars. One star broke free, and in the blink of an eye, crossed a million miles from east to west. *It's goin' the wrong way.* My mind, conditioned by a lifetime of left to right and right from wrong, protested. Before I could think another thought, the star incinerated in our atmosphere.

Remorse overwhelmed me. I broke the silence. "If Ted were here, he would scoop me up and save me too." I choked on the words. "If he was alive there'd be no need for me to be here. I'd be home, livin' my life, ignoring the memories of my mistakes, and avoiding all thoughts of the people who've hurt me." My words hung on burdened breath.

"Is this my destiny? The end I've earned for the story of my life?" Transfixed, Jim and Mabel listened to my emotionally charged tirade. "My mother swears that every detail of our existence is part of God's plan. If that's so, how could He allow Ted to die? I blame Him and the doctors. Maybe, I should blame only myself.

"I have to face my demons. I wanna be better, but I'm afraid. I'm scared of what I'll discover about myself. If Ted hadn't died, I'd still be living my 'out-of-sight, out-of-mind' mentality."

"Bette, tell us about when you learned to fly," Mabel suggested, in an attempt to change the subject. "What was the Aeronca like in those days?"

"It was the spring I turned 14," I explained. "Mac asked me to ride out to the airport and check on his Cessna. He had an old 172 at the time. The Champ was in the next hangar. When I went over to peek in the window, he asked me if I'd like to go for a ride. After we landed, while he was filling it with fuel, he told me it was his.

"I'm sure he didn't have much money back then. He must've made a heck of a deal. Anyway, I immediately loved that little plane. He insisted we continue my lessons in the Cessna, but I constantly begged him to let me fly the Champ.

"She looked pretty much the same, just not nearly as nice. Of course, there were no wheel fairings or electrical system.

"On the morning of my sixteenth birthday, my dad woke me at daylight. We were socked in, zero-zero with fog was so thick you couldn't see your hand in front of your face. By late morning, it was clear enough to drive, so my mom took me to get my driver's license. After lunch, like a gift from heaven, the ceiling lifted to 1,100 feet. Visibility cleared to 3 miles. My dad immediately came home from work.

"I got in my three required landings in the 7AC, but by my second approach in the Cessna, the ceiling had fallen below minimums. He flagged me down. That night they threw a surprise party for me. All my friends came. It was one of the most memorable days of my life." I touched my lips and realized that Jim and Mabel's smiles were a reflection of my own.

"Jim, how about you? What was the Champ like when you found 'er?"

"Nothin' unusual really." He repacked the bowl of his pipe. "I heard about her through a friend of a friend. The old bird was still in Indianapolis. She was in decent condition with serviceable fabric. The engine ran fine and mostly checked out within acceptable limits. I flew her home and landed on my new airstrip for the first time.

"I spent the next six months of Sunday afternoons and plenty of evenings, with two of my friends', restorin' every part. We shipped the engine to California and had it majored to factory-new specs. It was a busy 24 weeks, but it was fun. I know it was exactly 24 'cause Mabel kept track. Every time I ordered a part, she reminded me of how much over-budget we were."

Mabel took a theatrical swing at him.

"Lovingly reminded me," he added.

I AWOKE from an uncharacteristically deep REM sleep during the last few minutes of predawn. Birdsong, along with the mouth-watering smell of bacon frying and coffee brewing, filled the air. I massaged the scars on my legs where the doctors had inserted the pins. After a long hot shower, I slipped into khaki slacks and a pocketed shirt. I twisted my damp hair into a shoulder length ponytail and pulled it through the back of my baseball cap. I checked my look in the dresser mirror.

I hoped to see the face of a pilot. Instead, I found sad blue eyes in the beaten image of a confused Irish girl from Missouri.

The Reed's kitchen was too much like home, the same story with an altered backdrop and similar characters with different names. Jim sat at the table smoking his pipe and drinking coffee. Mabel hovered over a large skillet. It was déjà vu on a sliding scale.

"Mornin', dear." Mabel splashed grease over sizzling eggs and glanced up with a smile. "Sleep well? Today's the big day."

Jim strapped my duffel in the back seat of the recently washed Champ.

"There's one thing you have to tell me before you go." Mabel stepped back and took my left wrist in her hand. "Your watch—is it an antique? It looks like a man's watch. You've prob'ly touched it a thousand times since you arrived." She lowered her voice. "Sorry to be so nosey. Was it Ted's?"

"No." I smiled, unbuckled the black leather band, and dangled my cherished *Racine* in the sunlight. "My folks gave it to me for my thirteenth birthday. It was my dad's idea. He said I needed a stopwatch for timed turns during instrument flight. It was 1969. He couldn't find a ladies watch with a chronograph. So, he bought me the same style that they gave my brother on his thirteenth.

"Every May, I wear it for the whole month." I turned the watch slowly so she could see every detail. The worn stainless-steel case, cream-colored face, and phosphorescent hands and numbers glistened. "I can even tell you what we had for dinner that night, my favorites, fried shrimp and fried apple pies."

I cinched the strap securely around my wrist. "I wear it now to remind me of what's important, of where I came from. I guess I have two *Rosebuds* in my life, this watch and that airplane." I pointed to the Champ.

"What's that mean, dear, two *Rosebuds?* "

"I took a film class in college. We studied *Citizen Kane,* a forties film that Orson Welles made and starred in."

"I remember somethin' about that," she nodded, "but it's been a long time. I don't remember the story."

"The whole movie revolves around a reporter trying to find out what the super rich Kane's dying word, *Rosebud,* really meant. Turned out, it was the name of his sled. It was his only connection to a truly happy time in his life. Charles Kane missed out on his childhood because he was sent away to boarding school."

"Fly safe," Jim mouthed as he took hold of the aluminum propeller for the last time.

Time for my real journey to begin, I reminded myself when the engine sparked.

The Champ broke free of the grass within the first 200 feet and began a slow ascent. We passed the Reeds standing arm-in-arm in front of the barn. We climbed straight ahead to 400 feet, passed the end of the runway, rolled slightly right, and then banked hard left into a tight 180-degree turn. I pushed the stick forward and rolled out. We rapidly descended. The airspeed quickly hit 100 miles per hour. Level at 10 feet above the manicured strip, we flashed past my friends close enough to see their eyes.

I hauled the stick back. The airspeed slowed as we jumped upward into the morning sky. At 400 feet, I dropped the nose. We passed the downwind end of the runway. I started a shallow climbing right turn to the north-northwest.

I glanced back for one last look at the farm. My heart froze. My world blurred. Parked partially in the ditch along the county road, a cherry red Camaro was half-hidden behind tall corn. Binoculars glinted in the sunlight. A thickset man stood between the open door and the driver's seat.

He was watching me.

TEN

*E*LIZABETH ERASTELLA, be cool. I forced my breathing back to normal. My throbbing heart slowed. *No way—it couldn't have been him.* I tried hopelessly to convince myself. *Too far from home, too remote, how could he have known?* Unanswered questions rattled through my brain.

I calmed myself and used Pilotage to correct for wind and magnetic variation. Landmarks confirmed my calculations. Forty-six miles north of Reed's, we crawled past Arcadia, Florida. The altimeter's needles lay solidly on 4,500 feet above sea level. I eased the throttle back and set the airspeed at a fuel-sipping 75. One last minor course correction, I loosened my seatbelt and stretched.

It had been years since I had flown such a slow airplane. The terrain below changed at an agonizing pace like watching grass grow. In my beautiful Skylane, at 155 miles per hour, the world had seemed smaller. At less than half that speed and no navigation radios to keep me company, home seemed a lifetime away.

IN MY EARLY TWENTIES, I was content. I was alone, but not lonely. I reflected deeply upon my solitude and justified my life decisions by reminding myself of the emotional pain I had suffered at the hands of others. Somehow, within that rationale, I found a precarious peace.

Leon Berger taught me a lesson in human nature I shall never forget. What we see, learn, and inherit is the foundation of our personalities. Our decisions along the way mold our hearts and temper our reactions.

We are all what we are. We look different, sound different, think differently, and even smell unlike every other. We have minds with which to reason, hearts to fuel our bodies, and souls to power our beings. Even evil people have a soul. Somewhere within us, our essence links our hearts, minds, and souls, and inevitably determines how we lead our lives.

We can have our hearts transplanted and our psychosis evaluated. Nonetheless, our essence never changes. Unalterable, like our fingerprints, it is who we are forever. Gloves can be worn, and cruel people can be nice. Both are unsustainable disguises. I now know that Leon is a narcissistic sociopath with a black essence. He blindfolded me with stylized love, touched my heart with pseudo-kindness, and kept his true self hidden away.

When we separated, I boxed up the personal items he left behind and did my best to scrub away every trace. Behind some books in the back of a bottom shelf, I found an earmarked copy of a neuroscience textbook. The book opened naturally to a section that focused on the behavioral sciences. Of those, the reward system pages were obviously the most read.

I accept my shortcomings and frailties. I own and suffer with them every day. I too have a true essence. I pray it's mostly good. In the past, I reached out to others, opened my heart, and shared my darkest secrets. I spoke openly of my fears and my desires with those I trusted. I did so in the belief that what I whispered in confidence would remain so. I thought the details of a conversation, or some unrestricted act of physical love, would stay in context. I was wrong on all fronts.

With soft caresses and sweet words, Leon lifted the pain of my previous relationships. He caused me to feel wanted. Foolishly, I did not look well into his eyes. Stupidly, I ignored the concerns of others. Naïvely, I overlooked the darkness hidden in the depths of his soul. It was not until our wedding night, after I passed the point of no return, when he gave me my first real glimpse of the truth.

Reverend Jones had recently transferred to my mother's church. She asked him to perform the wedding ceremony even before we met. He insisted upon pre-marital couples counseling. Once a week for a month, he spoke with us in his dismal study in the parsonage.

On our first visit, the Reverend's young son hid behind his mother's skirt in the kitchen doorway and watched as the Reverend led us down the hall to the cloistered room. Like a battlefield general, he sat stiffly behind a scarred oak desk, littered with papers, and lectured us on the sanctity of marriage. He continually recited scripture to make his points. During the tedious sessions, I entertained myself by counting the antique Bibles on sagging homemade shelves against the wall behind him.

I rewrote our vows at least a hundred times and edited them a hundred more. Even in the last moment when the music began to play, I was unconvinced that everything was perfect.

The day concluded with an Irish reception. At my insistence, we slipped away before the party ended.

In a dingy motel room 60 miles from home, I saw Leon's true essence for the first time. As though the trap was sprung, and the facade no longer necessary, the real man stepped into the light. In the manner in which he spoke, in his touch, and reflected in his gray-black eyes, I found a thick indelible cloak that was not a disguise. It was who he really was.

The emotional burden of my wedding night and the continuing aftermath haunted me for four tumultuous years. Embarrassed, I concealed most of what happened from my family and friends. I blamed myself. When he beat me, Leon blamed me too. Every day, I asked God for guidance. I prayed for salvation. Sometimes, alone in the dark, bleeding and violated, I prayed for a merciful death.

He reveled in telling my secrets to his friends without discretion. With each strike of his verbal hammer, he forged a weapon, which he wielded against me without mercy. He convinced me there are things much worse than being alone.

JUST BEYOND THE WINDSHIELD, the thin brass rod, protruding from a one-eighth inch hole in the center of the Aeronca's chrome fuel cap, bounced and swayed. A cork attached to the base of the rod floated in gasoline and measured the level in the tank. The distance above the cap, of the rod's uppermost L shaped end, communicated the fuel level to me.

It had been two hours since my departure from Reed's field. The rod's L danced an inch above the cap. I was very low on fuel. A tinny voice crackled from my handheld transceiver with landing instructions and an airport advisory. Traffic was light at the Leesburg airport. Within minutes, the Aeronca's propeller spooled to a stop in the refueling area.

The terminal door burst open. A lineman sprinted a hundred yards across the hot tarmac straight to me. "You Liz-bet…?" he wheezed. "E-liz-a-bet Maa-Kenna?" He bent at the waist and supported himself with his hands on his knees.

"Yes," I grabbed the doorframe and swung out of the cockpit. "What is it?" I demanded.

"David wants you to call him." The red-faced boy

looked up. "He's called three times. Says it's urgent!"

I fumbled, dropped two quarters, and misdialed twice. In the middle of the first ring, it clicked. "Bette," he answered shrilly with a tense voice, "you alright?"

"What's wrong?" I half-shouted. Across the room, a pilot looked up from his book. I lowered my voice. "David, what is it—my parents?" I leaned against the wall.

"They're fine," he blurted out. "It's your hangar, your Skylane!"

"What happened?" I slid to the floor; the telephone cord stretched tight.

"Fire—early—hangar burned to the ground, lost everything. Skylane's gone. Bette, I'm sorry. There was nothin' anyone could do."

"How," I struggled. "What—what happened?"

"No details yet. Fire department put it out before it could spread. There's talk of an explosion. It's still too hot to get close. The cops blocked off the whole area."

"You sure the plane's gone?" I asked sadly. "Anything left, anything at all?"

"It looks like a pile of rubble."

"What about my mom and dad?"

"Saw your dad about an hour ago. He's fine. Told me your mom's home, shook-up, but okay. At least it happened early. No one got hurt."

"David," I cleared my mind and searched for the right words, "I think I saw him this morning."

"Saw who?"

"Leon."

"You're shittin' me. How's that possible, you sure?"

"Not a hundred percent. When I took off from Reed's, there was a red Camaro stopped on a side road and a man with binoculars. It sure looked like him." Recounting what I saw caused me to feel trapped inside a dystopian dream.

"This is a whole new can of worms," he said slowly. "I've been sittin' here all mornin' thinkin' I should tell the cops he threatened you, just in case. But, if you're right, if he's down there, he couldn't have set the fire."

"Shit," I railed. "Why're you so calm? An arsonist or a stalker, what does it matter? They're both shitty choices." I half-buried my face in the palm of my free hand.

"Bette, don't kill the messenger," David defended himself. "I'm as upset as you. We all are. Thing is, no one knows where you are except your folks and me."

"And the Reed's," I added.

"Your dad says they're great."

"You too—did everybody 'cept me know they were down here?"

The line fell quiet. After a time, David clumsily changed the subject. "If Leon Berger's down there, we've got a bigger problem than a burned up wreck."

An image of Mabel unable to contain herself popped into my head. I laughed.

"Bette, how's this funny? What in the hell's gotten into you?"

I tried to stop laughing. Pent up tension fueled my response. Slowly, I regained my composure.

"Sorry, it's just that name." I started laughing. "Mabel Reed told me—" I roared.

The two people in the terminal stared at me. I must have looked like a string puppet hanging from the cord of the wall-mounted phone flailing with laughter.

"Mabel told you what?" he demanded, angrily.

"Leon Berger's a dog!" I howled. Tears rolled down both checks.

"Okay, Bette, enough. What does that even mean? What's she know about Leon?"

"No, you don't get it," I forced the words between diminishing chuckles. "It's a dog breed. He's a Leon Berger," I snorted.

"Whatever," he said, disgustedly. "Let's get back to business."

"I guess." I controlled myself. "What do you think I should do now?"

"I don't know. Take some safety precautions until we get this mess sorted out."

"Like what?"

"Leesburg is a scheduled stop. If Leon really is following you and knew you were at the Reed's, he could also know where you are now. Your plane's not much faster than a car and doesn't carry much fuel. If he really stays after it, he can catch you again. If you run into any weather, it'll work to his advantage."

I interrupted, "Call him Dawg, okay?"

"Yeah, whatever. If it'll keep you on track, fine. If the Dawg really is following you, you should get movin'. Head north. Don't tell anybody where you're goin'."

"I wanna come home," I said flatly. The humor I experienced was completely gone.

"And I want you to. But, let's take this one step at a time. Get some place safe and call me in a few hours. In the meantime, I'll try to find out if Dawg's around—at work or whatever. I'll see if I can talk to the investigators about the fire."

"You stallin' me?" I demanded. "Are you tryin' to keep me away from home?"

"Shit, course not," he defended himself for the second time. "I'm just lookin' out for you. You've gotta trust me and quit kickin' my ass."

"Okay, I'll play along for now, but I still intend to come home." I softened my tone. "Do you think we lost all of the Skylane parts? Was it all in the hangar?"

"We didn't lose everything. Your dad sent what was left of the connecting rod and the piston to a metallurgist a few days ago. The sabotaged fuel line is at his house. We lost plenty, but we're certainly not done. Now, get back in the air and call me from your next stop. Make sure that wherever you go, it's completely random."

The name on the map caught my eye. I remembered that St. Augustine is the oldest city in the United States. It was within my range, on the coast, and most importantly way east of my planned route. I adjusted my course, took a series of deep breaths, and with trepidation, imagined all the dangers that awaited me on the ground. I felt safe in the air, at least until the image of my exploding Cessna flashed through my mind. Then, I didn't feel safe anywhere.

I WAS BORN and raised in Stanville, Missouri. It's a nondescript country town full of familiar faces, where people often know everyone else's business. I like country towns. I like the quaint look and feel of Main Street. I appreciate their history. I like when I go in a store and people know me. In high school, everyone talked about getting away and never looking back. I didn't think a lot about it then. Now, I know, every place is pretty much the same. They just have different names.

Maybe Stanville isn't special, but it is to me. Our street sweeper wasn't always a big machine with giant rotary brushes and a watering system that cleans the empty streets in the predawn hours. It used to be Walter, a little old man with a dirty gray fedora pulled down to the top of his ears, a wheelbarrow, a broom, and a brother who was Chief of Police.

Mac and Maggie McKenna have lived in the same white house, a mile from town, since I was two. I don't remember the move there. However, I've heard both versions of the story my entire life. My mom insists that the too-small-for-a-family-of-four house was not her first choice. She says my dad told her it was all they could afford. He sticks to his story. She claims he chose it because it was close to the airport. In fact, if you landed to the west, before the old airport closed, on final approach you passed right over our house.

When we moved in, there were only three rooms plus a bathroom, three screened-in porches, and a chicken coop. The tiny kitchen with painted plywood cabinets was sandwiched between the only bedroom and the living room.

My older brother, Danny, and I slept in metal bunk beds against an inside wall near the foot of our parents' bed. I was youngest, so I got the bottom. My dad piled his clothes on my bed. I was accustomed to crawling in under whatever happened to be there. A gas floor furnace was the only heat during the bitter Missouri winters. The only air-conditioning we knew was at the Berwan, a movie theater built inside a galvanized Quonset hut, where we spent our Saturday afternoons.

My sister, Susan, came when I was four. My dad added on to the house. He lengthened the living room and built a limestone fireplace. The pine floors were like ice in the winter. We used to crowd around the fireplace to watch television and talk. On Friday nights, they allowed us to eat dinner there on TV trays. My room was an icebox. Most winter mornings after my shower, I dressed on the hearth.

We always had used cars, at least one old airplane, and an assortment of battered motorcycles and scooters. A tomboy, I spent a lot of time with my dad. He taught me to weld and repair almost anything. I liked being with him more than hanging out with other kids. In some way, I made myself an outcast.

Because of the airplanes, people seemed to think we were rich. We weren't even close. My mother saved all year for Christmas. If my dad had to choose between avgas and food, the airplane always won the toss.

Danny was the social one. He was a senior when I was a freshman. We never knew how many of his friends would wake up on the floor of his bedroom on any given morning or show up for dinner. My mom always insisted there was enough. As I think back on those days, I realize the extra food usually came off her plate.

I don't talk a lot about Susan. It's not because I don't love her. It's just that I was a senior when she was in the eighth grade. I left for college right after graduation. We never really knew each other as adults.

When I graduated from college, my first job was in St. Louis. I settled in Kirkwood. It was the closest thing to small town living in the city. Stanville was only an hour by car. When I bought the Skylane, I kept it in an enclosed hangar one row over from my Dad's Cessna 172.

I worked my way up from Copywriter to Creative Director. With increasing responsibility came travel, mostly in the United States. My company allowed me to fly my own airplane, so long as I was alone, and it didn't cost more than commercial travel. I logged plenty of hours in the Skylane. Company reimbursements usually covered the cost of the fuel as well as the operating expense.

Most Sundays, I drove out to Stanville, went to church with my mom, and had lunch at home. I particularly loved when she fried chicken in her favorite cast iron skillet. In the winter, she cooked on an antique wood cook stove. Those days, more than any others, I was overwhelmed with contentment. On Sunday afternoons, my dad always insisted we go flying, even if it was for only a few minutes.

At times, I resented the fact that my dad treated me like a new student regardless of how many thousands of hours were printed in my logbook. I look back on those Sundays; the smell of chicken frying in my mom's kitchen and pipe tobacco burning in my dad's airplane, and it makes me sad. Not because those days have passed, rather because I didn't enjoy them enough. If he hadn't treated me like a student, I probably wouldn't have survived the crash. Maybe, just maybe, if I had listened better, Ted would be with me now.

Since the accident, I have lived with high anxiety. It wells up in my chest like a fully inflated balloon. In moments of panic, it swells to a point where I think I can no longer breathe. I really wish I had listened better.

THE MILES clicked by. St. Augustine was near. The permanent ball in my chest inflated against the inner lining. Nervously, I keyed the built-in microphone in my handheld radio and reluctantly told St. Augustine control the Champ's tail number. Broadcasting my identity certainly didn't feel like stealth.

On the ground, I fueled the Champ, and then taxied her to the transient tie- down area.

My duffel swung loosely from my shoulder as I threaded my way through the assortment of deserted airplanes. Every step was filled with dread as my mind raced with the myriad possibilities of news from David. I was prepared to spend the night or leave immediately. In that moment, I was indifferent.

David's answering machine picked up after the fifth ring. I hung up. "Shit," I bit my tongue. *I should have brought my cell phone.* I reconsidered the rash decision to cut myself off from the world. I reentered my access code in the payphone and keyed the familiar numbers for the Stanville airport.

"Good morning, Stanville Municipal Airport. This is Anthony." Tony was a tall, skinny, 30-something flight instructor/airport manager. He had to fold himself into the cramped Cessna 150 trainers and spent more time thinking about women than he did flying. Most husbands refused to let their wives take lessons from him. They all came to my dad. Any time one of Tony's students wore skirts to her lessons, we joked that she would never switch to my dad. Tony didn't like my family much.

"Hi, Tony, this is Elizabeth McKenna." I hoped he was in a good mood. "Have you seen my friend, David?"

"Hey, sorry 'bout your hangar." He sounded remorseful. "Do I know yer friend?"

"You've seen him out there with me from time-to-time." It occurred to me, when David and I went flying we seldom had a reason to go to the office. "He's 5'11", probably about 180 pounds, and curly brown hair. Oh, yeah, and he usually wears Carhartt jeans and shirts. Maybe you've seen him with my dad in the last few months."

"Yeah, hmm." His tone switched to one of recognition. "I reckon I know who he is. He was here earlier talkin' to the cops. He might've left with yer *ole man.*" He pronounced 'old man' with a hint of disdain.

"Okay, thanks, I'll track 'im down. If you see him, or my dad, please tell 'em I called."

"Right-o," he answered, trying to imitate a British aviator. It made sense. The last time I saw him he was with a brunette in a miniskirt. He was wearing a fur collared flight jacket and a long white scarf. He switched back to his Missouri boot-heel drawl, "Where're ye? Ya wanna leave a num—"

I dropped the receiver on the hook. *Why are people so nosey?* I kicked my own ass. *Not long ago you would've told him everything without even thinkin'. Your mouth and your faith in human nature always get you into trouble.*

My mother answered on the first ring, "Mo—"

"Hon, you okay? Where are you? Are you safe? When are you comin' home? I think—"

"Ma, take a breath. I'm fine, still in Florida. That's all I know. Are David and Dad there?"

"Yes," she answered, resignedly. "Just a minute, they're out back." She dropped the receiver on the small white desk, which I pictured next to the wood cook stove and strewn with the usual clutter of mail. An oversized calendar hung on the wall above the desk marked with birthdays and her Eastern Star meeting schedule. She was always after me to join. It was too much like a circle of multi-colored drones to interest me.

"Bette-girl," my dad's steady voice had a calming effect, "sorry 'bout the Skylane."

The line clicked. An extension phone lifted. "Bette," David's tone was exploratory, "your mom said you wanted me on the call. You okay?"

"I should get you all three on the phone so I only have to say this once." I sounded indignant. "I'm okay." I heard another click. My mother sighed. My wish had come true.

"I'm in St. Augustine. I'm fine. The plane's fine. No one, except the three of you, knows I'm here. What've you found out about the fire?"

My dad spoke first. "I've been diggin' through the wreckage with the fire department." He paused. "The investigator thinks it started in the metal cabinet under your workbench. Looks like there was an accelerant. I don't remember anything flammable in that cabinet. Was there?"

"No, 'bout the only things in that cabinet were used pistons and a coffee can full of odds and ends bolts and nuts." I pictured the contents of the hangar, which I hadn't seen since the August morning when Ted and I left for Florida. I visualized myself standing in the center. "I had some paint thinner and a little touch-up paint. It was on the opposite side in a tall gray metal cabinet."

"Anyway," he continued with a hint of discouragement, "there's plenty left to look at. They won't let me in there by myself. They haven't told me anything. It's obvious they're lookin' for evidence of arson." He paused again and lowered his voice. "Bette, David has somethin' to tell ya."

"I knew it." My heart pounded. "Now we get to the really bad news."

"Maybe," David answered, "but there's a lot we don't know."

"Spit it out," I demanded.

"I called Dawg's boss and then his sister."

The line was silent for what seemed like a minute. In the airport terminal around me, people went about their business as if nothing was wrong. I was appalled.

"His sister was outwardly nervous and wouldn't tell me anything. His boss told me he took vacation. Bottom line, Leon Berger, aka, the Dawg, is missing."

My heart thrashed the walls of my chest. I supported myself on the payphone. "Jesus," was all I could muster.

"Bette-girl," my dad took over, "we've discussed this, and we think you've gotta lay low for awhile."

"Shit, Pop, what the hell does that mean? If I lay any lower, I'll be in the Atlantic."

"Maybe, hang out where you are," David suggested. "See the sights."

"Why does she have to stay there?" My mother broke in with an unusually assertive tone. "Why can't she just keep movin'? She wants to fly to California. Let her. It sounds safer than he—"

"We just don't want her to come home," my dad interrupted, "not now, not yet. It'll take a little time to sort this out."

"I'm right here," I protested. "Don't I get a say in this."

"I vote for California." David ignored my complaint. "She just needs to stay off plan."

"Whatever," I reluctantly agreed. It was three against zero. I obviously didn't have a vote.

"Call us every day!" My mother insisted.

"Fine, I'll just get up every morning, close my friggin' eyes, and put my finger on the map."

"Good." My dad sounded pleased. He had always been oblivious to my sarcasm. "Spend the night there and get movin' in the mornin'."

My mom and David added sounds of agreement.

"Girl," my dad said sternly, "don't take chances, not in

the air or anyplace else."

"Got it. I'll call ya tomorrow."

"Bette," my mother's were the last words, "love you."

ELEVEN

St. Augustine, Florida, Thursday Morning, April 6, 2000

*D*AVID AND I MET *when we were eight. I felt something special when he crossed the vacant lot to help me with my kite. It's hard to describe how I felt in the moment, or how I feel about David today. Certainly, I love him. However, it's never been romantic love, at least not for me.*

Once, when we were something like 12, David ambushed me when I got off the bus. In front of our neighbors, he shoved a small white box in my hand. "This is for you," he blurted out and then backed away like a spectator preparing to witness a miracle.

Naïvely, I untied the string and removed the lid. Inside was a Five and Dime silver necklace with a tiny pendant. "Will you be my girlfriend?" he asked, like a lovesick puppy.

Shocked, I shoved the box back in his hand and ran home. David stood alone in the street between our houses surrounded by a gang of taunting kids with my older brother and his older sister leading the riot.

Later, I learned from my brother that David's sister had set him up. She told him I wanted to go steady.

He didn't speak to me for more than two months.

David trusted his sister. She blabbed the whole thing to my brother, and they used it against him.

Simple math:

Secret shared + trust betrayed = hurt feelings (or worse)

Eventually, he got over it. We became unconditional friends. He's always been there for me, and I've leaned on him plenty.

His sister died in a car wreck when she was only 19. We were 16 when it happened. Standing in front of a closed casket, I made a clumsy attempt to comfort him, but failed. The experience taught me there are situations in which we cannot be consoled. Some things we have to deal with on our own.

In his twenties, David married. She didn't like me in the least. There was something not right about her. I saw it plain as day. He did not. It angered him when I tried to tell him what I thought.

Their marriage ended badly after only a few years. Turned out, she had lied about nearly everything in her life. Her bizarre claim that she was a non-practicing medical doctor was my favorite.

EVERY MUSCLE in my body complained. The pins in my legs felt like rusty barbs. My thoughts, which had been on my mind for a day and a night, were finally on paper. I reluctantly pried my head out of my journal and steadied myself to meet whatever reality the day would bring. The local newscaster's monotonous report blared from the television and competed with the wretched ringing in my ears.

I cracked my knuckles and checked the time. It was nine o'clock in the morning. I had been sitting Indian style in the middle of the hard bed since before daylight. *Where did the hours go?*

In the hotel lobby, a maid was busy clearing away the last of the free breakfast. "Hi," I bent slightly forward and caught her eye. "Sorry I'm late. Can I get a little somethin' to eat, anything really?" I thought of my mother's disdain for my ability to get people to do what I want. In this moment, I didn't care if it was manipulation. I was hungry.

"No puedo, *Señora.*" The middle-aged woman answered in Spanish, looked nervously around the lobby, and then switched to broken English. "I no suppose to." She glanced at the distracted Front Desk clerk and pointed to the clock. "No puedo." She shook her head.

"¡Ay, Señora! Por favor, tengo mucho hambre." I tried to emulate the phrase for *I'm starving*, which I learned from my awkwardly gay high school Spanish teacher. "Por favor," I repeated, mustering my most forlorn expression.

The indifferent clerk disappeared through an open doorway behind the Front Desk. The woman muttered something else in Spanish and continued shaking her head. All the while, she went straight to the kitchen area and returned with a small box of Cheerios, a carton of milk, and a banana.

I couldn't prevent someone from beating me or saying incredibly hurtful things about me, and still, in another language, I could convince a stranger to feed me. How ironic.

The crudely painted yellow sedan had obviously been converted to a taxi when it should have been taken to the junkyard. A maverick spring in the threadbare backseat pricked my lower back. It was impossible to get comfortable. *Like my life*, I thought, *something beyond my control poking me.* I cranked open the window and turned my face into the salt air. Thankfully, it was less than 10 minutes from the hotel to the St. Augustine airport.

I paid the metered fare along with a two-dollar tip and was out of the car before it came to a full stop in front of the terminal. I longed to call home. I shunned the tempting bank of payphones as I passed. It was too soon.

With two fingers, I traced the Champ's molybdenum tube frame beneath its taut skin. "It's you and me against the world," I commiserated. "Out here on the road, it's just us girls.

"You need a name," I exclaimed. Surprised it hadn't occurred to me before. "How can we have a conversation if I don't know what to call you?" I glanced about hoping there was no one around to hear me talking to an airplane.

Nearby, a dark-skinned man in a broad brimmed straw hat skillfully maneuvered a green and yellow lawn tractor around the tarmac's edge. The distinct whir of multiple mower blades threw off an aromatic smell of freshly cut grass. It reminded me of a Missouri spring. I lifted my face against the blazing sun and closed my eyes.

At my home in Kirkwood, beginning when I first moved in, I cultivated what I call my *family garden.* Dozens of individually framed photographs are scattered across the weathered surface of a wide antique mahogany table. In a prominent place at the center, surrounded by three generations of family, is my favorite 8 X 10 black & white. Taken in central Texas during the summer of 1949, the year my parents married, a young Mac McKenna is perched in the doorway of an airplane, a converted crop duster. It was probably a Piper J-3 Cub.

In the picture, my dad is wearing a look of genuine satisfaction, a worn leather jacket, and a matching aviator's helmet with big goggles pulled up over his forehead. His right hand is hidden behind his back. I've never asked, even so, I'm sure he was holding his pipe.

Five words are painted on the fuselage above and behind him. The uppermost line reads, *The Kitten*, my dad's nickname for my mom. Below, on the second and third lines, *Pilot, Mac McKenna,* is also hand-lettered. The image is permanently engraved upon my heart and imprinted in my mind. The single detail I love the most is the cuff of his trouser leg caught in the opening of his engineer boot, which rests casually on the landing gear. One trademark pant leg is always caught in the top of my dad's boot. Anytime you look deeply enough into his eyes, you can plainly see, it simply doesn't matter.

"*Kitten* it is then." I stepped back and admired my airplane. In my mind's eye, as clearly as if he was there, my dad sat in the doorway. A mischievous grin plastered on his face. His pant leg caught in his boot. "I'll call you, *Kitten*."

The engine started on the first try. I monitored the instruments as the engine temperature and oil pressure rose in tandem and stabilized. One final check of the control surfaces, a radio clearance from ground control, and I rolled toward the runway.

A shallow S pattern back and forth across the centerline of the taxiway yielded a clearer view of the tarmac through alternating side windows. *The Kitten* carried her nose proudly in the air while her tail bumped roughly along on its small hard rubber wheel.

It was a long way to the threshold of the departing runway. I taxied past several access points. A woman's voice on the radio advised I could depart from any of the intersections, my choice. Certainly, my airplane would be airborne within the first few hundred feet. Like always, my dad's caution put a doubt in my mind; *"Runway behind you..."*

I stopped at the final intersection and checked for traffic before pivoting 90 degrees to taxi the last 100 yards to the runway. Before I covered half the distance, something was clearly wrong.

The Aeronca wobbled roughly from side-to-side. Wings flapped like a waddling penguin attempting to fly. A bone rattling flopping of tires was louder than the engine. I announced my intentions to ground control and headed for the taxiway's shoulder. Rubber wrenched against thin metal wheel fairings. We ground to a stop in the grass.

One wing was a foot higher than the other. *Both* tires were flat and squeezed out of mangled wheel pants like a broken toy. Within 30 minutes, three men arrived. They ignored the sickening sound of rubber tearing metal as they slowly winched my airplane up on a small trailer behind an aircraft tow-motor.

"David," I didn't give him a chance to speak, "you won't friggin' believe this. I've got two flat tires." The line was quiet. "You there?"

"I'm here." He sounded confused. "How can you have two flats? Were the tires dry rotted?"

"No, they were new. It makes no sense, one, maybe, but not two."

"Did you run over somethin'? It couldn't have been intentional, could it?"

"I don't know how," I replied, exasperated. "If you're thinkin' he followed me here, how's that possible? Only you and my folks know where I am. Even though it's both tires, it's gotta be a coincidence, right?

"Anyway, what's done is done. I'm tired of thinkin' about all this shit," I said with despair. "Any news 'bout the fire?"

"The powers-that-be seem to think it's a pretty big deal. The State Fire Marshall from Jeff City was down here last night."

"Did they find somethin'?" A sense of doom filled my chest.

"They say for sure the fire's point of origin was the

workbench. We lost the engine case and some other important parts. They were laid out on top of it."

"Whatever," I said, impatiently. "Point of origin—Fire Marshall—blah-blah-blah—big f'ing deal—what's it all mean to me?"

"What it means, Elizabeth," he said harshly, "is the fire was set where it could destroy the engine and any clues to what caused the crash. Plus, and this is apparently a big deal, it was unbelievably hot. The aluminum engine case completely disintegrated and the steel cabinet along with it. Where they were is a pile of dust. If I hadn't seen them the night before, I'd swear they were never there. Damn thing burned through the back and sidewalls of the hangar like paper. It's lucky the fire department put it out before it spread."

"How hot we talkin'? They sayin' it was a gasoline fire?"

"Bette, they're sayin' it was close to 5,000 degrees. That's a couple thousand degrees hotter than a gas fire."

"Holy shit," I spit out the distasteful words. "What do they think happened?"

"If they know, they aren't sayin'. They've got the whole area cordoned off. They're guardin' it 'round the clock. They bagged a bunch of debris. The Fire Marshall took the evidence with 'im."

"And my plane?"

"Partially burned, and scorched all over. It didn't see nearly the heat like the workbench. We had drained the wing tanks, and there were two full five-gallon gas cans on the floor between the workbench and the plane. They exploded. That probably did more damage to the plane than anything else."

"Shi-it." I tried to imagine the scene. "The Skylane's tanks were rubber bladders. Did they burn?"

"Yep, completely through the wings."

"David, as soon as the tires are fixed, I'm gettin' outta

here. Even if I only make it to the next airport, I really wanna be someplace else."

LEON BERGER'S surreptitious entry into my life disrupted my routine. Innocently, I forgot to tell my mother about him. By the time it occurred to me they should meet, it was too late to be nervous. Her *bad-dar,* as my brother called it, was unmatched. She could spot a bad boyfriend, bad friend, or a bad idea from a mile away.

On Saturday night, a few weeks after our first date, Leon took me to dinner. The next thing I knew, I was insisting he accompany me to Sunday lunch in Stanville.

I called early the next morning and shyly asked my mom to set an extra place at the table. She pried his name from me, told me she loved me, and hung up.

We drove through downtown Stanville and straight to the white clapboard house where I grew up. My parents were home from church and waiting in the kitchen.

My mom had fried the chicken before the service. It was in a covered bowl on the back of the stove. I made quick introductions. My dad invited Leon to sit with him while mom and I set out the food. Twice, while ladling mashed potatoes, gravy, and green beans into big miss-matched bowls, she gave me an unsettled look.

The day bumped by like a carload of acquaintances traveling on a rocky road. Everyone was uncomfortable. No one dared complain.

"Somebody's gotta fix the damn things." My dad took a friendly poke at Leon for being a mechanic as we rolled his airplane out of the hangar for a mandatory Sunday afternoon ride.

"Mac," my mother reprimanded, "language, not on Sunday."

Outwardly, it all seemed innocent. Nonetheless, I knew the truth. Finally, I got up my courage and managed a moment alone with my mom. "What do ya think?" I cautiously asked.

"Seems nice," she answered, unimpressed.

The profound tick of my biological clock disrupted my common sense. For the first time in my life, I decided to push the envelope with my mother. "What exactly does that mean?"

"I don't know, honey. It's just a feelin'. Nothin' I can put my finger on. Somethin' not quite right, but I'm overprotective. I don't need to get in the middle of this. At your age, you have to decide for yourself. 'Sides, if you ever wanna get married and start a family, you're gonna have to find someone."

"Mom, that sounds like settling. I'm only 25," I argued.

"I don't want you to settle, but I was 18 when I married your father and by my mother's standards, that was old."

"You're talkin' 'bout havin' kids. I'm not even sure I want any."

"Elizabeth EraStella McKenna." She put her hands on her hips and looked at me incredulously. "Children are God's gift to the world. Besides, I want grandbabies to spoil. You have ta find the right man, that's all."

"Yeah, that's all. You want me to choose well, and soon, but you never like anyone I bring home. Ma, you don't make this easy."

"Sorry, Bette," she said sadly. "You don't know how special you are."

IT WAS NEARLY TWO HOURS since they towed my Champ back to the maintenance hangar. "Miss, here're your culprits." The mechanic towered over me. I sat near the terminal's spotless windows. In his outstretched palm were two shiny 16-penny nails. "There was one in each tire," he added, dropping the scarred nails in my open hand. "Funny thing, they were in exactly the same spot in both tires. Even the angle of entry was 'bout the same."

I held the nails to the light and slowly examined every

marking. The shafts bent at identical angles.

"Can you patch 'em?" I asked.

"Tubes are ruined. Tires might be okay with a patch. I wouldn't risk it. The last thing you want is a blowout on landin'."

"You're right about that." I nodded, remembering the time I had a blowout while landing. "Do you have tires and tubes?"

"No, sorry. We can get 'em here by tomorrow." He tilted his head to one side. "You're lucky they went flat 'fore ya got off the ground."

"I know."

My invisible antagonist pressed her face to my ear and laughed.

On my knees, in the oppressive afternoon sun, I scrutinized the asphalt around the anchors where I tied the Champ the night before. Close to the coiled ropes, exactly as I had left them, were wooden chocks. Partially obscured beneath the blocks, which I had wedged against the backs of the tires, I found two more identical nails, one on each side. I arranged all four as I imagined they had been. With one unmarked nail behind each tire and one scarred nail in front.

Wouldn't have mattered, I reasoned. *Taxied forward or pushed backward, I would have picked up a nail in each tire no matter what.*

TWELVE

St. Augustine, Florida, Friday Morning, April 7, 2000

I WONDER *if writing in this journal will really help? How can spilling out my thoughts for no one but me to read heal me? I don't know the answers. To survive this ordeal, I must cause myself to write and pray every day.*

It's not yet daylight. I chose this motel because it's nowhere near where I spent last night. Kitten has two flat tires. It looks like someone did it on purpose. I'm stuck here. For the first time in a long time, I'm truly afraid of something other than my own heart. David thinks Dawg is following me. He might be right.

I awaken every morning way too early, somewhere in the neighborhood of three o'clock. From then until daylight is the worst time of my day. My thoughts hang between reality and nightmares. Sometimes, I can't even tell the difference between what's real and what haunts me. It all fills my mind and my heart with an overwhelming fear of failure.

Dawg most certainly despises me, and maybe always has. He didn't marry me for love. He did it for control. I've asked myself a thousand times how I missed it. Then I remember I didn't. I just wouldn't accept the truth. I wanted to trust him, to believe he was good.

This is my downfall, the curse of my family. I have always wanted to trust people. My problem is those that prove themselves trustworthy can be counted on the fingers of one hand.

In a few hours, the Champ will be fixed. I'll leave this place. When I'm airborne, I'll decide where I'm headed. Until then, I can't think about it, tell anyone, and I don't even want to write my destination here. It's as if someone knows my thoughts, as if some evil omniscient power is out there looking for me—waiting—watching, deciding when to hurt me.

Grandma Damon always said if I wanted results, I would have to ask God for his help. She said I have to confess my sins and ask for forgiveness. She told me, if I pray these things with a pure heart, then He will answer. She warned me, what I think I want and what God wants for me may not be the same. She said, what He wants is what's best. If I believe in His wisdom, then he'll give me the strength to accept His plan.

Grandma was a sweet, take-no-prisoners Baptist born in 1896, descendent of French Missionaries and Blackfeet Indians. She respected the ways of her Indian ancestors, but also read the Bible every day. She swore by 'spare the rod and spoil the child', was like an older sister to my mother, and adored my dad.

Granny was a profound influence in my life. She died before I had the sense to ask her what it all means. Her advice usually came from the Bible or the verbally passed down teachings of Blackfeet medicine men. She always knew what to do.

My dad told me the medicine men believed they had the

ability to become spiritually centered and heal others through the focused, quickening force of their own energy. I wonder if this power was only for physical ailments or if they also had the ability to heal emotional trauma.

If I am to keep my promise to myself and pray every day, then I must have a process, something that will allow me to open my heart and say the right things. Jesus obviously understood this when he taught His disciples the Lord's Prayer. If I repeat my prayer every day, perhaps I will learn to understand God's answers. Maybe then, I won't need a codebook.

I guess I've ignored His messages most of my life, especially when what He said didn't suit me. I was self-absorbed and expected others to be naturally sympathetic. I'm an emotional cripple.

I must redeem myself. If I wish to live, I must first find a way to survive.

I start today on this page. In memory of my grandmother, I commit my life to God with this daily prayer:

Dear God,
Thank you for this day, for health and happiness, and for my family and friends. Help me protect those who depend upon me. Forgive me my sins. Give me the strength to forgive those who hurt me. Please let me find happiness and become a real person.
Amen

IT WAS STRAIGHT UP ten o'clock. The tarmac was already slow roasting beneath the mid-morning Florida sun. The Champ waited patiently outside the maintenance hangar wearing a pair of unrolled tires. Her wheel pants, of which Jim Reed was so proud, lay on the ground next to the plane, damaged beyond use.

The mechanic, with a slow drawl, took his time explaining how difficult it had been to locate the tires and tubes and how expensive it was to get anything by overnight freight. I tried to listen in case he said something worth knowing. All I could think about was leaving St. Augustine.

He finished his memorized value statement and finally told me the price. I paid him in cash without a word.

I didn't care about the cost of tires or shipping. I did care about the nerve-wracking delay and the damage to Kitten's fairings. Unfortunately, there was no room for them inside the airplane.

"Can you UPS the boots?" I asked, realizing that other than 'good morning' these were my first words.

"Sure," he replied, "you want them over-nighted?"

We're still talkin' price, I thought. "No, no rush. Just send 'em the cheapest way. How much you think for packin' and shippin'? I'd like to pay you before I leave."

He made a quick phone call to the office. "They say it'll be 55 bucks," he apologized.

I pressed three twenties into his palm and climbed into my airplane without looking back.

THEODORE JOSEPH WILSON was my second chance. He was my second chance at everything: love, happiness, and self-fulfillment.

We met in college. We instantly felt a connection. However, it didn't work. It couldn't work then. He was in a relationship with someone else and life got in the way.

On a Thursday in the fall semester of my sophomore year, Bill Cook, a shy 'townie,' who sat across the aisle in my American history class and lived at home with his parents, changed my life.

Late autumn filled the Southeast Missouri State University campus with the promise of cool nights and warm fires. Alone near the windows that overlooked

Normal Street in the lower level of the Memorial Hall Café, I picked at my overcooked lunch.

Nearby, the glass entry door opened. My friend Bill blew in followed by a gust of wind, dry leaves, and a tall handsome stranger.

A sensation, which had nothing to do with the chill or the wind, fell upon me. My heart fluttered. My skin tingled. A tiny lump formed in my throat.

Bill smiled when he saw me, tapped the man on the shoulder, and in three steps, they towered over me.

"Elizabeth McKenna, meet my oldest friend, Ted Wilson." Bill delivered the introduction exactly as we learned in fourth grade. "We grew up in Jackson. We've been friends since kindergarten," he said, formally.

Ted bowed slightly and smiled. "Nice to meet you." His voice scooped me up and held me tight.

"Call me Bette," I answered, self-consciously. "Bill does."

How foolish I must have seemed, I thought, scowling at the brown waifs and strays from countless oaks, which swirled about my feet as I hurried to my next class.

Friday morning, Bill arrived for history lecture just after me, two minutes to spare before the bell. "Tell me about your friend, Ted Williams." I purposely misspoke his last name in an attempt to appear cavalier. Others streamed noisily in and took their seats. Soft unrelated laughter filled the room. Bill and I sat firmly upon an island of serious conversation amidst a tempest of indifference, for which I was grateful.

"Ted *Wilson's* my best friend," he answered, with a polite emphasis on the correct use of Wilson. "He's a math ed. major with an art minor."

"Sorry, I was in such a rush yesterday." I used my rehearsed excuse. "I would've liked to stay and visit. Your friend seemed nice."

"Have lunch with us today," Bill whispered as the bell

rang. "It'll be fun."

Big brown eyes twinkled. Ted Wilson's southern accent was sweet like honey on grits. "Just before my tenth birthday, my dad went out for a beer 'n' never came back," he explained. "It was me 'n' my mom from then on 'til after my eighteenth birthday. A few weeks before high school graduation, she was on her way home from a 12-hour day when a drunk driver crossed into her lane. They say she died instantly."

"Oh—Ted," I stammered, "I'm so sorry."

"It's okay. It's been awhile now," his eyes moistened, "but she *was* all I had."

"You've got me, brother," Bill chimed in.

Much later that night, we bumped into two of my girlfriends on campus. We all ended up across the river. The Hushpuppy, a cavernous, low ceilinged monstrosity, was once a small one-room liquor store. It evolved into a student bar in the early days of the gold rush when the state of Illinois lowered the drinking age to 19.

Wedged between Ted and Bill, I lost track of my girlfriends in the crowded room. Shortly after midnight, I found them bleary-eyed in a stark unpainted plywood and concrete bathroom sloppily painting their faces with uncoordinated strokes and dabs. I needed desperately to pee, but the stalls had no doors and the toilets had no seats.

"Lizbeth, you'll be okay with yuur dates, won't yaa?" Lisa, the dirty blonde, slurred as she stepped away from the filthy porcelain and inched up her tight jeans. "We're goin' to a par-tae. Next." She pointed at the stopped-up toilet she had just used.

"Lisa," I shook my head in disgust, "no way I'm usin' that. I'd rather pee in a port-a-pot at a Mexican fruit stand."

In the parking lot, unable to wait a minute more, I squatted between two cars. Their backs faithfully turned toward me, Bill and Ted stood guard.

Alone in the backseat of Ted's cramped Maverick, I leaned back and closed my eyes. My world spun. I felt nauseous. "Bill, crack your window," I pleaded. The frigid river valley air filled my lungs. The sleepy effects of the beer began to wear off as we drove through unfamiliar countryside.

Unexpectedly, Ted made a hard right turn. Pea gravel pinged car bodies as we slid to a stop. Harsh neon light flooded the car. I stooped forward between the bucket seats. A giant *BOWLING* sign hung from a long blonde-brick building.

Ted hopped out of the car and hurried across the crowded parking lot. Fifty or so feet in front of the building, he stopped. A tall woman with long dark hair and glasses appeared. She stood before Ted, her arms stiffly crossed and her legs spread.

"Who's that?" I whispered.

"Mindy," Bill answered reluctantly, "Ted's girlfriend."

I RELAXED my grip on the walnut knob and steadied the Aeronca's control stick with two fingers. A slight, inherent vibration continuously rippled through the airframe. The partially folded sectional chart in my lap fluttered in the wind, which forced its way into the leaky cabin. My plastic rotary azimuth plotter, which looked like a fancy ruler in statute and nautical miles, served as an anchor.

A little more than 4,000 feet below, a series of first Georgia and then Alabama towns, meaningless dots on the chart, crawled past at a snail's pace. My stomach growled. The Champ's fuel was low. Foolishly, I refused to choose an airport. The antagonistic voice in my left ear laughed and reminded me; even my thoughts were no longer private.

By this time, I had a feel for the trim tab adjustments, and the aerodynamically trimmed Champ practically flew herself. I unfolded the next chart and found my position on the eastern edge of the paper world. I closed my eyes. Using my index finger, I drew two crude circles just west of my location. I arbitrarily stopped. The town closest to my fingertip was Eufaula, Alabama, near the Georgia border. The name meant nothing to me. *There*, I decided, unwilling to give voice to the town's name. *I'll stop there.*

I began a slow on-course descent. Far below, like finely crafted toys, two modern biplanes, one milky yellow and the other bright blue, flew southbound in a tight side-by-side formation skirting the rippled surface of the *Walter F. George Reservoir.*

They know where they're goin', I thought. *They don't have to hide from their own lives. That honor is surely reserved for me.*

Eufaula was little different from the hundreds of airports I have seen in my life. I taxied straight to the fuel pump, prominently mounted on a concrete island surrounded by an asphalt apron. "Top her off," I instructed the attendant. "Full to the brim. As quickly as possible," I added, wanting to be ready if I had to make a fast get-a-way.

A large centrally located main hangar with a full width horizontal bi-fold door gaping open, looked like a hungry bird waiting for a worm.

There must be a bathroom in the back, I thought as I threaded my way through boxes and parts strewn about the unlit hangar. Two fuselages, parked side-by-side at an angle to one another, looked like skeletons. Shreds of fabric hung from tubular bones. Next to the entrance to the ladies room, in a back corner beneath a dust encrusted white canvas, the partially finished kit-plane nose of a miniature Bede jet peeked out like a shy dog.

When I landed a few minutes before, I had thoughts of spending the night, calling David, and catching my breath, but this place felt too much like an Indian burial ground. Inside the bathroom, I pressed my back against the locked door and gasped for breath.

Every forced step from the bathroom to the office was agonizingly slow, in the wrong direction. The urge to escape plagued me. I wanted to race to my airplane. *Run away from what and go where?* I asked myself a question for which there were no good answers. When he took my cash, the man behind the counter made some comment about nice weather. I contrived a polite nod and asked for change for the candy machine. I hoped to find comfort in the chocolate.

"Your tank's really full." The lineman pointed to the brass rod at full length above the fuel tank cap.

Free of the ground and level at altitude, I felt calmer. I bit off half the Hershey's bar, which was already beginning to soften from the warmth, and closed my eyes in satisfaction. The dark chocolate injected a shot of optimism directly into my brain.

In an hour, a small nondescript southeastern Alabama airfield appeared on the horizon. I began a long descent. Night pulled its seamless cover up over the earth as I taxied to the transient tie down area. New yellow ropes at every unoccupied parking spot waited like coiled snakes ready to strike. I looked away from the name of the town painted on the side of the building and refused to allow it into my mind.

When I circled to land, I spied the long narrow motel, which seemed close to the airport. It took 20 minutes at a half-run to get there. The neon sign with its damaged, partially lit M finally came into view, *Notel.*

Good, I thought as I passed the sign's posts at the edge of the gravel parking area. *I won't tell either.* Neon transformers buzzed loudly. Kamikaze bugs wildly circled the flickering tubes. Uncovered yellow incandescent lights, one above each room's door, dotted the full length of the poorly kept building's shallow porch. A strong smell of greasy hamburgers hung from a long gray tail of smoke that streamed from a blackened roof vent atop the greasy spoon next door.

My mother, the infamous Maggie McKenna, would have instantly turned away and refused even to have a look at a room. She had walked away from plenty of places much nicer than this one. I inherited her fastidiousness. However, in this moment, I didn't care. I would have slept in an oil drum if it were safe.

Without acknowledging the waitress's comments, I pointed at the day's chicken fried steak special on the chalkboard. *Maybe, I'll die of food poisoning*, I half-heartedly hoped. If it hadn't been for the people in my life who would suffer, I would have considered the list of least painful ways to take my last breath.

Ungrateful, self-serving bitch, I chastised myself. *Stupid, this is your reality. You made it. You face it.*

"BETTE," Ted said with thinly veiled mock disgust. "Buy the damn dress. We can't take it with us. Let's enjoy what money we have while we can."

It was our first Christmas season after nearly two-decades apart. Ted had given me my precious journal a few days before. We were planning our first New Year's Eve together. I wanted it to be perfect. The dress was a one-occasion slinky black sequined number with a split up the side that stopped just below my hoo-hoo. I admired myself in the full-length mirror and touched my thigh through the opening four times before he scolded me. I bought the dress.

Something like 16 years after I last saw Ted in college, we found each other for the second time. Everything about our lives had changed except how we felt. We had each made *'til death do us part* attempts at socially acceptable bonding and failed. After we were together for a while, I confessed to Ted about how he made me feel on the day we first met in Memorial Hall. I finally admitted I had never stopped thinking of him. One day, soon after my declaration, he brought his Algebra textbook to my house and asked me to open it. I asked what page. "Just open it," he replied.

I held the tattered burgundy book to the light. It practically opened itself to a page near the center where a brown, partially disintegrated oak leaf was pressed flat.

"I picked it up outside Memorial," he explained, "the day we first met. I didn't want to forget." He closed the text and lovingly took me in his arms.

Southeastern Alabama, Saturday, April 8, 2000

IT'S A COOL MORNING. The calling birds have not yet been able to summon the sun and dissolve the soft blanket of night. These words are evidence that I'm awake. I don't remember when sporadic dreams became waking. Yet, here I sit with what seem to be conscious thoughts.

I like not talking and not answering questions. I like my aloneness. The only way I would choose it to be different would be if Ted could fill this silence and wash away my sorrow.

I print these words because I long ago gave up writing. I like the scratch of pen on paper and the unique shape of each letter. I like that each has its own name and unspoken number, and when properly grouped, they have meaning.

Even with my eyes closed, it is not dark. I feel myself fall, and yet, I have perfect balance. I see a series of glowing words in the half-light. They speak to me in my own voice. Nevertheless, they are not spoken. There is no sound in the room. Still, I hear clearly spoken words in low tones of soft texture and disconcerting rhythm. My hand begins to move of its own accord as a planchette on an Ouija board. I resist finishing this thought. There is something else at work—an unwelcome gift from a faceless someone—a diaphanous entity that exists on

another realm somewhere between waking and dreaming,
loving and hating, fear and bravery, loneliness and
fulfillment. Someone, whose words rob me of hope.

OF LOVE AND LOSS
Loneliness, a cold boundless abyss, lurks nearby
-fueled by fear, loss, and longing-
Joy, an infinite pool of warmth and pleasure,
lies in obscurity
-out of reach-
-awash with the elusive glow of ever-present moons-
Affection and love might bring joy and fill the abyss
-if only they could find their way-
Their futile search is lit by the dim glow
of hope's tiny fires
I dream of joy's moons,
of hope's flickering fires
I long for an elixir, a cure
The elixir is love, the cure is joy,
but my love is lost

I reread the words shaped by my own hand. My misery surprised me. What was written had the shape of a poem, but no rhyme or measure, only offbeat despair.

I tossed my journal on the dingy bed and noticed that the covers were hardly ruffled. *How can I sleep so poorly and not rip the bed apart?* I wondered. My legs ached. Physician-installed steel pins seemed to pierce my muscles instead of the bones in which they were implanted.

In the sandy parking area outside the regrettable room, I experienced a temporary lightness-of-being threatened by the neon's harsh buzz. It spoiled the tranquility of the morning's rapidly unfurling light. Night's eastern canvas was awash with horizontal bands of crimson that emanated from a fiery ball as it raced from its hiding place behind the earth. Broadening, uneven brush strokes overwhelmed the dark sky with rapidly growing streaks of red and yellow.

I watched with awe as nature's verse wrote itself. Soft blue stripes quickly swallowed crimson and the marginal band grew white as a thin veil of broken overcast gulped down the colors.

"Red sky in the morning, sailors take warning." My Uncle Curtis's cautionary reminder replayed in my head. I often remember the expressions of my father's younger brother. He was once a sailor and always a second father to me. Taken by cancer before our time together was enough, I miss him still.

In my pseudo-poem, I read only sadness and dismay. In the dramatic watercolor sky, I saw God's hand holding the brush. I felt the warmth of His colors happily splashed upon our lives. I fell to my knees in the middle of the deserted parking lot, interlocked my fingers, closed my eyes, and repeated my prayer word-for-word, exactly as I had written it the day before. I added something about "please keep my airplane in the sky today." When I finished, I opened my eyes to a challenging, cloud-covered day. *God's will*, I reminded myself.

"Bette, thank God," David's strained voice was a cross between enraged and relieved. "We've been worried sick. Why haven't you called?"

"I'm fine." I knew I should attempt to explain that I hadn't wanted to talk, but how do you do that without talking? "I'm in Alabama," I answered, avoiding the town's name.

"Okay, good." He sounded relieved.

"What do you know?" I warily asked.

"Nothin' new about the fire," he answered guardedly.

"What's wrong, David? What aren't you sayin'?" I demanded. A sinking feeling began to build in my chest.

"Le—Dawg—"

"Shit, what now?"

"He's MIA. Nobody knows where." He paused. I sensed he was gathering himself to get to the point. "St. Louis County cops checked his house. He left it like he's not comin' back, and…" The line fell silent.

"You there, and what?"

He cleared his throat. "Two things, first, he left a note for his sister. Dependin' on how you read it, it's either a suicide note or goodbye. With that sick bastard, who knows? One thing's for sure, it's written in a tone of finality."

"And the second thing?" I asked, afraid.

"They checked his bank accounts and credit cards. He emptied the accounts a couple of weeks ago and hasn't charged anything since the day you left for Florida. The money, he stole from you before your divorce, is gone— all of it!" He paused again. "I told you then, you should have fought for it," he said angrily.

"I don't care about the money. Never did," I answered, confused by David's fascination with my money and sensing there was more. "What else did they find?"

"Some purchases he made with a credit card during the last couple of months," he answered reluctantly. "They're really strange."

I steadied myself against the payphone mounted on a short stainless steel pole just outside the Fixed Base Operator's office. Again, I wished I'd brought my cell phone so I could lie down and talk. Dizziness and doom worked its way down my unsteady legs.

"He bought a digital timer from Wal-Mart, a magnesium fire starter from Bass Pro, and—and a model rocketry electric match from the hobby shop in Kirkwood," David stammered.

"Bette, the Fire Marshal told the Stanville cops that those things along with some highly combustible materials could have started the fire with a three-day delay. Dawg could've started the fire and been at the Reed's farm at the same time. You're in danger."

I labored to breathe and frantically searched for a single clear thought beneath the dense fog blanketing my mind. *Surely, it can't get any worse*, I told myself, unconvinced.

David was intuitively quiet.

"What else?" My disembodied voice weakly asked.

"I'm worried 'bout your mom."

"Why, what happened?"

The line was deathly silent. Searing white noise clamored in my ears. "David, is she alright?" I demanded.

"She overheard us—your dad and me."

"Overheard what exactly?" A pressure on the backs of my knees threatened to collapse me.

"I talked to some of the guys Dawg works with. He caught a ride on a corporate jet to Florida last fall." There was another terrifying silence. "Bette, he arrived in Orlando on the evening of August thirteenth."

"You mea—" I gasped.

"Yeah, sorry, he was there when you went down, Bette. You weren't dreamin'. I think you *did* see him in the hospital."

"Oh, my God" I stopped myself and forced any concern for me out of my mind. "What about mom. Is she okay? The truth, David."

"Your dad says she's okay. I saw her yesterday. She was pale as a ghost. He's takin' care of her. We need to keep you safe. She'll be fine."

"David, what can I do? I wanna come home. I need to see her for myself."

"Bette, even she agrees. We want you here, but until the cops find him, it's not safe. You have to keep doin' what you're doin'. If he's behind you, you've got to put some distance between you. Get back in your plane and head west as fast as you can. Don't come home."

"Whatever, I don't like it, but I'll do it—for now."

"Bette," David's voice cracked, "watch your back."

THIRTEEN

ONE STOP and a second emptied fuel tank, after departure from the unnamed overnight, and I'd had enough. When I was in the air, I wanted to be on the ground. While on the ground, I couldn't wait to get airborne. No thing or place made me happy. Every muscle in my body throbbed. On the left side of my back, a fierce knife's-blade pain sliced above the shoulder blade.

My mind's only image was of my mom's tortured face. Once, I saw her when she looked exactly as David described. It was in the hospital after the doctor removed adhesions from a years old hysterectomy. She was a breathing corpse whose complexion was whiter than the sheets upon which she lay.

Relieved when the second tank of gas was finally gone, I slammed my airplane on a secluded runway as though swatting a fly with a fuselage. Kitten cried out in protest at my unseemly treatment and hurried to the grass tie down area. We were still barely in Alabama.

Disgusted upon not finding tie downs, I fished three braided nylon cords out of a canvas bag that Jim had strapped down next to the battery in the small area behind the backseat. From force of habit, I wiggled the battery cables and then checked the connections on the Emergency Locator Transmitter also mounted on the fuselage. On the far side of the battery, almost obscured from sight, I noticed an additional hand formed metal box. *You should know what this is*, I thought.

The mildly oxidized rectangular aluminum container, half the size of a woman's shoebox, matched its surroundings. I considered removing the four corner screws from the professionally formed lid. *The airplane runs*, I told myself. *Leave well enough alone. Next time I talk to Jim, I'll ask.* I apathetically promised.

Before I finished securing the Champ, a Cessna 150 landed. The young pilot sauntered over to say hello. He lashed down the Aeronca's tail without me asking, and I helped him push his Cessna into the hangar. He offered a lift to town. I broke two of my own rules by gratefully accepting a ride from a stranger and not bothering to fuel my airplane or ask about fuel availability.

Alone in another gloomy motel room, I collapsed fully clothed on the bed.

Northwestern Alabama, Sunday Morning, April 9, 2000

GOD, WHY HAVE YOU forsaken me? Is it not enough that I suffer for my past? Must You also bring my family into this? Why punish my poor mother? If this is part of Your plan, what else do You have in store for me? What lesson will You teach me tomorrow?

Embarrassed by what I wrote, I read the indelible words aloud and hastily clapped my journal shut and tied it tight. I regretted my insolent note to God, and hoped it wouldn't make matters worse. I hid the book under a stiff foam pillow. I cringed as I cautiously stepped outside expecting a lightning strike. To my amazement, there was no lightning. Rather, it was a glorious day with a perfect cloudless sky and sweet, still air. *Maybe God's setting me up,* I thought suspiciously. *Just because He's God doesn't mean He's all-forgiving.*

The parking lot was empty save a half-dozen cars and a couple of semis. Other than scratching a few disrespectful words on a page, splashing a little chlorine-laced water in my face from a corroded tap, and pacing the grimy carpet of my 12 by 12 room, I'd done nothing since I arrived mid-afternoon the day before.

When I set out from St. Augustine, where I had passed a long night riding a rollercoaster of emotions ranging from fear to despair, I had felt close to God. I prayed a prayer of gratitude for His blessings and was certain He was listening. Kitten's new tires had arrived on time. She ran great, and I got away without a hitch. However, a short conversation with David, a few hours alone to think, and my contentment turned against me.

A sound like rocks being crushed between steel gears shattered the serene morning. The driver of a shiny stainless-steel tanker warmed his engine. I must have looked like a lost puppy because he rolled down his window and offered me a lift. "To the airport?" I asked without considering the risk of accepting a ride from a second stranger in as many days. *Don't tell mom,* I reminded myself realizing what I'd done. At 43, I was still subject to my mother's lectures.

The airport's solitary fuel pump was locked. The place deserted. *Broke your own rule!* I chastised myself for not asking for fuel the afternoon before. I walked down the row of galvanized tin hangars and considered siphoning a few gallons from somebody's plane and leaving a note and some cash. Without a can and a hose, there was no way. I couldn't believe my luck when I found a chubby gray-haired pilot changing his oil in the very last hangar.

"I'd he'p ya, miss," he began apologetically after I

explained my situation, "'cept tha pump ain't worked for a week. I reckon tha' new un's still on back order."

I knew it, I thought, looking at the sky. *God couldn't let this pass.*

"I kin ma'be he'p ya though," he said when he saw my reaction. "I kin spare a few gallons outta my plane. It'll least git ya to the next airport."

Three gallons is a quarter tank, I thought, pointing the nose northwest. *I have plenty of time to find fuel.*

I crossed into Mississippi and checked my sectional chart for the nearest airport large enough to be open on Sunday morning. There was nothing close by. I continued on course, measuring distances and weighing my options.

The morning sun was behind me. With no rear window, only indirect sunlight filled the cockpit. I squinted against the harsh glare, pushed my Ray Bans up the bridge of my nose, and turned my attention to the airport directory in my lap. My head was down for no more than a minute or two when the names on the page became obscure in an unsettling darkness. Before I could raise my head, a flash as bright as a thousand white suns devastated the cockpit. A thunderous crash followed. Next, a wind shear tossed the Champ sideways like a cork in the ocean.

I tore the glasses from my face and hurled them over my shoulder. Inky black night in the middle of the day devoured my plane. *This is what God was waiting for,* I thought, banking into a hard left turn. I counted the spinning numbers on the Directional Gyro until we had turned 180 degrees. With wings level, on a reciprocal course, I waited, hoping to break free of the dark clouds, which completely engulfed my airplane.

The airplane shuttered. Seconds felt like an eternity. We popped out of the cloud cover. "Shit." The involuntary declaration leaped from my lips. No more than three football fields directly ahead was another wall of ominous black clouds. We were boxed in. I had seen this before.

There was no escape. A second flash of lightening blinded me. The clouds took on a greenish tint. "Damn it, hail!" I yelled.

Once, when I was nineteen, I saw the exact same conditions. My dad and I were flying through the Missouri Bootheel headed home from Tennessee. The weather rolled in just as quickly. I wasn't afraid because he was in the right seat. Then, I looked over and saw his pipe clinched between his teeth and the color drained from his face. I knew we were in serious trouble. Luckily, Sikeston was two miles ahead. We made the airport before the storms trapped us. My dad's face said it all that day. There's no fleeing from this kind of weather.

The Champ's fabric was no match for hail. Our featherweight made us helpless against violent winds. I dropped the nose, banked hard left, and began a tight spiral. My only hope was shelter on the ground.

As we fell through 600 feet, I spotted an open cow pasture with power lines on the north end and tall trees on the south. There looked to be something like 1,000 feet between. I'd landed the Champ plenty of times in less space than that. *I'm glad the wheel fairings are gone*, I thought, scanning the possibly hazardous terrain. The grass appeared short, but I knew how deceptive looks could be.

No choice, I resigned myself to whatever fate awaited. I made the last turn and lined up on the field from the south end. I was too high. I forced the stick over to the left and forward. Simultaneously, I pressed hard against the right rudder pedal. With radical cross control, we slipped almost straight down to the end of the rapidly approaching field.

Newly budded tree limbs brushed the tires as we dropped through the last few feet. I rolled the plane out on an imaginary centerline, held my track with the rudders, and kept the left wing down into the wind. I pulled the nose up into a flare. In the last few feet of ground effect, the wings stalled. The Champ dropped to the ground with a harsh thud. Rough terrain reverberated through the fuselage. We rolled less than 100 feet to an abrupt stop. I had used far less than half of the available distance. Had Mac been here, he would have patted me on the shoulder, taken a contented drag on his pipe, and smiled.

A barbed wire fence bordered the field on the west side. Beyond that was a small white country church with an imposing steeple and stained glass windows. The scene was something from a Norman Rockwell style picture postcard. At the back of the gravel parking area, between the church and the near fence, was a tiny brick house with a closely cropped lawn. On the far side of the church, just beyond a white picket fence with a pink-honeysuckle draped trellis arched over a small matching gate, was an ancient cemetery. Behind me, on the other side of the line of trees we had kissed on approach, was a narrow blacktop road.

One of the wooden double doors of the church swung open. A short rotund man with a graying beard appeared. Leaning into the howling crosswind, he hurried across the empty parking lot in my direction. One hand kept his jacket tightly closed against his chest. With the other, he clamped a black full-brimmed hat on his head. Using throttle, rudder, and brake, I swung the airplane around 90 degrees to the left, and bounced through the grass toward the approaching man.

Against the fence on the church side, with strands of wire embedded in its thick bark, a massive oak reached out with long black arms like a beckoning guard. There was some danger of falling limbs in a windstorm. However, I decided to take my chances with the lesser of two evils and stopped beneath the tree. *Might give me some protection from the rapidly approaching hail,* I reasoned.

"Looks like ya had a good co-pilot." The man shouted as the propeller took its last turn.

"I'm sorry, what?" I asked.

He pointed at the colliding black clouds. "I watched ya land. Praise the Lawd, looks like you had he'p." He reached skyward with open arms.

"Can I tie 'er down here?" I asked in a pleading voice. "Rain and maybe hail'll be here in a minute."

"Ya need rope?" he asked with a sugary southern accent. "Don't know much 'bout planes 'n' sech."

"I have rope and stakes," I shouted, over angry howling wind. "I can swing her 'round and tie the tail to the tree."

"I'll help ya, missy," he volunteered, already nimbly astraddle the fence.

I tied the last knot. The sky opened. Rain pounded the Champ's tight skin like pebbles on a drum. Stooped uncomfortably, I took shelter beneath the wing. The stranger joined me. Relaxed and happy, he stood fully erect with room to spare.

"Pastor Fid," he offered, reaching for my hand. "This is ma cherch."

"Elizabeth," I answered, returning his firm grip. "I really appreciate your help. It's a little late to ask permission. Is it okay I landed here? I didn't have a chance in this storm." A backdrop of lightning crashed and sizzled followed by a deafening clap of thunder. "It came outta nowhere."

"It'll be jest fine. Looks like it's gonna be a toad strangler." A toothy smile appeared through thick salt and pepper whiskers. "This here's Brother Elmer's field. He'll be here in a spell for Sund'y service. He won't mind a-tall. God bless us; he just moved tha cows yesterd'y. I reckon He's watchin' out fer ya."

"I suppose," I reluctantly agreed.

"Sounds like you 'n' God have issues," he said loudly over the pounding rain. A broad smile and a look I didn't understand followed. "Lucky for you, He's a good lis'ner. Let's get outta this weather."

Inside the austere church, tall stained glass windows

were a kaleidoscope of storm muted light. The immaculate oak tongue and groove floor was two shades lighter than the polished pews. I guessed there was room for something like 80 parishioners.

"I have another problem besides the storm," I confessed as he led me to the front pew. "I need fuel."

"Folks 'll start 'rivin' soon," he answered, without a hint of surprise. "I'm sure we can he'p ya with whatever ya need. My flock always comes through." He smiled again. "Ye'll see. You might's well stay fer church? If'n it's God's will, the storm'll pass, and we'll git ya on yer way."

"Thanks, that'll make my mother and my grandmother, God rest her soul, very happy."

"Praise tha Lawd." He raised both arms straight up and opened his hands as if he expected someone to toss him a ball. "Praise tha Lawd for bringin' ya here taday."

"I'm not sure He brought me," I answered, unimpressed. "I don't think He's been too interested in anything good for me lately."

"Sounds like I was right. You do have issues," he said with a concerned tone, his accent for a moment gone. "Elizabeth, if you like, we can talk."

The back wall on both sides of the doors soon teemed with open, dripping umbrellas. Pastor Fid introduced me to every member of the arriving congregation as though I was a visiting cousin. Several of the men complimented my airplane. The women praised God for my safe landing in the storm.

"God guided you to us like He did Paul to the Greek Island of Rhodes on his way to Ephesus." A tall deacon commented as he flipped through the pages of his heavily worn Bible.

I squirmed at the analogy, smiled politely, and nodded. *I already have enough trouble with God,* I thought, glancing nervously at the ceiling. *He won't like me being compared to the Apostle Paul.*

Resounding bells filled the sanctuary. The last few people slipped in. An usher closed the double doors. Every pew was full.

I weakly protested when Libby, the Pastor's wife, insisted I sit with her in the second pew from the front. A little earlier, she had told me she loved singing in the choir. Now, I felt badly because she gave it up to sit with me. *Something else to feel guilty about,* I thought as we settled in. She slipped a hymnal into my hands.

I felt his breath on the back of my neck before I heard his voice. "I kin he'p ya with fuel." A man in the pew behind whispered in a kindly baritone rasp.

I felt like a sore thumb in damp khakis, boots, and a denim shirt, an out-of-favor sinner surrounded by good people.

I hadn't set foot in church since Ted's standing-room-only funeral. It was probably 30 years since the last time I crossed the threshold of a Baptist church with Grandma Damon supporting herself on my arm. It was the summer before she died. We arrived late because when I picked her up, I was wearing a pants suit. She made me swing by home and put on a dress. "No good Christian would…" was how she always began a stern reminder.

Pastor Fid finished the announcements. I sighed with relief. He hadn't mentioned my plight or me. He freed the microphone from its cradle, stepped down from his low stool behind the pulpit, crossed to the center of the sanctuary, and stopped in front of the altar.

From the moment he took up the microphone, Libby began to shift uncomfortably in her seat. When he moved away from the pulpit, she let out an audible gasp. The speakers popped loudly. She jerked back as if she'd been shot. I looked around. Astonished faces followed his every move.

"He never leaves the pulpit!" Libby whispered, her lips

close to my ear.

Pastor Fid smiled warmly, looked straight at me, and began to speak in a soft, comforting, unaccented voice.

"In a week, we will celebrate Palm Sunday," he began. He closed his eyes and lifted his face as though waiting for inspiration. "On the pulpit," he pointed at it without looking, "every word of my sermon is written." He opened his eyes and scanned the room. "I've worked on it every day this past week. It was to be something special because in these holy days of Lent, we must remember that our Savior was troubled as He reluctantly prepared for His supreme sacrifice. He had doubts, but He always knew He would carry out His Father's wishes and give Himself for all of us. Even for Jesus, the Christ, it was difficult to accept.

"At times, those who wish to live the life God has planned for us question *His plan*. We struggle with our personal tragedies and doubt.

"Today, something special happened. In place of the sermon I prepared, I want to talk about this event. God brought us a special visitor. Although I do not know the details of her life, I feel she is here for a very specific reason."

He looked at me. My face burned. Libby took my hand.

"Elizabeth," he said decisively.

Although I was embarrassed, I found comfort in my name on his lips. I relaxed. A content silence filled my mind. The ringing in my ears stopped. Everyone, including me, could have heard a pin drop.

"This morning, I watched you literally fall from the sky between two thunderstorms that came out of nowhere. You landed in a place on God's earth where no airplane has ever put a wheel—all just in time for church. I do not wish to embarrass you. However, I believe God brought you here for a purpose. When we first spoke, I sensed something very profound in you. Since then, I have been praying. Now, I know what God wants me to say. Let's begin with Psalms 6."

Libby flipped to the page without searching, and laid her open Bible partially in my lap.

"[1]**O LORD**, rebuke me not in thine anger, neither chasten me in thy hot displeasure." Pastor Fid recited the scripture flawlessly from memory.

"[2]Have mercy upon me, O LORD; for I *am* weak: O LORD, heal me; for my bones are vexed.

[3]My soul is also sore vexed: but thou, O LORD, how long?

[4]Return, O LORD, deliver my soul: oh save me for thy mercies' sake.

[5]For in death *there is* no remembrance of thee: in the grave who shall give thee thanks?

[6]I am weary with my groaning; all the night make I my bed to swim; I water my couch with my tears.

[7]Mine eye is consumed because of grief; it waxeth old because of all mine enemies.

[8]Depart from me, all ye workers of iniquity; for the LORD hath heard the voice of my weeping."

He looked around the sanctuary. "We ask ourselves, why do good things happen to bad people and bad things to good? When we do not get our way, when God's answer is not what we prayed for, we too often turn our backs. We blame Him. We ignore Him." Pastor Fid raised his arms in an open embrace of the heavens. "Sometimes we are angry with God," his voice grew smaller, "because of His choices for us.

"Brothers and sisters, God does not mind that we are angry. Rather, the opposite is true. He gave us the gift of freewill. He wants us to think for ourselves. He knows it sometimes includes anger. In some way, His only Son was angry with His Father for sending Him to the cross.

"He gives us anger because it makes us stronger. He gives us disappointment because it balances us. He gave us each other because He wants us to find strength and understanding in the comfort of others."

Soft shouts of "Amen," came from throughout the room.

"Accept the plan that God has for you." The Preacher's voice rang out. "Open your eyes to all that lies before you. Be grateful Jesus sacrificed Himself that we might have eternal life..."

He finished with a short story of Palm Sunday. The choir began to sing.

"Elizabeth," Libby whispered as her husband left by the center-aisle to wait at the open doors through which warm freshly washed spring air rushed in. Sunlight shone brightly through multi-colored windows. Every trace of a storm was gone. "Join us for lunch. The men will bring your fuel later. I think you and Fid must have a lot to talk about."

"Why do they call you Fid?" I asked, anxious to break the silence. In a homey basement room, Pastor Fid sat across from me on a dark brown sofa, which matched the overstuffed chair with a hollowed out spot in the seat that was trying to swallow me.

He smiled a shy, barely-noticeable smile through rebellious whiskers. From behind the sofa, he retrieved a worn and polished fiddle. "Little odd fer a Baptist Preacher I reckon, but I love it so." He laughed, wedged the instrument beneath his chin, and in one seamless motion, drew a heavily rosined bow across the strings. A mournful wail echoed against green concrete walls in the rectangular room. He grinned and flawlessly began playing both parts of *Dueling Banjos* from the movie *Deliverance.* "Wouldn't wanna disappoint, given our geography," he said impishly as he drew out the last note and nestled the fiddle between two throw pillows on the sofa beside him.

"Tell me," he began, without his southern drawl. Again sounding like the man who two hours before had delivered an impassioned sermon. "What has God done to make you so angry?"

"I think I finally know," I answered. "But before I say, I'd like to know how it is you're always so happy?"

"Happiness is easy." He smiled broadly. "Around here we operate on the honor system. We honor God, and He fills our every need.

"Happiness, Elizabeth, starts with the sixth letter of the alphabet," he said factually. A mischievous grin crossed his face. "It's the most important thing in our lives."

I pictured the alphabet in big white letters inked on green cardboard squares above the chalkboard in Mrs. Downright's First Grade classroom and counted to six. "But Pastor, F is the sixth letter. H is the eighth." I pointed out.

"Exactly," his face disappeared behind sparkling white teeth, "F is for Faith. That's where it all begins—with Faith!

"Now, it's your turn to answer my question, Elizabeth. Why are you angry with God?"

"I am angry," I confided, listening intently to my own disembodied voice with the hope of hearing what I really thought. "Before today, I didn't know who I was angry at. I thought my anger was directed at the two men with the biggest impact on my life. I thought I was mad at Ted because he was the love of my life, and he left me. I have no doubt, I'm furious with my ex-husband because he abused me, and won't leave me in peace."

I sat in awe of the steady voice, which sounded like mine and seemed to know more about my life than I did. My fingers tightly laced in my lap, and my hands pale from a lack of blood flow. "Today, you've helped me see that I'm angry at God because He allowed an evil man into my life and left him there. Then, He gave me only a glimpse of my one true love before spiriting him away."

"I understand." He nodded. "You think God is punishing you. That's not necessarily true. Can you tell me what you've done that's so awful you believe you should be punished?"

I didn't have to search for the answer. "I've failed to be the kind of friend we all should be. You said yourself; we are here to comfort each other. I'm self-centered and self-serving."

"Why self-serving?"

"Maybe I wasn't always this way. I think it happened gradually. I've always worn my feelings on my sleeve. I'm too quick to say what I really think. I'd tell somethin', to someone I thought was a friend, in confidence, and they'd use it to hurt me.

"My dad says our family's always been this way. Before the civil war, the McKennas owned a prosperous North Carolina plantation. Story goes that my Great-Great-Grandfather, George Washington McKenna, Senior, hid all the family's gold before he left with the Confederate Army's 25th North Carolina regiment. Anyway, long story short, he was wounded in battle. The surgeon told him he was gonna die. So, he told his best friend about the gold and asked him to get it to the family after the war. The friend went AWOL, took the gold, and disappeared. My grandfather survived. Our family lost everything. They struggled. Finally, destitute, they moved to Missouri with little more than the shirts on their backs.

"They call it the family curse because we all seem to have a propensity to trust people with the secrets of our lives. In the end, we're always betrayed. My dad's generation is so paranoid they don't even trust each other."

"How does your desire to be open make you self-centered?"

"I was married before Ted. I told you." I stiffened in my seat. "Nearly every day for almost four years, he told me I was conceited, self-centered, and arrogant. In our final year together, he must have learned a new word because he called me a narcissist." I covered my face with my palms.

"He said my private thoughts were no big deal. I'm not necessarily talking about deep dark secrets. I'm referring to the personal thoughts we all have—embarrassing moments—the little things we don't want to make public knowledge."

"I understand," he said sincerely. "What you call your secrets are things you sometimes need to share with one other person, but don't want them broadcast to the world at-large."

"Exactly," I said, relieved. "Thank God, someone finally understands. He turned everything into a weapon against me. He told me that when I expected people not to repeat my secrets it meant I thought myself superior. He constantly reminded me that I'm no better than anyone else. Rather than feeling sorry for myself when people talk about me, he wanted me to return the favor and talk about them, even if I had to make something up.

"I could never do it. However, he wasn't one to let a sleeping dog lie, so he did it for me. He told people things about me I'd never said or done. He twisted everything and made it all sound wicked.

"Pastor Fid, do you think God is punishing me for being weak, for not being able to buck-up and carry my own load? Or is it just as my ancestors thought, a family curse?"

"Elizabeth, God filled our world with people and animals of all types. Good and evil is everywhere. What you describe is not your punishment; it's others letting evil control them. It is they who sin. They are the ones betraying your confidence."

"Thank you. I understand. What you say makes sense." My voice no longer sounded surreal. "In church this morning, you said God brought me here. If that's true, do you think it is so I could talk to yo—"

"Elizabeth, when was the last time you had a real conversation with your folks?"

The question surprised me. We had not talked much about my family. "Couple a days, I guess. I've been avoiding my mother. My friend, David, said she's really upset. I have no idea what to say to her."

"Why don't you let me give her a call?" He rose from the sofa as though my answer was a foregone conclusion. "I'd just like to tell her you're alright. I won't betray your confidence. Maybe I can help ease her suffering."

"God bless you," he said, finishing a five-minute conversation. He handed me the phone.

My mother's voice was clear and calm. "God is with you, honey. I'm glad you found someone to talk to. Don't worry about me. I'm fine now. I know everything will be okay..."

FOURTEEN

LATE SUNDAY AFTERNOON, the man who whispered in my ear during church arrived with three other men from the congregation, their wives, and more than enough high-octane avgas to fill the Champ's tank. Brother Elmer brought a monstrous green and yellow cab tractor and mowed a strip, 18-feet wide, straight as a string, dead center down his pasture.

Mothers, husbands, Libby, Fid, and I walked shoulder-to-shoulder the length of the makeshift airfield. Laughing children played tag among our ranks. We raked, scooped manure into wheelbarrows, and picked up rocks. "Amen." From time-to-time, someone enthusiastically hollered as they held up a large rock, limb, or dry cow pile as though they'd caught the prize bass in a fishing tournament.

After a Sunday supper of abundant leftovers, just before dark, Libby invited me to explore the cemetery. Nearly every tombstone prompted a family story as far back as 150 years. She explained how everyone related and why each person and family was remembered. At the bottom of the hill, on the west end, we turned back toward the gate.

"He's a good man," she commented, for no apparent reason.

I scanned the tombstones searching for the name of the man to whom she referred. I must have looked confused because she faltered.

"I—I mean Fid," she explained. "I've no idea what ya'll were talkin' 'bout in the basement this aft-ah-noon," she said, with charming southern diction and an ever so slight rasp. "And I nevah will. He's like a tomb, my Fid. Tha's what makes him—him. He listens ta people. He tells 'em what he thinks. If'n they ask, he tells 'em what he thinks God would say. He nevah tells anothah soul what othahs tell 'im. I spect whatever you need, hon, you kin get from Fid. Aftah his faith and his fam'ly, 'bove all else on this earth, he cares 'bout people. He told me you're somthin' special, nothin' moah. Liz–beth, even though ya'all just met, he cares 'bout ya."

Finally alone, with no regret for having bared my soul to a stranger, I crawled under the fragrant covers in Libby's cramped spare room. An indignant calico cat gave me an unwelcome look and then curled up in the corner of the single bed. I slept peacefully for the first time in months.

Early Monday morning, actually rested, I left the sleeping cat and ventured into the quiet parsonage.

"He's waitin' for ya, downstahs." Libby met me at the kitchen door with a cup of coffee and a warm muffin on a chipped plate. "Says he figuahs ya wanna talk 'fore ya leave."

The swale in the chair seemed to fit my bottom better than the day before. The warmth from the cup displaced a little of the cold that filled my chest where my heart should have been.

"Elizabeth, if you want, why don't you tell me the rest of your story. Tell me more about the two men you mentioned yesterday." As Fid began, it was again clear. When he preached or counseled, he spoke with no accent.

I swallowed hard. "Okay—I'll get the bad news out of the way first. I've only been legally married once. His name is Leon Berger…"

With compassionate hazel eyes intent on my every word, Fid sat across from me in the center of the brown sofa. Occasionally, he nodded in agreement or understanding. *If he truly disagreed, would he say so?* I wondered. He balanced his coffee cup in his lap, but never drank.

"I tried to fix whatever was wrong with us. I cooked his favorite foods. I watched football and went to bars. I had sex with him anyway and anytime he wanted." My candor astonished me. "None of it made a difference. Every day he treated me a little worse. His mood swings became more frequent and harsh until I was truly afraid.

"For the first time, I wished I could escape. I began to think about divorce, but I couldn't find the strength. My life became a comedy of catastrophic, emotional tragedies. He told the same lies so often even he believed they were true.

"When I first told him how others had betrayed my trust and hurt me, he seemed sympathetic. He said I was entitled to my secrets. It wasn't long before my friends knew everything I told him. He had repeated it all to his drinkin' buddies. He berated my every thought. He made believing in soul mates, intangible connections, and true love sound like a bad thing.

"I read somewhere about a Chinese belief, *Yuan*."

Pastor Fid nodded with a knowing smile. "I've read of it." He set the cold cup on the low table between us. "Yuan is what the Chinese call an imaginary red thread, which connects true love across time and space, no matter what, right? They believe if two people are meant to be together, they are always and absolutely connected by Yuan."

"Do you believe in it?" I asked, scooting forward in my chair.

"I believe in something that transcends all limitations and is not restricted to the love between two people." He paused and smiled. "We call it faith. The question is what do you believe?"

"That's just it. I'm so confused I'm unsure of what I believe. Being here with you and Libby has been somethin' special. The people in your church are wonderful. Yesterday, I came as close to contentment as I've been since before the accident. You and your congregation give me hope. I even slept last night. Today, my problems still exist. I feel them trying to catch up with me."

"It sounds like you're leaving something out," he said as if he already knew what it was.

"Talking about my ex has dredged up some horrible memories. I remember what he did to push me over the edge—the things that finally gave me the strength to fight for my freedom."

"Would you like to tell me what they are? Sometimes, when we give voice to our burdens, we feel better."

I breathed deeply. "I mentioned earlier that I tried my best to please him sexually. It came back to haunt me."

"What did he do?"

"The first thing he did was tell everyone I was promiscuous. Of course, that's not how he said it." My face burned with humiliation.

"What else?" Fid asked in a consoling voice.

"Two other things were all I could stand. It didn't happen overnight. In our third year together, he accused me of being a lesbian. Turns out, he made a pass at my best friend. She turned him down. In some twisted way, he interpreted it to mean she and I were lovers. I guess he thought any woman who could resist his charm, and he could be charming when he wanted, was either stupid or gay."

"And the straw that broke the camel's back?" He gently probed.

"Eight months into our last year together, late on a Tuesday night after his bowling league, he came home reeking of beer and cigarettes. He dragged me out of bed and told me he was leaving me for another woman. Then he left."

"That was when you decided to divorce him?"

"Not exactly, stupid me, I laid there all night thinking about the sanctity of marriage and what I could do to win him back. It was like I had forgotten all of the horrible things he did."

"What finally changed your mind?"

"The next morning, I went into the bathroom to wash my face." Turning away, I stared at a blank wall. "I found a used condom on the vanity; it was tied in a knot—"

"Lunch is ready, ya'll." From the top of the basement stairs, Libby's raspy voice saved me from the humiliating end to my Leon story.

Chicken fried steak with milk gravy may have been the biggest Monday lunch I'd ever eaten. I wolfed it down and told myself I didn't want to hurt Libby's feelings. The truth was I was starving.

Half-dozen feet to my right, in the front pew of the church, a broad smile covered Pastor Fid's face. "We've got our bellies full, so let's get to the good part of your story, Liz–beth. I know there has to be one."

With my right leg drawn up under my left and my right arm draped over the back of the pew, I rested my cheek on my elbow. Fid, relaxed in an unassuming slouch, faced me. *It's amazing how comfortable you make me feel,* I thought.

Brilliant columns of sunlight slanted in through the church's open doors. An occasional car whizzed by on the paved road out front. A soft breeze filled the room with spring air.

"Ted Wilson was the love of my life." His name stung my lips. "We became friends in college. He had a girlfriend, so it was never more than friendship. Some years after my divorce, we bumped into each other in a store in St. Louis. He had married the girlfriend. It also ended in divorce. He told me it didn't end badly; it just ended. They were good to each other. However, there was never any passion.

"We picked up where we left off, as friends. It was as though we had been together all of our lives. We both felt it. There seemed to be no boundaries. It wasn't long before I began to tell him all of my innermost thoughts, my secrets. I told him I believed we were connected from the first moment we met and always would be. I told him about Yuan. He didn't laugh. He never laughed at me. Best of all, he never betrayed my confidence.

"We dated for a year. He told me he loved me. During this time, although we were intimate, we neither one mentioned marriage. Even though I never wanted to be away from him, I couldn't bring myself to suggest living together.

"He got me. He understood my paranoia. He encouraged me to believe in people, to trust. He said life and relationships have risks. By burying my head in the sand, I was only hurting myself. He insisted I not deprive the people who really care about me the opportunity to prove their loyalty.

"Like a lot of what Ted said, I remember his exact words. 'Elizabeth, brilliantly cut diamonds are to be worn, not locked away. It's true. When you wear them, you chance losing them, but it's worth the risk. Your feelings are brilliantly cut and unique. Give the world the opportunity to know the inner Elizabeth.'" As I spoke, I found strength in Ted's words given voice after so much time.

Fid nodded in understanding.

"Pastor, I love those words. I want to fulfill Ted's hopes for me, but without him, I'm afraid."

"Elizabeth, you aren't alone. We're all afraid. We have to take risks if we want to succeed. Making a difference means putting yourself out there. Every Sunday morning, before I take the pulpit, I ask God to give me the wisdom to lead my flock. Even with Him in my heart, I'm apprehensive.

"I'd like to hear the rest. I want to know Ted."

"Two months into our second year together, he told me he thought we should take our relationship to the next step. It scared me because I thought he meant marriage. I already knew how bad I was at that. I was relieved when he suggested we invite our family and friends and commit ourselves to each other without a legal ceremony. That spring, on the bank of the same river where I was baptized at fourteen, we promised to love each other forever."

Dozens of memories of Ted flooded my mind. I was determined to tell Fid everything.

"I hope you're not disappointed in me because we didn't get legally married," I apologized.

"Elizabeth, this isn't what the church would have me say. However, it sounds to me like you were married in the eyes of God."

"Thanks for saying that. I felt like we were. We wrote our own vows and a Christian friend presided. Afterward, it was kind of a joke because I'd memorized what I wanted to say and Ted hadn't. I was disappointed when he took out a sheet of paper and began to read. In the first line, I knew exactly what it was."

From beneath my leg, I produced my leather journal, unbound the cord, and took a folded paper from inside the back flap. Shaken by emotion, I slid across the pew and handed the paper to Fid.

He opened it, and read the words aloud.

"Wondering, watching, wondering
Each within, curious of the thoughts of the other
Each alone, until the moment
When one or the other ends the aloneness
Breaks the silence,
Begins a new time,
A time of interaction"

Fid finished and slowly folded the paper. "Did Ted write this for you?" he asked, passing it back.

"No, that's what makes it special. I wrote it for him when we were in college. I hid it in the pages of one of his textbooks. I always thought he'd never found it. He had, and even though it was unsigned, he knew it was from me and kept it all those years. It was proof we felt the same."

"He sounds like a wonderful man. What happened to change it? What did he do? Why are you so angry with him?"

"I'm furious because he left me—he died!"

Fid fell to his knees in front of me and reached for my hands. "Pray with me," he whispered. "Then tell me the rest…"

The most ancient marble headstone stood at the center of the Crossroads cemetery. Topped with carved angels, it was also the tallest. Libby had told me the family story. It was the teenage daughter of the church's founder. A mule and wagon had run over her the same week they finished the church.

I sat with my back against her monument for more than an hour before the Monday afternoon sun kissed the treetops. Emotionally and physically exhausted from my conversation with Fid, I futilely tried to clear my mind. Libby's rendition of buried family histories played repeatedly in my head.

A vivid image of my name next to Ted's on the double

tombstone at the end of a row of family markers, which included my grandparents', weighed heavily upon my heart.

The telephone rang only once. "Bette," David answered with a wounded voice, "you okay?"

"How'd you know it was me?" I asked, taken aback. I had made the decision to call only moments before. He should not have expected me. Sitting alone in the center of the brown sofa, Fid's indention tried to swallow me. Libby had refused to let me help with Monday evening's dinner dishes. She suggested I *check-in.*

"Just had a feelin' you'd call. Your mom said she talked to ya yesterday. I figured today'd be my turn. 'Sides, my phone isn't exactly ringin' off the wall these days," he said, dismayed. "You still in Mississippi with the preacher and his wife?"

"Yep, I'm leavin' early tomorrow. I actually hate to go. They're super nice. Pastor Fid's sharp and a great listener. We talked a lot today. It seems I'm able to open up to a stranger better than a friend, present company excluded, of course."

"Course." David laughed. "It's always easier to pour your heart out to someone you don't know, especially when they aren't judgmental."

"Amen. He understands me. He lets me talk. It felt good to show my thoughts the light of day. It was cathartic. I actually slept all night last night."

"You still sound tired."

"It's all the emotional stuff. I feel like I'm on the *Tilt-A-Whirl,* and the Carney won't let me off." I grimaced with the reminder of a carnival ride that caused a much younger neighbor girl to throw up in my lap. "I haven't done anything today except walk in the cemetery and pet Kitten."

"You don't like cats. You're always comparin' 'em to insensitive people."

"I don't, and they are. There's a calico here. She's mad 'cause I'm sleepin' on her bed. Anyway, I'm talkin' about the Champ. I named her Kitten after my dad's crop duster. She was his plane when he was workin' in Texas in the forties."

"I remember that picture. Haven't I heard your dad call your mom Kitten?" "Yeah, pretty sweet, huh?" Suddenly weary from small talk, I sighed. "David, what's goin' on there?"

More than a minute, which seemed like an eternity, passed. "Not much, we haven't heard a word from the Fire Marshall since he took the evidence to be tested. As far as the engine parts, the metallurgist who's testin' 'em says it'll be at least another week."

"What about *him*?"

"The cops are monitoring his credit cards. He's not usin' 'em." He lowered his voice to a whisper. "He's totally off the freakin' grid."

"What aren't you tellin' me?" I demanded.

"Nothin'," he said defensively. "There's nothin' else to tell."

"I wanna come home."

"Your folks and I think you should keep doin' what you're doin'. Whatever the preacher said to your mom yesterday really worked. She's bakin' and singin'. She's her old self. You planned to be gone for some number of weeks, so stay gone. Give us time to sort this out. Let the cops catch him—then come home."

"I suppose." I tried to mask my disappointment. "It almost sounds like you don't want me there."

"Bette, that's unfair," he said indignantly. "I want to do what's best for you. Don't attack me because you're unhappy."

"I'm havin' a hard time gettin' enthused about this trip."

"I understand, but it's for the best. Where ya headed

next?"

"I've decided to stop in Cape and visit the campus. I have some memories to confront."

"Like what?" he asked. "You haven't said a word about Cape Girardeau or SEMO for a long time. What's up?"

"I haven't felt like talkin' about it, no big deal."

"Where'll you stay?" he probed.

"Don't know." *What happened to, 'let's be careful about what we say on the phone,'* crossed my mind. "A motel I guess. I don't have any close friends still there."

"One of the hotels out on the interstate would probably be best," he suggested.

"David, what difference does it make, why all the questions?"

"I only wanna know you're okay," he answered, still obviously indignant. "I worry about you, that's all."

Crossroads Baptist Church, Mississippi, Tuesday Morning, April 11, 2000

I WISH I COULD ERASE my last entry. I am ashamed. I blamed God for everything wrong in my life. I guess I'm lucky He's forgiving. I'll take Sunday morning's thunderstorms as a blessing embedded in a warning. He planted me here in a field next to a church and a preacher who could help. If I was previously unconvinced of divine intervention, I am today converted.

Pastor Fid and Libby along with Brother Elmer and the other members of this church have shown me the goodness in strangers. They prove Ted right. There are people in the world that can be trusted. I will forever be grateful for my time here.

There's something else wrong. Something I can't put my finger on. If Dawg is following me, what does he hope to gain? How is he even able to find me? I have to be like a needle in a haystack.

Pastor Fid says I have to confront my demons and cast them out. I think I have to find them first. If, and when, I do confront them, what if I'm among them? How do I forgive myself for Ted dying on my watch?

PASTOR FID, Brother Elmer, and two other men had the Champ untied by the time I exited the parsonage. It was barely daylight. If I was to spend the night in Cape Girardeau, it promised to be a long day. Libby waved from the fence when she saw me. I waved back, dropped my bag in the grass, and hurried to the empty church.

Next to the pulpit, I knelt and said a short prayer. Mostly, I asked forgiveness for my sins. I genuinely wanted to pray. Moreover, I needed a reason to be alone in the church. I didn't want to lie to my friends.

From inside my shirt, I took a yellow envelope and hid it in the pulpit beneath Fid's huge Bible. It was open to the book of Job. I made sure the envelope's corner was barely visible from where I knew he would stand the following evening at Wednesday's service.

Earlier that morning, I had written only four words on the outside of the envelope.

To: Crossroads
From: Elizabeth.

With Fid, I was sure an explanation was unnecessary.

My Tuesday afternoon descent to Cape Girardeau, Missouri, from the south was easy. The tower assigned a straight-in approach and reported no traffic. We crawled down the slow 10-mile final at a rock solid 60 miles per hour. Crops stretched as far as I could see to the west and ended on the banks of the Mississippi to the east. After so many years away, it felt like homecoming.

I eased the airplane down the last few feet and gently touched the runway with the main gear. With forward pressure on the stick and the throttle cracked, I flew the tail three feet off the ground in a high-speed taxi toward the distant turnoff.

On the tarmac for less than half a minute, a sense of trepidation tore away my fragile joy. For no obvious reason, an image of a rabbit with a beagle hot on its heels flashed through my mind. I slumped in the seat as if it would help. *Focus,* I chastised myself. One tiny error during high-speed taxi with the tail flying and the airplane would have rewarded me with a ground loop and serious damage. I put my mind to the rudders and ailerons.

I couldn't shake the feeling of being pursued. I rapidly neared the turnoff and backed off the throttle. The tail began to lose lift. I glanced across the open field toward the airport buildings. As I passed the southerly end of a long narrow hangar, a spot of red glinted in the sun. I froze. The airplane veered to the right. The left wheel lifted from the runway. Reflexes threw my fear aside. I corrected our track. My heart pounded the walls of my chest like a crazy woman locked in a closet. My hands trembled. Barely visible behind the hangar, was the rear end of a red Camaro.

FIFTEEN

MAGNETOS OFF, the Champ rolled to a stop at the edge of the refueling area. A tempest of fury replaced fear-fueled paralysis. I kicked open the door and was out and running before the propeller finished its last turn. My apprehension reflected in the lineman's face as I blasted past him like a terrified woman escaping a burning building. I had no regard for my own safety. *I'll put an end to this,* was my only thought.

I sprinted across the apron, ducked under parked aircraft wings, and dodged tie down ropes headed for the place where I knew the Camaro to be. From the bottom of a shallow ditch, I scooped up a softball size rock and covered the last few yards to the hangar without breaking stride. Dread welled up in my chest as I rounded the corner. A low cable barrier caught the toe of my boot. In slow motion, I plunged face down in thick pea gravel. The rock flew out of my hand. Ignoring the pain, I rolled over and covered my face to ward off an onslaught of blows. Nothing happened. The place was deserted—no Camaro—no Dawg—nothing.

"Bette, slow down." David's frantic voice grew louder with every syllable. "What in the hell are you sayin'?"

I hung on the low payphone mounted on the outside wall of the pilot's lounge. "I'm tellin' ya he was here. I saw his car. I didn't catch him, but he was here." I looked nervously around.

"Bette, that's impossible," he said, seeming too soon calm. "No one knew you'd be there."

"You knew," I answered with an accusatory tone. "David, who did you tell?"

"Bette, I haven't told a soul. You're paranoid," he answered angrily. "You need to dial it down a notch." He paused. "Besides, the preacher and his wife knew."

A drop of blood fell from a gravel littered gash just above my right elbow and spotted the concrete at my feet. "I'm standing here bleedin', and you want me to dial it down."

A hundred yards away, the lineman, standing on a short ladder refueling a Beechcraft, looked up. I lowered my voice. "I may be paranoid, but not about this. I'm tellin' ya. The S.O.B.'s here. I don't know how, but he is. He's a lot of things. Clairvoyant isn't one of 'em."

"Bette, I'm sorry you're hurtin'. I don't have any answers and I don't know what you saw. You have to believe me. I told no one—not even your folks."

"Don't worry about me." I lashed out, drowning in frustration. "I'll take care of myself." I slammed the receiver down.

At my wits end, I was bloody, angry, and terrified.

The woman looked up questioningly. "No one's ever asked what colors we have." She shook her head and checked her computer screen again.

I chose a white four-door Chevy and signed the rental agreement without reading a word.

Normal Street bisects the Southeast Missouri State University campus. Near its center, at the highest point of a steep hill, Academic Hall with its copper dome and Kent Library with its classically columned portico, face one another across the broad divided thoroughfare.

I permitted myself a furtive glance toward Memorial Hall to the left of Academic and remembered the long Vietnam Vets' table near the center of the basement cafeteria. One row over, at a table next to the door was where I first met Ted.

From the duffle in the trunk of my car, I took another of the thick yellow envelopes. I double-checked the trunk lock and headed down Normal Hill toward Sprigg Street. In less than twenty steps, flooded with doubt, I returned to check the trunk.

At the bottom of the hill, I turned left and walked hurriedly to the Wehking Alumni Center. Indifferent to my presence, the receptionist looked up from her purse. "What?" she twittered after I announced myself for the second time.

"I want to leave an anonymous gift," I explained and slid the envelope across her desk. "Please, give it to the head of the Alumni Association."

From the top step of Kent Library, I deliberately scanned the street for red cars. Students hurried in every direction. Invisible amid the turmoil, with my head down, and my Airport Directory clasped to my breast, I slipped into the library and found an isolated table near a rear window.

In a soft chair with my back to the wall, I sighed with relief. Even with large bloodstains on the elbows of my shirt, no one gave me a second look. I had told Dawg very little about my favorite places on campus, mostly because he never cared. In the library, I felt safe.

Within every haven, we remain ourselves. There is no escape from our reality. Hidden by the thick masonry walls of Kent Library, my past gnawed at me. A tumor of malignant memories quickly spread. Debilitated by danger lurking in the shadows, I saw no future. For every good decision I had made, three bad ones followed. For every person I had successfully trusted, 10 betrayed me.

IN ROSE THEATRE, just down the hill from Kent, I met the man to whom I willingly gave my virginity.

A Southern Baptist English major from Poplar Bluff, he was five years older than I was. He didn't drink, smoke, or swear, and liked to say he "held no truck with those who do." I trusted him. He was sweet. His kisses were sensual. I was head-over-heels in love for the first time in my life.

Don insisted we go to church together every Sunday. He said my friends were too "secular." I quickly became isolated. Weeks became months, our intimacy never went beyond kissing. "It wouldn't be right outside marriage," he insisted. Eventually, it was I, who was truly desperate. I made my feelings known.

He took me to dinner at a restaurant he could not afford. When we returned to his apartment, he hung his necktie on the outside of the door. By candlelight, he got down on one knee and asked me to marry him. Before I could answer, he removed first his shirt and then my dress. Ravenous for the experience my friends loved to describe in detail, I gave myself to him completely without a second thought.

"Don, I need a few days to think," I answered when he insisted for the third time. Embarrassed by my nakedness and still in pain, I covered myself with my rumpled dress. "Marriage is a big deal. I love you, but I need some time."

After three sleepless nights, I saw Don's younger brother in the Physical Science building.

"Hi," he said cheerfully. It had been two weeks since we had seen each other. "Congratulations." He offered his hand.

"What?" I answered, perplexed. "Congratulations for

what?"

"Sounds like Don's gonna make an honest woman of ya."

"What do you mean?" I demanded, backing him against the wall. Only the textbooks, which I held tightly to my chest, separated us.

"I just mean," he stammered, "that ya'll 've moved to tha next level."

I stepped back, turned, and ran.

"YOU TOLD YOUR BROTHER!" I screamed, shoving past Don into the apartment. "What happened was between us, our secret. You betrayed me—you betrayed my trust!"

THE LIBRARIAN emerged from between tall bookshelves and startled me. She tapped her watch. Astounded by the passage of time, I twisted in my seat. My muscles were stiffer than normal. It was dark outside.

There were no red cars in the street. Even still, it wasn't until I was inside my car with the doors securely locked that I breathed a sigh of relief. David had suggested a hotel out on Interstate 55. With an overabundance of caution, I found a motel on Kingshighway instead.

"You okay, girl." My dad's voice was comforting.

I was anxious to speak with my mother. However, I still didn't know what to say. "I'm okay, Pop." He could read me like a book, so I saved him the trouble. "A little unhinged."

"How so?" He asked calmly.

I told him about the Camaro behind the hangar. In the background, my mother bombarded my dad with questions. Occasionally, he covered the phone and shushed her.

"Doesn't sound good," he said when I finished. "You're safe in the air. You've gotta keep your head down and keep movin'. There's somethin' else botherin' ya.

What is it?"

"I can't put my finger on it. There's somethin' up with David." I swallowed hard. "When we talked earlier today, he wanted to know exactly where I would spend the night. He was pushy. With me, he's never pushy."

"He cares about you, Bette. He wants to know you're safe."

"That's what I keep tellin' myself. Only, there're two problems."

"Like what?"

"He was defensive for one thing." The words wedged in my throat. "And other than the preacher and his wife, only he knew I was stoppin' in Cape."

"Are you sayin'," my dad's tone was slightly off kilter, "you think David's talkin' to Leon?" My mother gasped.

"I don't know what I think." Something crashed to the kitchen floor and shattered. "Pop, please tell ma I'm fine. We'll talk soon," I said, still unsure of what to say to the dish breaker.

"You may have to do that yourself," he answered resignedly.

"How does he always seem to know where I am, and where I'll be? He's stayin' ahead of me in a stinkin' car."

"All he has to do is drive the speed limit and only stop for gas." He confirmed what I already knew. "You've spent a whole lot more time on the ground than you have in the air." Poof, his lighter sparked. "In the mornin', don't tell anyone where you're headed. Just go. I'll keep tabs on David."

Cape Girardeau, Missouri, Wednesday Morning, April 12, 2000

DIDN'T SLEEP. I feel like a broken record. I lay in this disgusting bed for five hours unable to corner a single wink. I accept who and where I am in my life. I got myself here. I don't understand why I can't find even a minute of peace. Yesterday, I visited the SEMO campus. Four years of great memories and all I can think about is what went wrong.

I was optimistic because Pastor Fid and his flock showed me the goodness in others. Yet, here I am today back at square one. Whom can I trust? Are my feelings and fears even safe in these pages?

What choice do I have? Ted is dead. Fid is behind me. I dare not go home. Now, I question the motives of my dearest friend.

IN THE PREDAWN, lit only by yellowish halogen lights high above the parking area, it took me three times longer than normal to preflight the Champ. I removed the cowling. With my Mini Maglite® clutched in my teeth, I checked every nut, bolt, and wire. Normally, I would have drained an ounce of fuel onto the ground, with the presumption that there was little overnight condensation in the tank. Instead, I completely filled a soda bottle, carefully examined it for water, and even tasted it.

"Cape tower, Champ 8-2-6-5-0, ready for departure to the northwest," I announced with no declared destination, no flight plan, and no thought of my next stop. The Aeronca climbed slowly through the pre-sunrise sky. I leveled off at 4,500 feet, calibrated the directional gyro to the magnetic compass, and took up an arbitrary heading. I positioned the grommet at the center of my plotter's rotary azimuth over the blue symbol for the Cape Girardeau airport and drew a line along my heading. To my chagrin, I had unwittingly assumed a course direct to Stanville. Like a horse to the barn, I was headed home.

I repeatedly told myself to change course, yet I didn't. Instead, I maintained cruise altitude and overflew the Stanville airport. My hangar looked like a burned out miniature you might find in an authentic model train set.

There was a gaping hole where half the roof had been. David had not accurately described the extent of the damage. The three hangars with which I shared common walls were empty. Those airplanes were tied down outside.

I circled twice. It was like being outside the funeral home not wanting to enter because you know what's inside. I asked God to keep me conscious. As always, I begged for forgiveness.

In less than a minute, I crossed town and overflew my parents' house. I followed what once had been the traffic pattern of the old airport where I learned to fly, now converted to a fairground. I hoped my dad would hear me. As I expected, he appeared in front of the carport, crossed to the center of the driveway, and waved.

The bobbing brass rod marked my fuel level at 45 minutes of flight time remaining. As was our custom, I waved my wings by jostling the ailerons and rolled out to the northeast. In three seconds, I overflew David's banana-yellow two-bedroom in a sleepy neighborhood. A few blocks away, Main Street looked much like it had for the last hundred years.

Bordering David's back yard, an alley connected two side streets. David's driveway was empty. Pushing my luck, with only 40 minutes of fuel, I should have been preparing to land. I circled once more. Just off the alley, nosed into the backyard of the house next to David's, was a red Camaro.

Disoriented, I slammed the throttle forward against the stop and rolled out on a westerly heading. I meant to escape like a striped ape. Instead, we crawled away at a dishearteningly slow pace. Vibrant sky stretched out as far as the eye could see. It was a magnificent blue shawl draped upon the shoulders of the Ozark's rolling hills. However, in my state of mind, I could not have cared less about the morning's natural beauty.

The oppressive cockpit was devoid of air. I looked

longingly at each of the dozens of perfect spots beckoning me to drill the Champ's nose into their rocky landscape.

"We can help. We'll put an end to your misery," they tempted me like Greek sirens from the depths.

With both hands, I choked the control stick as if killing a snake. I threw it roughly forward. The Aeronca's nose pitched violently down. Wind howled in the struts. Ceconite fabric hummed in protest like the teeth shattering twang of a Jew's harp. I aimed the Champ's nose at a high river bluff and steadied my fatal course.

For more than a minute, a lifetime of memories taunted me. From a place, squirreled away in the most remote corner of my mind, the name of my target peeked out— *Gap Holler on the Big Eddy of the Meramec River.* When he was a boy, my dad camped there with his dad and brothers. Grandpa pushed a handmade wooden wheelbarrow piled high with their kit through the woods from the family farm. Using salted jowl, they cooked meat and greasy beans on a campfire and caught catfish for the family table.

My legacy no longer mattered—at least not to me.

The gray water-carved wall of stone rapidly loomed. *I don't deserve to live,* I scowled, *but Kitten does not deserve to die. Pop would never forgive me if I take my own life, especially in this place!*

I released my hold on the controls. *Kitten 'll decide her own fate, our fate,* I reasoned. She lifted her nose, slowed, and slipped past the highest tree branches atop the bluff. Adrenaline surged. My world turned red.

The impact blasted through the Champ's sturdy airframe and jerked me out of a mindless stupor. I reacted. It was too late. We were already careening across a narrow span of asphalt. I yanked the stick back and slapped the magnetos off. We bounced off the asphalt. The freewheeling propeller thrashed tall weeds like a lawn mower set on its side.

I locked the brakes, the tail lifted high in the air, and the propeller tips came dangerously close to the ground. Nose down, balanced, we hung in midair. I held my breath. An inch lower and she would flip on her back. "NOT AGAIN," I screamed at the top of my lungs. A second longer, the tail fell safely to the ground.

Vomit spewed uncontrollably across the inside of the partially open door. I sat safely on the ground. Between now and a fuzzy image of the beckoning river bluff dead ahead, I remembered nothing.

Dangling from the open doorway, the seatbelt cut harshly into my waist. Unable to free myself, I sobbed until I ached. Revived by the fresh air, I loosed my binding and fell into an acrid pool of puke. Using the strut for support, I lifted myself to my feet. The place was familiar. I was 15 miles west of Stanville. Thankfully, the airport was deserted.

Embarrassed beyond words, I parked by the 1970's style fuel pump and examined my airplane. The propeller was heavily stained, but undamaged. The cockpit reeked. I pulled some weeds from the cowling and looked back toward the windshield. The fuel gauge rod hung by its end. *That can't be,* I thought. *I'm out of gas.*

When I crossed over David's house, I had 45 minutes fuel. I began making mental calculations. *The river bluff was four minutes away. Getting here should have taken another eleven minutes.* Incredulous, I checked the gauge again. *What happened to the other 30 minutes of fuel?*

"Walking coma," was what David called the condition that beset me in times of high stress. He had seen me this way on more than one occasion during the first couple of years following my divorce. I think the spells began while I was still married. All I remember is passing out when Dawg threatened me. David described what he saw as, "eyes wide open and lifeless." He said that sometimes I even walked around like a zombie.

I found the phone number for fuel service crudely scratched on the side of a weathered payphone that hung catawampus on the outside of a rusty tin building. After more than 30 minutes, a stooped-back man with a full head of glistening white hair arrived and unlocked the pump. I ignored his questions about the smell of puke and the few remaining weeds that hung from the horizontal stabilizer.

Standing on a short rickety stool, I filled the tank myself. The pump hummed, and the gauge clicked until avgas gurgled from the tank's neck. I released the trigger and handed the nozzle down. The old man looked first at the 14.6 gallons registered on the pump, then at the plane, and finally up at me. "How much does that little bird hold?" he asked, obviously puzzled.

"Fourteen gallons," I answered, without looking down.

SIXTEEN

OUT OF MY SKIN, back in the air, and westbound, the hair stood up on the back of my neck. *His car was at David's.* The memory of what I saw tormented me.

The engine screamed in protest against the full throttle. I held it against its forward stop with such pressure that my hand throbbed. The propeller beat the air. Ninety miles per hour registered on the airspeed indicator. Still, it was too slow to suit me. I was determined to put miles between the horrid red car and me.

Why would he betray me? Maybe Dawg hurt him. David's always been there for me. The only time we ever had a disagreement was over the necklace. He's never been jealous of me, I rationalized. *He wouldn't do anything to hurt me, would he? Why was he so curious about where I stayed in Cape?* Then I remembered—*hmm, there was the flower incident.*

IN AUGUST, the second summer after David's family moved in across the street, my parents took us to

California on vacation. We mostly followed *Route 66* in our dark green 1958 Mercury station wagon. It was the five of us and enough camping gear and groceries for two weeks.

In the sweltering desert without air conditioning, my brother and I rode with our heads hanging out the open windows. It ended with chapped and bloody lips. Filled with block ice, a galvanized washtub wedged between the seats helped. Still, we were miserable.

At a gas stop in Arizona, my mom made us lock the doors while a Navajo filled our tank and washed the windshield. I begged until she finally let me out to pee. She insisted we go together. When she realized the Indian had the key, she told me I could wait. It was too late. He'd heard us and had it out of his back pocket before she could drag me back to the car. I grabbed for it. When I touched his hand, an unearthly sensation resonated through me. One look at his face, and I knew he felt it too. My mom saw it happen. She jerked me away and dragged me to the bathroom.

I tried to distract myself by reading. No matter where we went or what we did, the Indian's face haunted me. There have been times, in all the years since, when it haunts me still.

Tired and cranky, we arrived home late on the last Sunday night of the month. David was waiting in our driveway. The instant I opened my door he thrust a bunch of wildflowers into my hands. "I'm really glad you're back," he whispered.

Irritated, I looked blankly into his eyes, muttered a displeased "thanks," and left him in the driveway. I followed my little sister into the house, dropping the flowers just outside the front door.

IN MY HASTE to leave the place where I ran off the runway, I climbed into my airplane without organizing my gear. It wasn't until after takeoff that I realized the 1960s road maps were in the back seat. I loosened my seatbelt and stretched until I finally retrieved the bundle. I settled back into my seat. We were 10 degrees off course and had lost 500 feet.

THE NIGHT BEFORE I left Stanville headed for the Reed's farm, I found my dad with only his lower body protruding from a trap door in the ceiling of his home office. He was standing on a stool, which he had positioned in a cleared spot atop his desk. Looking like an upside down Jack-In-The-Box, he groaned and muttered when he heard me.

He flashed a *cat that ate the canary* smile and handed down a rumpled brown paper bag. Inside, I found a dozen tattered maps that I had last seen strewn across the front seat of the green Mercury.

"If you're gonna follow *66*, you'll need original maps," he said, climbing down. "These are from our vacation to California, remember?"

We spread the maps out on the kitchen table. With a red Sharpie and plenty of recounted memories, he traced the route we had followed in the 60s.

FROM THE TOP of the ordered stack, I removed the Missouri map. It tore slightly in a couple of creases as I unfolded it in my lap. I descended to 1,000 feet and began to follow remnants of the old road.

Sixty miles west of Stanville, I flew directly over the scarred ruins of a burned out motel. Only broken and uneven brick walls remained. Rusting appliances and charred furniture littered the overgrown parking lot. I winced. It was where I spent my wedding night, where Leon Berger first revealed his true essence. It was the time and place where my nightmare began.

When we first met, I had no interest in him. Although I

didn't know it then, his was a methodical and premeditated plan of seduction, which he carried out with unmatched patience.

My mother recognized his dark side the first time they met. She even told me what she saw. I was blinded by the need to find a soul mate. On my twenty-sixth birthday, May 5, 1982, he got down on one knee in a restaurant and asked me to marry him.

We married in early August of the same year. *This is what happiness feels like,* I thought, walking down the aisle. *I'll never be alone again.* Inside a small motel room, what began as a perfect day, ended badly. With the closing of the door of room 101, I sensed a change. His gray eyes narrowed and glazed.

"What's the matter, Sweetie?" I asked, throwing my purse on a chair and crossing the room with open arms. "You upset 'bout somethin'?"

"I'm sick of you and your family." He said in a mean voice, which I had never before heard. "You McKenna's think you're so fuckin' special. You treat me like the help." He put a clinched fist in my face, and backed me against the wall. "Let's get somethin' straight. From now on, things 'ill be my way. I'm the head of the house. You'll do what I say—when I say it."

"Leon, I don't understand," I sobbed. "What'd I do?"

He clamped my shoulders with vice-like hands, and threw me roughly on the bed. Loathing covered his face. His voice grew harsh. "You belong to me. I know what you need, and by God I'm gonna give it to ya." He ripped the white silk honeymoon skirt from my legs. My panties cut into the backs of my thighs as they tore free. Grunting, he mounted me and took something that 20 minutes earlier I would have readily given.

In the morning, he acted as though nothing had happened. His newfound air of superiority remained. For many years, I remembered that night as the worst of my life, until the night Ted died.

KITTEN WAILED beneath the pressure of my thumb on her throttle. Resolved to escape my past, I forced her to fly wide open. The engine temperature hovered near the red mark. The oil pressure fell a quarter-pound an hour. We flew out of Missouri, across Oklahoma, uneventfully through the Texas panhandle, and into New Mexico.

I ignored my father's continuous words of caution, which grew louder each time I checked the tachometer. *If I can take it, so can she!* I argued with the imaginary voice. I stopped for fuel only when necessary, and always at small out-of-the-way airports. I spoke only when spoken to, volunteered nothing, and took a wide berth of every telephone. I subsisted on stale candy bars from vending machines.

Ever-changing terrain rolled past at a pace still too slow. All that mattered was the number of miles between the red car and me. With little to do, other than stare into space and think unpleasant thoughts, every few minutes I mentally recalculated my groundspeed against fuel consumption. The brass fuel rod danced in the wind. Too often, it gave me no choice but to stop.

The vibration of the overtaxed engine seeped into my soul. Hills, pastures, and coarse terrain slid by. What lay ahead was often a fraternal twin to that which fell behind. Occasionally, like leaving one planet for the next, everything changed. Thousands of acres of lush crops dotted with irrigation circles stretched to the horizon and beyond. Before I could count all the circles, agriculture gave way to desert. Leapfrogging from hill and hollow to flat and barren, my course intermittently touched the old road keeping us on a westerly track.

At times, *Route 66* was hard to find. Short stretches of ancient asphalt disappeared into the earth then reemerged some place further on like a losing stream. Other times, it gradually turned to gravel as though the ink in the pen that drew it had sporadically run out. I found where it was the outer road for the Interstate in one place and a small town's main street in another.

We passed the Painted Desert and the Petrified Forest, bordered the likes of Tucumcari and Albuquerque, and somewhere in western New Mexico, flew head-on into night's gaping mouth. Still unwilling to expose myself on the ground, I pushed ahead in the dark until I could fly no further.

As though summoned from the darkness, a beat up green sedan emerged from behind a hangar. It inched across the aircraft parking area. High beams trained squarely on me as I secured the Aeronca's left wing. I moved to tie down the right wing. The car turned and backed up. Headlights followed me like a spotlight on a stage performer. I focused on my work, careful not to acknowledge the driver.

Dawg could not have beaten me here. I argued against my fear. *I covered more than a thousand miles today.* My logic went unanswered. The car seemed to wait. Too much thinking, too many hours flying, and blinded by the headlights, unwavering, I marched straight to the car.

"Need a ride, miss? Welcome to Holbrook, Arizona," the driver said, in a strangely calming voice.

Yellow spots caused by the bright lights distorted my vision. I leaned in and looked through the open window. A dark skinned face smiled back. "Don't look like much, but it's a taxi." He patted the brightly colored beads covering the steering wheel.

I rubbed my eyes. My vision cleared. "You blinded me with your headlights," I explained, almost apologetically.

"Sorry, I was just tryin' to help. Figured you needed the light."

I settled into the back seat next to my duffel with my flight case beneath my legs. Rapidly cooling evening air filled the car and forced out a thin smell that fell somewhere between body odor and garlic. I breathed in deeply through my nose and traced the odor to a string of threaded cloves interlaced with grape-size beads of glass that hung from the rearview mirror.

"Sorry, I just need a place to sleep," I answered after the second time he asked me where I wanted to go. "Let's drive through town. I'll let you know when I see it. Holbrook is right on *Route 66,* isn't it?"

"Sure is. I'll take ya wherever you wanna go. Just tell me when." Lit only by the dim light from the instrument panel, his dark eyes shone brightly in the rearview mirror. "Firewalker," he said. With a missing front tooth, his was a broken comb smile.

"Sorry, what?" I asked, unable to shake a feeling of déjà vu.

"Firewalker, is what people call me. I'm John Firewalker. I'm Navajo, the last male in my family—the last Seer," he added in an official tone. "The name and the visions die with me."

"What do you mean, Seer?" I asked, thinking I already knew.

"Some call me Medicine Man and others say Shaman," he answered without bragging. "There are those who believe I can heal the sick. A few think I can see inside their souls. Fact is, I see and feel things yet to happen. The gift has been passed down from generation to generation through first born sons." He paused and looked at me with captivating eyes. "My granddad taught me how to use my gift. I learned I could *feel* certain people. It's not magic. It only works if it's someone I have a natural connection with. It's a force of nature that goes beyond physical boundaries. Finding someone special, someone who's linked to you is like finding a needle in a needle stack." His gaze intensified. He paid no attention to the road ahead. "Fact is, it's only happened to *me* once before."

The words hit me like a bat between the eyes. "What do you mean?" I shivered.

"It was more'n 30 years ago. That summer, I was helpin' out at the big gas station in town, right on the old highway. A little girl and her mom asked me for the key to the ladies room. When I gave it to her, our hands touched. I saw her future. It's been clear in my mind ever since. I've been waitin' for her to come back. I knew she would. I saw it."

"What'd you see." I felt as though my life depended upon the answer.

"Think about it. You know as well as me." He answered vaguely without sounding evasive.

Like narrow river canyons in the desert, deep lines creased his sun-browned face. A beaded string tied his coal black ponytail. From behind, I would have guessed him at 30. His face gave him away. He was at least twice that.

"What do you think I know?" I asked bewildered, but not surprised. "By the way, people call me, Bette."

"I know." He nodded. "I knew when I heard your plane that it was finally time." Air whistled through the gap in his teeth like a venturi. "My vision has nearly caught up with itself. I only saw a little past now. I'm glad you're back. It was a lifetime to wait."

Strangely unafraid, I smiled.

Fifteen white concrete teepees came into view. "This is it, the Wigwam Village Motor Court, right?" I leaned forward. "I'll stay here."

"I was sure you would." He nodded. "Office is in the Texaco," he said, pointing at the gas station next door.

"When we were here in the 60s," I said, not wanting to get out of the car, "we couldn't afford two rooms for the five of us. We camped outside town."

"I remember."

"Firewalker, tell me what you remember." I touched his

shoulder. An unearthly sensation resonated through me. *My mother would never understand!* I thought as I compulsively pulled myself up against the back of the seat and kissed his coarse cheek. "My Grandma Damon was half Blackfoot," I blurted out without reason.

"I know that too. I saw her through you. She was somethin' special. You were our link. I'm sure she saw me too."

"It was me, wasn't it? I was the little girl at the gas station, my mom and me. You touched my hand! I'm the needle in the needle stack!"

"You are." He smiled.

"I know every important thing that's happened to you since that day, starting with the boy and the flowers. I don't know exact times, names, or places, but I saw everything. I wish I could've kept you from sufferin'. The gift just doesn't work like that. I'm sorry you lost your man."

From the flapped pocket of his faded western shirt, he took a string of beads. He tied the leather bracelet on my left wrist next to my birthday watch. "I made this for you a very long time ago. I've carried it with me always waitin' for the day you'd come back."

Firewalker twisted in his seat and studied my face. Penetrating eyes, which were not dark at all, enchanted me. Vibrant green irises sparkled like similarly colored swirls of paint stirred in a glass jar. "The marbles," he squeezed my hand, "show me the marbles."

Startled, I tried to draw back. He held me tighter. "I feel them close," he persisted. "The Blackfoot, she gave them to you. I saw it in my vision." He released my hand.

I hadn't thought the marbles since I left home. Bringing them with me was a spur of the moment decision. I noticed the jar when I started to leave my room for the last time. Without knowing why, I took three off the top and stuck them in my pocket.

I took them out and opened my hand for him to see. Three hand-blown marbles of variegated colors and slightly different sizes captured the light from the car's dome.

"I knew it," he said gleefully. He touched each one. Then in the same order, he examined them one by one. "What'd she say when she gave them to you?"

"Only that her father gave them to her." I remembered Grandma Damon's sly smile when she gave me the antique jar. "She played with them as a child."

"There's more. She told you somethin' else!" Firewalker insisted.

"She kept them her whole life." I searched for her exact words. "She said they're magical. I was a little girl. I figured she was teasin'."

"They are magic," Firewalker said slowly. "This one," he held up the smallest of the three, "the Blackfoot sent this one to me."

"His was lost on the beach," he added, touching his marble to his cheek.

Strangely, I understood what he meant. "I never told anyone I gave Ted a marble when we started dating," I said, amazed at the detail of Firewalker's vision. "He carried it with him always. I searched his clothes after the accident and never found it."

"I saw you," he answered. "Don't worry. It'll never be found. It's safe. The Spirits took it back."

I nodded. I knew it was true.

"Little Blackfoot, there's somethin' else." He wrapped my fingers around the remaining two marbles. Firewalker's blue and brown marble was nowhere in sight. "I had to wait until you were old enough to understand."

Knowing I had been guided back to this place to hear what he would tell me, I hung on every word.

"Your present is merely a flash in the pan, and then it's gone. Don't confuse it with your past. The same with your past and your future, they were never meant to be the same. They are what they are. You believe you're safe in the shadows, protected by not sharing your feelings. Bette, you're special. Your future lies in the sunlight. What you have is meant to be shared. Those who have hurt you were part of the plan. It's how we learn. Evil people are the Spirit's way of telling us to be careful.

"You call your Great Spirit, God, but he has many names. Some say Yahweh and others Allah. What I call him is unimportant because it's all the same. There's only one true God. He sent you here this night so I could tell you—" Firewalker squeezed my hands tighter still, and smiled, "to live your life for you. Bette, don't be afraid of anything or anyone. Take chances and reap what you have sown. Enjoy your blessings."

He reached down past my knees and touched my flight case. With eyes closed, he hummed softly through tight lips. "The old woman, she sent you back. Her voice has been in my head since I felt you as a little girl. I should have known all along—it was the Blackfoot…" His voice tapered off. "She left something for you inside!" He took my hand and pressed it against the case. "She wanted you to know it was real. When you find it, you'll understand."

Firewalker released me and turned to face the front of his car. "It isn't over. We'll both suffer before we see each other again. There's no way to change our destiny. Don't be afraid; follow your heart."

From behind the iconic wigwams, laughter drifted up into the night air. A family of transients sat in a circle at the back of an abandoned Salvation Army truck. The clerk, who checked me in, told me they were harmless Oklahomans migrating west to work in the fields. Gajes living like gypsies, they had been camped there for a week working odd jobs for gas and food. A rusty black pick-up sat nearby. Laundry hung from weathered sideboards.

There but by the grace of God go I. My mother's

expression along with Firewalker's admonition about my future took on new meaning.

I wiggled the key with one hand and shook the door handle with the other. The door finally popped open. Behind me, braking tires slid through pea gravel. I threw my bag and case through the doorway. An old green station wagon drove slowly by and turned on *Hopi Drive*. In my mind's eye, I saw a little girl's face pressed against the side glass, inquisitive eyes between open palms. *Your past isn't your future,* Firewalker's reminder rang clear. I imagined the little girl was an innocent Elizabeth checking on a self-ruined Bette. Regardless of what John Firewalker said, my haunting mistakes influenced my thoughts.

Headlights faded into darkness. "Goodbye, Elizabeth," I said aloud, hoping my words would travel across the decades. I wanted the younger me, who existed on a different plane, to hear me. I hoped she would make better decisions in her life.

I dumped the contents of my flight case in a pile on the colorful Navajo bedspread and sorted them by category: road maps, flight charts, flashlights, rotary azimuth plotter, manual flight computer, and a Heuer stopwatch. Nothing was out of place. It was all mine, everything packed by me. *Firewalker seemed convinced I would find something,* I thought. *It doesn't make any sense. Grandma's been dead for a very long time. She never saw this flight case. What message could she possibly have sent?*

Weary beyond comprehension, I lay upon the bed. Eye level with my worldly possessions—too tired to put them away, brush my teeth, or even undress. The bundle of musty road maps was just beyond the tip of my nose. Arizona, poorly folded, beckoned me from the top of the stack.

I hoisted myself up on one elbow, unfolded the map with my free hand, and pushed it into the light from a driftwood table lamp. Holbrook was a dot in the center of the fold. The only unusual mark was the thick red line my father had drawn. Disappointed, because I found no clue to Firewalker's riddle, I sat up and spread the map on the bed.

I started to fold it, got the first crease wrong, and tried again. An out-of-place mark, at the bottom, in the narrow border caught my eye. A crudely printed word in faded blue ink, I held it to the light. Written in a right leaning cant, it was unmistakable, a name formed by Grandma Damon's unsteady hand.

Helter-skelter, like a runaway drum in my inner ear, my heart throbbed. I clutched the map to my chest. No longer tired, the high-pitched whine in my head amplified. The small air-conditioner jerked and wheezed. Amid the chaos, I was alone with my thoughts. *What does it mean?*

The telephone felt grimy. I held it away from my ear and mouth. "Collect call from Bette," the operator announced in a tinny monotone when my dad said hello, "will you accept?"

"You okay, girl," he asked, clearly concerned. "We've been worried sick."

"Pop, I'm fine. Sorry, I'm in Arizona. You should see—" I caught myself. I couldn't tell him about the Wigwams without saying where I was. "Dad," I searched for the words. "Somethin' happened this morning."

"What? I saw you fly over."

"It's so unbelievable. It makes no sense. I need your help." I swallowed hard.

"What happened? What do ya need?"

"The Camaro was parked behind David's neighbor's house."

The line was quiet. My mom whispered in the background.

"Oh—my—God," he finally answered.

More silence, "What can I do?"

"Check on David. Make sure he's okay. If he is, find

out what he's up to. I need to know if he's on our side."

"I'll go over there as soon as we hang up," he declared.

"One other thing, where'd you get the state maps you gave me for this trip?"

"Hmm, it's been a long time. I guess I bought 'em." He covered the phone and said something to my mother. "Mother says we got 'em from Grandma Damon. They were originally Uncle Albert's. Why?"

"Do you know anything about a name written on the bottom of the Arizona map?"

"No, whose name?"

"Not someone you know. It's a long complicated story. I'll show you and explain everything when I see you."

"Honey," my mother's pleading voice came on the line, "there's so much goin' on. Are you really okay? "

"Ma, I feel—," my voice quivered, "I feel like a tethered goat…"

SEVENTEEN

*B*LACK, I THOUGHT. I touched my eyes. *They're open,* I told myself. I pinched my arm. *I'm awake.*

I ground my fists into my unseeing sockets. I reached out. "Ouch!" The driftwood lamp drove a splinter into my fingertip. "Shit." I located my flashlight. A narrow beam penetrated the darkness and illuminated the inside of the white conical structure. I recognized the inside of the wigwam. *I know where I am.*

I drew myself up against the headboard and wedged a stiff pillow in the small of my back. It was an hour before sunrise. The air-conditioner popped loudly and rattled. Cool air flooded the room. Goose bumps covered my arms.

I extinguished the light. "Ted," I called out. "Ted," I said again.

Not here. The air-conditioner rattled an answer. *Never again*, it grumbled indifferently.

The whine in my ears stabbed the backs of my eyes. I slid down the pillow and buried my face in the blanket. *Please stop.*

I chose Joe and Aggie's Café because I could walk from the wigwams. The packed parking lot I took as a sign of good food. The place bustled with anonymous faces, also a good sign. A long white paper banner, announcing their fiftieth anniversary, hung above the kitchen door.

No one gave me so much as a second look as I waited for a table. The Formica™ was still damp when I settled in with my back to the wall. Alone in my misery, I hid in plain sight.

"Coffee, hon?" a bubbly copper-haired waitress asked when she finally arrived at my table after filling every cup between me and the kitchen. A thin smile rode every exaggerated chew of her gum.

"Yes, please." I visually traced her long pale arm and stopped at the white plastic tag pinned to her blue shirtwaist uniform. "Augie," I tried her unusual name.

"That's me," she answered. Like a rabbit from a hat, she produced a heavy ceramic mug. From high above, she filled the cup with a dramatic Niagara Falls pour without spilling a drop. The coffee stopped a centimeter below the brim. "What'll ya have this fine mornin'?" She looked at me with devouring green eyes.

Although it looked and smelled good, I had no taste for the food. I picked at the eggs and sausage and ate very little. Augie stopped by often, always with a kind word and a smile. She kept my cup full and seemed not to notice I wasn't really eating.

The conversation with my dad from the night before persistently hammered the backs of my eyes demanding to be set free. I ignored it until the pounding threatened real damage to my emotional balance.

After he told me the maps had been Grandma Damon's, my discovery made more sense. Even still, it, along with Firewalker's knowledge of my life, was too strange to be true.

When I was with Firewalker the night before, I felt at

ease, convinced, and reassured by his words. In the light of day, it was all surreal, unbelievable.

I chose not to pursue the subject with my dad. There were already too many unexplainable events in my life.

After he wrested the phone from my mom, his questions came fast and furious. I described my landing in Cape Girardeau. We speculated about what Leon was doing at the airport and why he was at David's the following day.

Occasionally, my dad grunted in agreement or added an *"oh"* or a *"gosh"* to let me know he was listening. Had my mother not been there, he would most certainly have used expletives. From time-to-time, my mother's sighs filled the background. My dad sounded as though he was talking into a tin can. I pictured them side-by-side at the kitchen desk with the telephone squeezed between them.

"Bette, I saw David early this morning before you flew over. He seemed completely normal. He didn't even mention Leon—uh, sorry, I mean Dawg. He comes over here nearly every day. He's been nothin' but helpful.

"Do you think the red car could've been somethin' other than a Camaro or maybe somebody else's? From 4,500 feet everything's pretty small. It's easy to make a mistake."

"Pop, I can't explain it, but I know it was his."

"Okay, if you believe it, I believe it. So the question is, what was he doin' there, and why didn't David tell us?"

I took a sip of the rapidly cooling coffee and attempted to push the conversation to the back of my mind. A dozen or so motorcycles roared by on *Route 66*. Augie stopped at my table. The voices in my mind hid. "You okay, hon?" She looked at my full plate. "Can I warm that up for you?" She gestured with the orange handled pot.

"Please, regular not decaf." I nodded.

She filled my cup and left. The voices reappeared. The conversation in my head resumed.

"Bette," my dad signaled the close of the subject, *"we'll do everything possible to find out what David's up to. I hate to say this, though it'd explain a lot if he's involved. Dawg seems to always know where you'll be."*

"I don't wanna pass judgment until I see what you find," I agreed, drowning in disappointment. *"What else?"*

"Well," he took a deep breath, *"the Fire Marshall called this mornin'. He thinks the arsonist planned a much bigger explosion."*

"Why? What else'd they find?"

"There was residue from magnesium scrapings, iron rust, and aluminum powder in the ashes. Those are all materials Dawg could have gotten from his job."

"Pop, I don't understand. They're just ferrous and non-ferrous metals. Don't people make bombs out of fertilizer and stuff like that."

"The Marshall called it homemade thermite. When mixed together, those materials create a highly volatile oxidation reaction."

"Holy—shit." The words fell from my lips. *"I know he's sick, but when did my ex become a bomb maker?"*

The idea echoed through cluttered chasms of my mind. The café was nearly empty. It was already nine o'clock. I didn't want to be there. I didn't want to be anywhere.

Augie filled my cup with increasing frequency. "Am I holding you up?" I asked politely.

"Oh no, hon, not at all. I'm a little hyper. My customers are mostly gone." She filled my cup. "I didn't mean to disturb you. It's nice, sometimes, to be alone," she said, looking me over.

I must be quite a sight, I thought, touching my ponytail, which protruded from the hole in the back of my baseball cap. *My mother would say I look like a tomboy.* I self-consciously fidgeted with the rolled up sleeves of my denim work shirt. My boots desperately needed a shine, and my khaki trousers hadn't been washed since

Crossroads. *She would really kick my butt if she saw me like this.*

Augie looked at my left hand. *Probably looking for a wedding ring and wondering why all I have is my great-grandfather's Claddagh ring,* I thought.

My Grandmother McKenna gave me the ring at my grandfather's funeral. I gave it to Ted when we exchanged our vows on the riverbank. It went missing after the accident. I asked the nurses about it and they brought me Ted's gold peso and chain. I quizzed them again about the ring. They avoided the question. The morning of Ted's funeral, my mother slipped it on my finger. My mom and dad had it sized to fit me. It's never left my hand since.

Could be she's lookin' at my birthday watch.

After she checked out my hand for the third time, I forced myself to ask. "Do I have somethin' on me?"

"Oh, no, I'm sorry." She stepped back. Her porcelain face turned bright red. "I didn't mean to stare. I was just wonderin' how you knew him." She held out her hand. A bracelet, nearly identical to mine, dangled from her wrist. "Firewalker—did *he* give it to you?"

"Yes, yes, he did." I answered, surprised. *Small town,* I reminded myself. "He gave me a ride from the airport last night."

"Wow." She glanced nervously around the room. A chubby, blue-haired woman in Bermuda shorts and a toothpick husband laughed loudly. They were crowded around a table in the far corner playing cards with two other Snow Bird couples. Otherwise, the café was empty.

"May I sit," Augie whispered, already pulling out the chair on my left.

"Please." I wanted to hear what this irresistible personality had to say, and I needed a distraction from the beleaguering conversation raging in my head.

"Does he make the bracelets to sell?" I asked, remembering the ultra-strange conversation that surrounded Firewalker giving me the bracelet.

I took the leather knot between two fingers and rotated it all the way around my wrist. The hand-drilled stones varied in color and fit one against the other perfectly.

"No—that's the thing." She leaned forward and lowered her voice even more than before. "As far as I know, you and I are the only people he's given a bracelet to since his wife and daughter died."

A chill crawled up my arms and left a sea of tiny bumps in its wake. "What happened?" I whispered.

"Car wreck—must be more'n 30 years now. A drunk plowed into 'em and pushed their car through a guardrail up near Flagstaff. Car exploded and they burned to death. Cops told Firewalker they died instantly." She shook her head sadly. "He says it's bullshit. He says his girls' screams still haunt him."

"That's horrible. Poor Firewalker, I had no idea." My own emotional wounds opened wider. "What'd he do? Did he ever remarry?"

"Nope, just lives out there," she pointed to the west, "all alone. Doesn't associate with anybody 'cept my little girl and me. Still blames himself for their death. Says if he's supposed to be a Seer, how come he didn't see that comin'. He drives his old taxi 'nough to survive, and that's all. He says people got nothin' he needs." Augie touched my bracelet.

"What do you think it means?" I asked.

"That he gave it to you?" She mindlessly tapped the crystal of my birthday watch twice with her fingernail. The hair on the back of my neck stood up. "Bette," she said my name, even though I didn't remember introducing myself. "You must be somethin' special. Firewalker's an exceptional man. If he took to you, it means a lot. To the town's folk, he's an outcast. To Violet and me, he's a Godsend.

"More'n once, he's paid my rent. I don't know how he

knows, but anytime I'm short and don't have enough for groceries, a box of food shows up on my back porch. It's always the stuff we like. He never expects anything in return. I've invited him to my house many times, and he always says no. He's never even been inside. Says it wouldn't look proper."

The blue-hair in the corner must have made a joke; the table roared. They looked like wrinkled baby birds with their beaks in the air crying for food.

"Augie," I rolled her name around my tongue, "hope you don't mind me sayin', it's kind of an odd name."

"Yeah." A shy smile crept across her face. "My folks are free-spirited hippies. They named me August Autumn. What a handle to hang on a chick, right? I'm the fifth of five girls born in consecutive summer months and consecutive years. We were each named for the month and season in which we were born. My eldest sister is April Spring. You can guess the rest. I grew up in a Volkswagen van. We were all born in the same tent, but a different state. My dad delivered us." She laughed; the tinkle was how I imagined fairies ringing their tiny bells would sound. "Firewalker calls me Copperhead." She touched copper-colored hair. The fairies rang their bells again.

"Were you married?" I asked, feeling like a friend without limits.

"Yep." Sadness marred her smile. She looked down at the table. "For all the good it did me. S.O.B. was a lazy drunk who thought contributing meant reminding me to go to work. I was eight months pregnant when he went out for a beer and never came back. It seems like a lifetime ago. I hardly ever think about him. 'Cept now Violet will be six in a couple of days and she's startin' to ask questions about her dad. I don't know what to say."

"You don't want him back?"

"No freakin' way. It was a nightmare. Besides, what would I tell Violet? Between you and me, my greatest fear is he does come back. There are a lot a things worse than bein' alone. He's at the top of that list."

Her wisdom struck my core. "Isn't that the truth!" In my mind, I saw Dawg towering over me as I lay weeping on my bed.

Reluctantly, Augie and I said goodbye. I headed back to my concrete wigwam. It was nearly noon. Even though I didn't eat my breakfast, I wasn't hungry. I wanted to organize my thoughts and call home.

Holbrook, Arizona, Thursday Morning, April 13, 2000

I MET A NAVAJO YESTERDAY, John Firewalker. He spoke to me in something like a secret code that he expected me to understand. He acted as though he had known me my whole life. It was all very strange, very personal. Somehow, I did understand a little. I do feel connected to him. When I touched him, I experienced the exact same feeling I did when I was here as a child. I'm sure he and I met when we traveled through Arizona on vacation. He talked about Grandma as if they were old friends. She wasn't with us that trip. The only way they could have been connected was through me. I was skeptical until he said there was a message in my flight case, and I found "Firewalker" written in Grandma's hand in the margin of my dad's old Arizona map. It's either real, or I'm losing my mind. The facts are there. I want it to be true.

I'm too exhausted to finish.

FATIGUED BEYOND REASON, I didn't want to deal with the telephone and an operator. *Should've brought your cell,* I chastised myself again for my decision to leave it behind. It was of no use hidden in the bottom of my underwear drawer at my mom and dad's house. When I buried it beneath a stack of folded panties, it seemed like the right thing to do. I wanted to be alone in a wilderness of my own making to face my demons and find my true self. Lent was nearing its end, and the irony of Jesus in the wilderness was not lost on me. It was not a comparison. The Messiah was steadfast in *His* suffering. I only suffered.

After a fashion, I found the strength to pick up the phone. My mother answered on the second ring. She accepted the charges before the operator finished saying my name. "Hon, you alright?" Her tone was urgent. "Talk to your dad."

"What now?" I asked as soon as he said my name.

"Your house—"

"NOT FIRE," I screamed hysterically. A weight crashed down upon my chest. Squeezed against the hard mattress in my Wigwam, I labored to breathe.

"No," he answered without hesitation, "it was ransacked."

"What'd they take?" I asked, relieved it was anything other than fire.

"That's the thing, nothin'. They turned the place upside down. As nearly as we can tell, nothin's missin'. Bette, what would someone be lookin' for?"

"I don't know." I bit my tongue. I hated lying to my dad.

"Okay." He sounded tentative. I was sure he knew it was a lie.

"Do you think it could have somethin' to do with Ted's life insurance?" he probed.

"Maybe," I answered evasively.

"Bette, it must have been a lotta money. You didn't have cash stashed at your house, did ya?"

"Of course not, Dad. But you're right, it's a lot." I struggled beneath the weight on my chest. "I haven't told anyone how much."

"What'd you do with it?" he asked innocently. "We

talkin' more than a hundred thousand?"

"Many times more." I rolled up on my side, pulled the canvas duffel from under the bed, and felt the remaining stack of thick envelopes inside. "Pop, I don't wanna talk 'bout this on the phone."

My mom's frantic whisper was indecipherable in the background. "Dad, tell mom to get on the extension. This one step behind your husband thing is losing its quaintness," I said, irritated at my parents' chain of command.

"Mom says that David was dating a girl at the bank." He relayed her message ignoring my remark. "You know anything 'bout that?"

"Yeah, a little. She's one of the Barton girls. A Financial Service Rep I think, but David told me it's over. What're ya thinkin'?"

"We're wonderin' if this girl could have talked about your accounts."

"Surely not. It'd be against the law for her to tell anyone what she knows about customer business. 'Sides all of this is conjecture and predicated on the idea David is complicit. We don't know that. As far as I'm concerned, he's still my best friend, innocent until proven guilty."

"Did you deposit the money? Could she have seen the transaction?"

"I didn't deposit it. I cashed the check and put it somewhere safe." *I should've rented a safe deposit box in a different bank,* I thought. "The amount was kind of a big deal. Pop, what do you know that I don't?"

"David's missin'."

Remaining rays of the late afternoon sun skulked from the cloistered motel room. Spellbound by my own demise, the Wigwam no longer fascinated me so I fled.

In the half-light of early evening, I aimlessly wandered the streets of Holbrook until I found myself in front of a small church. Through open doors, a rich singing voice rode the spring breeze into the night sky.

"Victory is mine." The voice triumphantly proclaimed.

"I told Satan…Victory today is mine."

The beat was more like a rock opera than a hymn and inexplicably drew me inside.

With eyes closed and arms outstretched, a tiny woman belted out emotion packed notes from a bottom step in front of the altar.

"When I rose this morning, I didn't have no doubt; I knew that the Lord would bring me out."

In a cramped space between the back wall and the last pew, I fell to my knees and clasped my hands together.

"Please, God," I whispered, "forgive my sins. God, if it exists for me, help me find 'Victory in Jesus.'" Seeking strength, I mimicked the singer's words.

No television, no telephone, no food, and no sleep, I passed a second night of self-imposed exile in the caricature of a wigwam in Holbrook, Arizona. I spent some time on the bed and some on the floor. I sat in a chair, brushed my teeth, combed my hair, and repacked my bag, twice. Within random, tumultuous thoughts, I continuously searched for a lifeline or a low hanging branch with which to save myself from the quicksand of my present. Every third or fifth thought included either Augie or Firewalker, or both.

I recounted the envelopes in the bottom of my bag. Eight of the original ten remained. Two from the middle of the rubber banded bundle slid out easily. *It doesn't matter which two,* I told myself. *They're all identical.* I had counted the ten stacks of hundred-dollar bills at least a dozen times in the privacy of my room in Stanville before I was satisfied. I'm the one who always doubts myself and checks doors three times before I'm convinced they're locked.

On the first envelope I wrote,

Augie,
For helping me remember the importance of
unconditional friendship.

On the second,

Firewalker,
Thanks for waiting, and for pointing me away from
my past.

Before the ink dried, I zipped the two envelopes safely inside my flight case and returned the remaining six to my duffel.

At seven o'clock in the morning, I checked out and walked to *Joe & Aggies* for breakfast. I never looked back.

As I emerged from the tangle of parked cars in front of the restaurant, Augie burst wild-eyed from door. She caught my arm and pushed me against the wall. "He's missing!"

"Who?"

"Firewalker. Friday breakfast, it's our thing. He hasn't called. Nobody remembers seein' him yesterday." She tightened her grip on my arm. "Bette, I think you were the last person to see 'im."

"Has he ever missed before?"

"Never, and tomorrow's Violet's birthday. He wanted to plan somethin' special for her. He wouldn't miss that for anything."

"Can we go to his house?" I looked around the parking lot wondering if the daughter of hippies owned a car.

"Yeah," she answered, already running. Her apron streamed behind her like a banner in the wind.

The battered Dodge whined like a mini turbine then coughed and started. Augie's seat was all the way forward. Still, she could barely see over the steering wheel, which she clutched with white knuckles. Gravel pelted parked cars as we slid sideways onto the highway. It took ten harrowing minutes to reach Firewalker's secluded two bedroom.

Augie hit the front door like a battering ram, throwing it open so hard she buried the knob in the inside wall. "Firewalker, Firewalker!" She ran screaming from room-to-room. There was no answer. Within seconds, we knew the house was empty. She slammed through a screen door at the back of the narrow kitchen with the same vehemence as before and leaped over two steps into the backyard.

I followed across barren soil to a large igloo shaped structure of woven branches and saplings. A bark covered pole protruded through a blackened opening at its apex. Tattered brown canvas covered a low arched entrance.

Augie threw the flap aside and disappeared. Before I could enter, she let out a blood-curdling scream followed by my name.

Inside, assaulted by a smell of sweat and burned wood, I groped across the dirt floor. My eyes slowly adjusted to the darkness. Finally, able to make out the scene, I froze in disbelief. Lifeless, swollen, and bruised, Firewalker hung from the center-pole, doubled up, and slumped forward. His face nearly touched the dirt. His arms, awkwardly wrapped around the scorched pole, stretched behind him. His hands bound.

"HE'S ALIVE!" Augie held two fingers against his carotid artery. "Help me untie him," she cried. "Let's get 'im outside. He needs water."

It was all we could do to drag Firewalker from the sweat lodge. I tore the flap from the entrance and spread it on the ground just outside. We gently rolled him onto the canvas.

Flat on his back, he took short shallow gasps. His left eye was swollen shut. His right was barely a slit and looked like a dying ember. Augie poured water into his mouth; most of it ran down his bare chest and formed tiny pools across the canvas.

"What happened?" she whispered with her face an inch from his. "Who did this to you?"

"Bette," he looked at me. "Ge' outta he'—he's afta you."

"Who?" Augie glared at me. "Who's after you, Bette? What kinda shit have you brought down on us?"

"Red," Firewalker wheezed. Blood trickled from his swollen lip. "Camaro, told 'im you wen' to Flag'taff, in renta' car—go now, no' much time." He spit and looked at Augie. "Copperhea', I'm oka'. Ge' Bet' ta the airport. Hurry!"

"We'll get you inside." I hooked my hands under his arms. "Augie, help me."

"No time," he twisted away. "Go now!" The slit opened wider. I saw a glint in his eye. His final words were clear. "He stole my family talisman." Firewalker touched his neck. "Get it back for me!"

"Augie, what talisman?" I asked as we raced recklessly down the road sliding onto the shoulder through every curve.

"It was prob'ly inside his shirt when you saw him," she yelled above the howl of the wind. "He never took it off. It was passed down through the generations along with the *gift*. Firstborn Seers have worn it since forever. It's a blue stone, shaped like an arrowhead. Firewalker says it's not manmade. His ancestors found it in a creek bed before the settlers came. He says even the hole where the strap is tied is natural."

The airport came into view. Augie looked at me with a woeful gaze. "You'll know it when you see it. Please, Bette, get it back. He believes it's the source of his power." She slowed for the turnoff and looked at me again. Hers was the face of an overprotective mother bear. "Since his family died, that rock and my little Violet are all that keep 'im goin'."

I shouted instructions while I freed one wing and the tail. Augie untied the other wing and threw my duffel in the backseat. I ignored the need for a preflight and instead said a quick prayer against sabotage.

One foot on the tire, I turned to say goodbye. Augie threw her arms around my neck and kissed my cheek. "Get outta here. Be safe."

I put my left leg into the cockpit. "We'll see each other again." I forced a smile and pulled myself in. "Oh, yeah," I remembered, unzipped the inside pocket of my case, and pulled the two envelopes from their hiding place. "For you and Firewalker, for a better life."

"I—I don't understand." She looked from me to the envelopes.

"Not from me." My voice quivered. "It's from Ted. I'm the courier. From him and someone else." I glanced upward. Suddenly, I understood my own actions. I knew what Firewalker meant when he said we would both suffer.

"Firewalker will explain. I was sent here to learn from the two of you, to bring you this gift, and deliver a message. Augie, we all have our own path. Mine is littered with the rocks of my enemies. You and Firewalker are the soft grass that aids my passage. Our friendship gives me strength.

"Tell Firewalker not to fret. I'll find my way. I'll bring back his talisman. Tell 'im Little Blackfoot sends her love." I switched on the magnetos and reached for the starter handle. "Don't worry, Augie." I raised my voice in anticipation of the engine's din. "We'll see each other again!"

EIGHTEEN

THIN MOUNTAIN AIR reduced lift and reluctantly permitted me to free Kitten from the Holbrook runway. Slowly, we climbed straight ahead. Once above 1,000 feet, I double-checked every instrument and sighed with relief.

In some way, I wished I could have been there when they opened their envelopes. In my mind's eye, I saw Augie, perhaps even at this very moment, examining each of the 200, hundred-dollar bills and crying all the while. I saw a battered and bruised Firewalker smile and nod with understanding as he opened his treasure. *Perhaps,* I told myself, *someday he'll tell me how Grandma Damon came to write his name on the map.*

I would have liked more time to tell them the story of my life with Ted. Happiness begets happiness. If I couldn't find it for myself, I could surely give it to others.

I pictured what it must have been like inside Crossroads Baptist Church when Pastor Fid found his envelope. I imagined him falling to his knees and praising God. It was all there in the forefront of my mind;

ephemeral images of happiness and faith, like a camera without film, gone before captured. Alone with my hopes and dreams, inside my airplane, I was an unimportant speck in the western sky suspended in a gooey mixture of fear, disappointment, and remorse.

My Grandfather McKenna, now 23 years in a cold Ozark grave, was a tortured, creative soul. Although he was born in the final years of the century before me, I remember him well, his mischievous smile, his kindness, and most of all, the intuitive way in which he turned an artful phrase. I suppose I understood him better than most, maybe even better than his eldest son, my father, did. I saw past the contraptions he built for amusement to the imaginative genius that presided at their core.

He died slightly more than a month before Christmas in 1977. As was the custom of the time, his body laid in an open casket for three days.

An Irish wake at the hand-hewn log house where he was born followed. On a screened in porch, I sat alone in a rocker he had made of split sassafras saplings and looked across the ridge past the Hoot Owl Tree to the Waterin' Hole Hollow. In the top drawer of a battered chest of drawers, buried beneath a 10-year's supply of Kentucky Twist chewing tobacco, I found a yellowed scrap of lined paper. There were three paragraphs written in my grandfather's hand.

I wanted to believe that grandpa wrote the words for me. I always thought he knew we were the same person born of different generations. I would have been more certain if what I found had begun with *Dear Elizabeth* and ended with *Love Grandpa*. It didn't. Nonetheless, I have no doubt. He wrote it for me.

From a secret compartment inside my wallet, I extracted the brittle parchment and painstakingly opened each fold. Seeming to understand the delicate nature of my task, Kitten steadied herself. I focused on the roughly inscribed words. I knew every one by heart. All the same, I read them aloud because I wanted to see and hear them. The sound of the engine and propeller drowned each one as it passed my lips, although my soul heard every syllable.

Sometimes I lie awake in a languid pool of loneliness, embraced only by darkness and utter quiet. The silence is devoid of comfort, an abyss without strength, love, or structure.

I must learn to kneel and anoint myself in the pool, to drink in the loneliness as a vaccine against illness. When I feel immunity's force, I shall move forward one step at a time always ready to compromise when compromise is good.

I will disregard loss and focus on gain. So it shall go— so I shall go— forward with my family, overcoming diversity. Always hoping, always dreaming, and always looking for silver linings. Breathing is automatic; the rest is up to me.

In the fourth grade, Grandpa McKenna left his friends in the one-room country school and took his place on the opposite end of his father's crosscut saw. In unison, with measured strokes, the blade sang its song from daylight until dark.

I love the words he wrote. Although sad, they are poignant expressions from his heart. They hold the wisdom of a lifetime and elegantly describe my own emotions.

From Ireland's County Cork, to England, and then to Transylvania County North Carolina, and finally Missouri, the McKennas sought happiness. For generations, they ran from some nightmare or toward a dream.

In 1881, financially devastated by betrayal and the lingering aftermath of the Civil War, the McKennas abandoned their once-splendid Appalachian plantation and joined a group of sixteen families headed for a hardscrabble life in Missouri.

As a family, we have never escaped the curse that dogs us all from the cradle to the grave. We carry our burden throughout our lives. From our deathbeds, we pass it on to the next unsuspecting generation.

If what I say were true, and not the hollow musings of a foolish girl, and if they expect me to shift the tide and free us of the family curse, they have left the responsibility to the wrong person.

The Aeronca's fuel and my emotions stretched to the limit, I entered the landing pattern at an unattended airport just northwest of Seligman, Arizona. There was no answer to my request for a landing advisory. I scanned the sky for traffic and landed of my own accord. As the Champ's tail lost the last remnant of lift and dropped to the tarmac with a thud, a familiar wave of dread washed over me. On the ground, I was vulnerable and within reach of an evil force that knew my every move.

A polite but determined man on the other end of the phone explained he would be happy to help me with fuel. However, I would have to wait an hour and a half until he was free.

If Dawg drove to Flagstaff and doubled back when he didn't find me, he could already be halfway here, I reasoned. I hoped he was completely unaware of when I started or which direction I took. *He's a mechanic. He knows the range of the Champ. It won't take a genius to figure out how far I've flown. If he knows I'm still headed west, he'll find me.* There was no comfort in my rationale. Like a bloodhound on a hot trail, he had tracked me or beaten me to nearly every place I'd been.

Firewalker's battered face haunted my thoughts. My second call was to the café in Holbrook. A friendly girl answered. I couldn't put a face to the voice. Without an image, it was like talking to a shadow. I didn't like shadows. She volunteered that Augie was at the hospital and even knew the number. I wrote it in pencil on the heavily scratched glass of the phone booth, thanked her without ever saying my name, and hung up.

A clueless shadow curtly answered the hospital phone and dropped it on a desk with a metallic thud when I asked about Firewalker.

Like a magic elixir, Augie's voice instantly lessened my anxiety. "Bette," she began before I could speak, "it's too much. The money's just too much!"

"Hardly," I snapped, "look what I've put the two of you through. How is he?"

"The doctors say he'll be fine." She paused. "A dozen stitches in his face, a couple broken ribs, and an injured pride for letting someone get the best of him. But he's good. He's pissed 'cause he said he knew he was comin'. He just didn't know when."

"Can I talk to him?"

"They just wheeled him down to x-ray."

"Did he tell you anything," I swallowed hard, "about the guy—about what happened?"

"The guy never said his name. From your description it was your ex. Somebody must've seen you get in Firewalker's taxi the night you arrived. There's no other way he could have connected John to you.

"Firewalker saw the red Camaro drive by his house several times. He said it stuck out like a sore thumb because of a weird homemade lookin' antenna thingy stickin' out of the passenger's window."

"What'd it look like, exactly?"

"He described it as tubing shaped like a sideways basketball hoop."

I shook my head in disbelief. "Sounds like a directional tracker." I remembered seeing something like it when I was a cadet in the Civil Air Patrol on practice Search And Rescue missions.

"Firewalker was walkin' around the outside of his

house when he was hit over the head from behind with a bat or somethin'. When he came to, he was tied up in the sweat lodge."

"What did he want to know?"

"Where you were stayin' and what you were doin'. He asked about your bags. He was super interested in exactly what you were carryin'. Bette, what's he lookin' for? Is he after the money you gave us?"

"I don't know, maybe. I don't have anything else of value, only my clothes, and a few more envelopes. Even my folks don't know how much money I have with me. 'Sides, it's not worth all this. He's been followin' me since Florida."

In the background, someone shouted the details of a two-car pileup.

"Augie, I've gotta go. Tell Firewalker I'm sorry. Please take care of him."

Shaking, I dialed the operator again. My dad sighed with obvious relief when he heard my voice. "Bette-girl, where are ya?"

"I can't say. Dawg's close. He beat up a friend at my last stop."

"O—my—God, you've gotta call the police," he ordered.

"Pop, they can't help. They'll tell me to call back if he shows up and threatens me. It was like that when I was married, and he beat me. The cops were useless. No, this is on me."

"There's more you should know," he continued in a funeral voice. "Looks like David left in a hurry. His house is a mess."

"Do you think he's alright? Pop, Dawg tied up my friend and nearly beat him to death. You think he could have hurt David?"

"Don't know, girl. David's house is in the foreclosure announcements in today's paper. I tried to call him at work. They told me he's been laid off for a year. Did he tell you anything about that?"

"I thought he was goin' to work every day."

"We peeked in his mailbox. Most of it looks like past due bills. Your mother's really upset. He's been like a son to us. We can't believe he'd be mixed up in this mess."

My dad's words roared through my head like an out-of-control freight train. "Dad," hoping to regain my equilibrium, I changed the subject, "my friend said Dawg has some kind of crude circular antenna mounted on his car."

"Sounds like something you'd use to track a radio signal, possibly from an Emergency Locator Transmitter."

"That's what I was thinkin', but there'd have to be a signal to track. I only turn on my handheld transceiver during takeoff and landing. If my ELT was transmitting on 121.5, every emergency crew between here and Florida would be searchin' for me. Do you think my ELT could be set to a different frequency?"

"It's not impossible. It'd have to have a different crystal though. I don't think there's any way to tune an ELT."

"Or if I had a second transmitter," I yelled. "There's an odd metal box mounted in the back of the Champ next to my ELT. I noticed it a few days ago and brushed it off as something Jim installed for the new electrical system. I kept meanin' to call him and ask."

"If it's a transmitter, it'd have to be set to some obscure frequency. He'd have to be pretty close to pick up the signal, especially if the airplane and his directional antenna were both on the ground. He'd have to already know about where you were—"

"I'll call you back tonight." I said before he could finish.

With a screwdriver from my leather tool roll, I removed the lid from the aluminum box. My dad was right. It was an ELT. A light on top was blinking; it was transmitting.

A loud bang followed the initial whoosh. The explosion nearly knocked me off my feet even though I had finally managed to hit the bucket of avgas on the fifth try from something like 30 feet away with a rock wrapped in flaming newspaper. I watched with satisfaction as the flames danced over the bucket of fuel, the transmitter submerged at the bottom.

A few minutes before, as I cut the wires with my pocketknife and literally ripped the device from my airplane, I considered the many ways to destroy it. Smashing it with a large rock came in second to burning, in the end a fiery death seemed most appropriate.

I replayed my first memory of the box mounted in my airplane until I was absolutely convinced it was not there before St. Augustine. *The Dawg must have put the nails under my tires and installed the box at the same time,* I thought. *It's all premeditated right down to putting a nail in front and behind each tire to make sure he didn't miss. He's crazy like a fox.*

The flames from the bucket were still licking the sky when I taxied to the runway and turned for departure. I jerked the Champ into the air before she reached flying speed and wallowed down the runway riding an invisible cushion of ground effect.

I threw the bundle of antique road maps over my shoulder and took a sectional chart from my flight case. Before opening the map, I banked hard left, rolled out on a heading of 180 degrees, and followed the nap of the earth at full throttle. I chose Wickenburg, Arizona, 100 miles due south of Seligman as my destination.

A place to hide and regroup, I told myself. *It's time to go on the offensive.*

No more credit cards, I thought as I paid cash for two nights at the motel furthest from the airport and signed *Evelyn Crown* with a fictitious street address in Des

Moines, Iowa. No one knew where I was.

RAIN POUNDED the windshield of my dad's Cessna and poured in like a leaky bucket. He sat stoically beside me smoking his pipe and waiting for me to react.

I awoke to the sound of rain pelting the motel room's only window. *It was a dream,* I thought, remembering where I was. *With my luck, it only rains in Wickenburg one day per year.* I slipped from under the covers and crossed the room. With my wrist between the curtains, in the window's yellow light, my chronograph showed five minutes past four in the morning. My night was over. I knew from experience, I could not sleep another wink. I wound my watch tight. From force of habit, I pressed the button, which started the stopwatch function.

The bedside lamp's paper shade cast a shadow across the blank page of my open journal. The white space stared at me. I held my fountain pen poised above the page. I wanted to record my feelings, but I was blocked. Even the date escaped me. I closed my eyes and counted the days. The pen's nib waivered and touched the page. I opened my eyes. A rapidly spreading blotch of bluish ink had become my entry's start. *Bad stuff is always indelible,* I told myself, remembering it was my second wake-up in that room. I knew the day and date.

Wickenburg, Arizona, Palm Sunday Morning, April 16, 2000

I'M A WRITER. Sometimes I think it's a bad thing because I prefer my pen to people. However, solace and serenity only go so far until they begin to isolate me from civilization. At that point, they are no longer symbiotic. They become parasitic.

My pen knows my heart. It often helps me drag away the dense underbrush of my imaginings and uncover my true feelings. My pen knows where to find my emotions and the tricks that draw them out and expose the inner me. For that, I am grateful.

I am at an impasse in my life. Other than my parents, I am unsure whom I can trust. For this reason, I must muster what strength I have left and make my own way.

I pray God will guide my thoughts and my actions and help me find answers. I ask His help to uncover my true adversaries and reveal them for the demons they must surely be. Today, I pray for the strength to do what must be done to survive. If happiness is anywhere within my reach, I beg for guidance to find it and be once again well. Please, God, help me.

PALM SUNDAY, I reread the heading of my journal page and reminded myself of the day's meaning. I searched through the contents of my duffel and found my last clean shirt. From the back of my mind, my mother's voice called through the partially open door to my bedroom and urged me to hurry with my new Easter dress so she could see how I looked.

"Don't wrinkle it," she reminded me with a mixture of sweet sternness. I modeled the pink dress in front of the fireplace. *"You have to wear it both Sundays."*

I asked the taxi driver to take me to the nearest Christian church. I slipped through a side door as the last bell tolled and found a place in the back pew. Dressed in slacks and boots, I felt out of place in the packed sanctuary. At least, I'd taken the time to iron my shirt and comb my hair—no cap, no ponytail.

The preacher was no Pastor Fid, although he seemed smart. I liked the way he recounted the events of Palm Sunday. He included some speculation about how Jesus must have felt the week before He died.

I'm no martyr, yet I understood the feelings the preacher described. I was a woman alone in an emotional wilderness, weary with fear, tired of running from my past, and scared shitless of the future.

The preacher droned on setting the stage for the resurrection story. I only heard part of what he said as I replayed the events of my life, especially the last several months. He finished. The congregation sang. I again begged God for guidance. I dropped a hundred-dollar bill in the brass offering plate and reminded God that I was running out of time.

The pianist hit the first notes of the last song. I gazed at the plain wooden cross, which hung high on the wall behind the altar. In a miracle of understanding, it came to me. I scribbled some notes on the back of the bulletin. Before the hymn was finished, I slipped out the same way I came in. I left the church with a palm frond and a plan.

NINETEEN

"**M**ORNIN'." The bleary-eyed desk clerk staggered from the motel's back room after I clanged the counter bell for the third time. "Help ya," he asked, rubbing the sleep from his eyes and popping his neck with a roll of his head.

"Good morning." I forced a smile. "Is there a used car lot nearby? I'd like to do some Monday morning tire kickin'." I focused on making my story casual and plausible. It was clear I would have to lie about everything for the next few days. I had to learn to live the part.

"Oh, sure." He shook his head from side-to-side as though trying to knock something loose. "Friend of mine has a lot just down the road with plenty a cars. He should be open by now."

I had spent Sunday afternoon shopping for a rental car company that would take cash and had struck out on every call. Everyone required a credit card. Using my cards was out of the question. Every phase of the plan I had prayed up the day before began with, *be smart*!

"Can I walk?" I asked. I turned and tried to follow his

sightline into the distance.

"It's like two miles. Guess it depends on how far you wanna walk." He scratched his head, leaned over the counter, and looked at my boots. "I get off in half an hour," he added. "If you wanna have some breakfast first," he motioned toward the three-table breakfast area next to the front door and a plastic display case filled with Saturday's pastries, "I'll drop you off on my way home."

"Sounds good. Thanks, I could stand some coffee." My stomach growled. It occurred to me, the cream cheese, beneath the crust of the only Danish in the case, might still be moist.

There weren't more than 15 vehicles in the gravel lot. The trailer-office was locked and dark. *Good thing he has a nice selection,* I thought sarcastically.

"He'll be along shortly," the young man assured me. "You wanna wait or can I drop you somewhere else?"

I had plenty of time to examine every vehicle before the owner arrived and introduced himself as Jack, the same name as the sign. I pointed to a green four-door Chevy pick-up. It didn't look at all like something I would drive. "How 'bout that one?"

"Good choice." He smiled with first sale-of-the-week used car salesman confidence and went after the keys.

"Eleven thousand one hundred dollars," he added in a low voice after a ten-minute pitch.

The truck had low-mileage, good rubber, and started on the first try. "Can't pay more than ninety-nine hundred," I offered shyly as I dug a furrow with the toe of my boot in the pea gravel. "Cash," I added, hoping to make a difference.

"I see," he answered with an understanding smile. "This isn't my first rodeo," he said, inferring he didn't like the IRS cash purchase reporting rules any more than I did. "How 'bout we split the difference. Pay me ten-five in cash, and I'll write the bill-of-sale for ninety-five?"

"Deal." I reached for his hand. "I'd like to register the truck in Frisco when I get home." I picked the city at random from a list of my favorites, none of which was my destination. "Do you have an unexpired license plate 'round here I can use?"

"Sure," he grinned, "for cash, I've got anything ya need."

After three phone calls, each of which yielded another name and number to try, I finally found someone who could help.

"You're in luck, miss," the emaciated man with a profound stoop said as he slid down from his pick-up and fitted a sweat stained straw cowboy hat on his baldhead. "This here's the first fully enclosed hangar to open up in years. The guy sold his Luscombe last week."

"Guess someone's watchin' out for me." I glanced at the sky. *Good thing I got my butt to church yesterday.*

He talked nonstop while he helped me lift the Champ's feather-light tail and pull her into the shadows of her hiding place. Dual sliding doors were the only way in. I secured them with a heavy-duty padlock from my tool kit.

"Not more than a month, but I'll pay for three." I told the man as I peeled off five crisp hundred-dollar bills, which was fifty dollars more than he asked. I stopped him with my open palm when he told me he'd have to go somewhere for change. "Thanks for the help."

For the first time since Crossroads, the food the waitress brought tasted pretty good. I realized I was famished. I thoroughly chewed each bite and wondered how I managed to burn up a whole day buying a truck and hiding my airplane.

My leather journal bumped my forearm as it fell from my upended bag to the king-size bed along with everything else I owned. It was Tuesday morning and too early to get out. I ignored the journal. I didn't feel like writing. I was piddling.

I had found a beauty salon and a western store the night before, neither opened until nine o'clock.

One at a time, I examined each object from my bag. If it opened, I opened it. If it could be turned inside out, I did. If there was another transmitter, or any kind of bug hidden in my gear, I was determined to find it. Satisfied I was bug free, I finished by organizing my belongings into two categories: things I would repack in a suitcase, and the remainder I would store inside the Champ.

The idea of leaving my airplane behind filled me with remorse. However, it was clearly the only way. It had to be done. The Dawg nipping at my heels gave me no choice. Still, I didn't like the change.

Perched cross-legged on a cheap chair in front of a cracked mirror in my dismal motel room, I combed my long sandy-blonde hair and deliberately counted each stroke aloud as if delivering a eulogy.

In 40-plus years, since I was a toddler, my hair had never been shorter than my shoulders. With Grandma Damon's encouragement, my mother didn't even allow a trim until I was 12. By then, it reached my waist. The kids at school called me Rapunzel. "Two hundred." I slowly drew the last stroke from my scalp to the ends and studied my disappointment in the mirror. "I'm glad Grandma isn't here to see what I'm about to do," I told the image.

With the face of a 12 year old, she peeked out from behind my head. "Mikey," the sexy girl in a green miniskirt with a white midriff top and one bare shoulder answered my question. She tottered on four-inch heels as she combed my hair with long fingers. "Nice." She smiled. "My dad wanted a boy so they named me Michaela." Without me asking, she answered my quizzical expression. "People ask me all the time." Purple streaked hair bordered deep dimples. A cubic zirconium on a silver chain dangled from her naval.

I grimaced. *Hope she doesn't ruin my hair.* I

considered making a run for it. Instead, I swallowed hard and settled in. "I'd like it short like Amelia Earhart," I said as she sized me up from every angle.

"Who's she hang with?" I checked her expression in the mirror to see if she was kidding. "She a movie star?"

"No, she was a famous pilot, a hero of mine." Her face was a blank slate waiting for the punch line. "Can I see your style book?" I asked resignedly.

Like the rings of a tree, long strands of my life rained to the floor beneath Mikey's surprisingly skillful comb and scissors.

The result was close enough to the picture I had chosen from the book. I nodded in satisfaction at the Amelia look. Mikey returned a pleased smile.

"Let's make me a platinum blonde." I said, remembering a whole day I had spent with friends playing the opposite game. Everything we said and did was supposed to be the exact opposite of the truth.

"Whoa." Mikey stepped back and looked at me with surprise.

"What? Can't you change my color to blonde?"

"Well, I'm actually pretty good with color—the top of my class. But platinum blonde is very eighties. Besides, you have beautiful hair."

"Thanks," I blushed, "but I want to look exactly the opposite of how I did when I came in here."

"You're already mostly blonde. If you want the opposite, you need ta go black, but still—"

"Black it is then," I said, not letting her object again. "I want the whole package, eyebrows too!"

"State board says we can't do that," she said apologetically. "Too close to the eyes."

"I understand." I held her gaze and lowered my voice to a whisper. "They're my eyes. State board's not here. I have plenty of money. Let's make this good for both of us, shall we?"

Mikey smiled.

There was plenty of time while I waited with wet coloring agent on my hair, so I agreed to my first ever manicure and pedicure. I pride myself on taking good care of my nails. I've always done it myself. I like them longish, yet not so much to interfere with the things I really like to do. When I paint my own nails, it's usually a soft pink.

"Bright red," I instructed the manicurist.

"You really are pretty," Mikey said matter-of-factly as she finished combing my hair. "A little too Morticia maybe," she added, smiling.

"How is it you know the *Addam's Family* and not Amelia Earhart?" I asked.

"Amelia isn't on Nickelodeon."

For the second time since I arrived, a girl in a bikini entered and went straight to the back of the salon, down a long hallway, and disappeared. "Is there an electric beach in the back?" I checked my reflection. Mikey was right. In contrast to my black hair, I was one skin tone above ghostly, very Morticia Addams.

"No, we have something much better. We have spray-tanning booths. They're new." She stretched a perfectly bronzed arm across my chest and rotated it for me to see. "A tanning bed would take you weeks to look like this. We can fix you today!"

HALLOWEEN WAS ALWAYS a big deal at our house. One year I was a wrangler. My mom and grandma made my cowpoke costume using a tobacco stained straw hat from goodness-knows-where and a plaid shirt from the same place. I balanced the repulsive hat on my head like a loose bucket with ten years of hair stuffed inside.

There must not have been much competition because I won first prize. I keep the picture with all my favorites in the photograph garden in my house in Kirkwood. I think it's cute. However, in the picture, I look more like a sharecropper with toy guns than a cowboy.

ON THE RACK, which stretched the full length of the western store, I found a straw cowboy hat that fit perfectly. It was brilliant white and a size smaller than I would have worn before my haircut. The reflection in the full-length mirror didn't look so much like a sharecropper this time. However, neither did it look like any Elizabeth I remembered.

Inside the cramped dressing room, I shimmied into skintight boot cut jeans and examined my backside in the mirror. *More than I want to reveal*, I thought. *Certainly not my style.* "That's the point, goof. You're not supposed to look like you!"

I wore the jeans, picked up another pair, and then found a rack of plaid western shirts. I chose one red and one blue, both with white snaps for buttons.

The man in the boot department explained horsehide would be an easy break-in and good for walking. I forced the image of innocent horses out of my mind and pulled on a black pair with fancy white stitching. He was right. They felt like I'd been wearing them my whole life. He brought out a matching belt, and I chose a huge silver and brass rodeo-rider buckle from the glass display case.

I replaced my retro Ray Bans with an oversized pair of burnt red tortoise shell sunglasses. Between the dark gray lenses and my cowboy hat, most of my face was hidden.

The clerk cut off all the tags as he checked me out. I changed into the red shirt in the dressing room and started to leave.

Halfway out the door, as I struggled to stuff my change into impossibly tight pockets, it occurred to me, without my flight case, I needed a purse. The clerk grinned when he returned with a large black horsehide bag with Conchos, and an abundance of fringe.

He stooped over the cash register for what I hoped was the last time. I admired the reflection of the tan cowgirl starlet in the huge wall mirror behind him. *Perfect,* I thought. *No one will recognize me like this.*

My new truck had an extra big tank, and I had to go back inside the station for a second time to prepay for gas. When it was finally full, I went in for the third time under the pretense of buying a candy bar and a soda. When I paid, I nonchalantly asked the clerk if there was a gun shop close by.

Long guns of every style, gauge, and caliber lined the walls. Grip to barrel, handguns crowded the glass case, which also served as the counter. Certain that pistols required extensive paperwork and a waiting period, I went straight to the shotguns.

Two middle-aged men were discussing ammo with a man behind the counter. Based upon his comments, and because he wore a brown leather shoulder harness with an ivory handled stainless steel Kimber 1911, I decided he was the storeowner.

On the wall behind the counter, a synthetic stock shotgun caught my eye. I studied the short barrel and mat black finish until the two men left.

"Help ya, miss?" the man asked as he walked toward me. "Benelli Super Black Eagle," he said as though answering a question. "Hell of a semi-auto. Bury it in the mud, drag it behind your car, do what you will, and then take it huntin'. The son-bitch 'ill bring down everything in sight."

He took it from the rack and handed it to me. "Guy that traded it in hunted ducks in Mexico." He reached across and touched a long tube mounted on the underside of the barrel. "It's an eight shot extender. Comes right off. With a three-shell plug, she's legal most everywhere."

I turned away and threw the twelve gauge to my shoulder. It was light and fit me perfectly. My eye was drawn to the fluorescent orange sight at the end of the barrel. "How long's the barrel?" I asked, pulling down on a mounted Pintail duck, its wings spread wide against the opposite wall.

"Twenty-six inch, damn good in a tight blind."

"Perfect," I laid the gun on its side on the counter, "how much?"

"Guy only hunted three days a year," he said with a smile. "I can let ya have 'er for a grand." He picked it up and opened the chamber. "She'll handle up to three and a half inch shells."

"I'll take it, and four boxes of Double-aught three and a half inch magnums."

"Shit, missy. They're hell for stoppin' power, but they'll kick the beejeezus outta a whisper of a girl like you."

"Sounds good to me." The words slipped out before I realized how bizarre I sounded. "Uh, it's for my boyfriend. He's goin' hog huntin' in Arkansas."

"Sounds like fun." He didn't bat an eye as he lined up the shell boxes on the counter and pulled out an official looking clipboard. "Just need to do a little paperwork."

Goosebumps raised on the back of my neck. "Ya—ya know," I stammered, "I'd really rather skip all that. It's my boyfriend's gun. I want to surprise him. How 'bout we let him come in later and do the paperwork. That way it'll be in his name."

"Sorry, miss, state requires paper on ever sale."

From the inside pocket of my purse, I retrieved the same yellow envelope I'd been using since I bought the truck the day before and counted out 10 bills on the counter. "A grand." I forced a wanton smile, pulled my sunglasses down the bridge of my nose, and added three more bills to the stack. "And we can say that federal paper trumps state."

He returned my smile. "Let's say, three more pieces of

federal paper would definitely beat state."

I added the bills plus one extra. "How 'bout throwin' in that rod case?" I pointed to a tubular blue-water fishing rod case with a leather shoulder strap and a snap-on end cap.

In a nearby second-hand shop, I found a slightly used carry-on suitcase with wheels. In the deserted parking lot behind the store, I folded my clothes and packed them. The shotgun fit perfectly in the rod case with two inches to spare between the butt and the lid. A box of shells, less the eight already loaded in the gun, easily fit in the bottom of my purse.

I stowed my old clothes, along with the rest of my unneeded gear, inside the Champ and slid the heavy hangar door closed for the last time. I snapped the saw-proof lock in the hasp. The finality of the metallic click ignited an emotional calamity inside my head. I leaned against the galvanized door and slid to the ground. The final shred of Tuesday's daylight disappeared behind the facing hangar. I buried my face in my palms.

"Ma, please put dad on the extension." I forced a sweet voice and braced for the lie I was about to tell.

"I'm okay," I blurted out as soon as I heard him pick up the phone in the living room. "I've been doin' a little sightseein'. Tomorrow, I'm headin' over to Kingman 'bout noon to look around and then on to L.A."

"But, Bette—"

"Don't worry. I'm safe." I interrupted my dad. "I'll call again soon, promise. Bye." I hung up.

"What are you doing with Bette?" the tiny voice in my right ear demanded.

"Alright, it's about time," the mean voice in my left ear cheered my ability to tell a lie.

I didn't need the voices to tell me. Duplicity was changing me.

Beneath a breathtaking star drenched midnight sky, I

raced across Arizona in my truck. I had plenty of fuel and arrived in Kingman well before daylight. Throughout the long night, I counted four shooting stars. The last of which scorched into the atmosphere just as I stopped a half mile from the airport. My truck partially obscured, I had a clear view of the entire field.

My nap lasted no more than 30 minutes before the sun spilled out. The excruciatingly slow countdown to noon began. On edge, empty stomach, and half-sick, cold coffee and a stale breakfast sandwich didn't help. My head pounded. I leaned out the window and threw up.

Midmorning felt more like day's end. I slid across to the passenger's seat, opened my journal to a blank page, and wrote a letter to my parents, which I had been mentally composing since I hung up on them the evening before.

April 19, 2000

Dear Mom and Dad,

If you are reading this, I was right. Your home phone is bugged, and Dawg is somehow listening in.

It's Wednesday morning. I am sitting in a pick-up truck within sight of the Kingman airport. Forgive me for lying last night on the phone. I had to set a trap to see if he would hear our conversation and follow me here.

I destroyed the transmitter he installed in my plane and checked everything I own for bugs. With no way to track me, and no one but the two of you knowing where I am, he has to be listening. This ruse was the only way to be sure.

I will have sent this letter overnight after I know for sure he followed me. For the time being—I AM SAFE!

Trust me to do what's best. I prayed for an

answer to my dilemma. Now, I am going to carry out a plan, which came to me in church on Sunday morning. I hope it means God is with me. Either way, I have no choice. I must put an end to this. Only I can stop him.

The Aeronca is safe in a hangar in Wickenburg, Arizona.

I hope we can talk again soon. When we do, please do not mention this letter. If you happen to find the bug on your phone, leave it alone. Feeding him false clues is the only way I can control this situation.

I don't know anything about David. I assume you don't either. I'll deal with whatever is going on with him later. For now, this is only about stopping Dawg. I am focused and will persevere.

Pop, there are no pigs in the cockpit.

Be well and pray for me.

All my love,

Elizabeth EraStella

USING THE BLADE of my Swiss Army knife, I carefully cut the pages along the spine of my journal. I folded them once and sealed them inside a Wickenburg motel envelope.

In the distance, a glint of red caught my eye. I put up my binoculars. A Camaro, with the antenna Augie described sticking out of the passenger's window, slowly entered the airport and parked behind a building at the far end of the arrival area.

TWENTY

"**H**EY, POP." I forged a cheery tone.

"Bette-girl, sure glad you called. We were worried. You hung up on us. You in Kingman?"

"Sorry 'bout last night. I had a lot on my mind." I began my carefully scripted lie. "No, I took a detour at the last minute and flew up to the Grand Canyon instead. Since I'm not comin' home, I'm goin' wherever the wind takes me."

"You still headed for California?"

"Yeah, I definitely plan to be on the beach in Santa Monica by dark on Friday. I wanna follow *Route 66* all the way to the end, see the Santa Monica pier, and wiggle my toes in the sand.

"Pop, I don't mean to be rude again, but right now, I need to get movin'. I need to find a place to tie down for the night. Tell you what though," I continued setting the stage, "I can call late tomorrow morning." I wanted to ensure I could speak with my dad right after the postman delivered the overnight letter I had mailed from Kingman a few hours before. "Tomorrow's Thursday, right?" I double-checked my scribbles on the back of the church bulletin to be sure I had followed my script.

"Yeah, Thursday. We'll be here when you call."

There were plenty of short segments of *Route 66* west of Kingman, all of which I avoided. I stayed on Interstate 40 and never drove more than a mile over the speed limit. I headed toward Barstow where I planned to rest for two nights, collect my thoughts, and ready the final phase of my plan. Friday would be Good Friday, the day I would bring Dawg's war to him on my terms.

A narrow ray of impertinent sunlight assaulted a breech in the corner of my tightly closed eye and bore a hole into my sleeping brain. Frantic, imagining I was under attack, I popped up from the backseat of my pickup and groped for my shotgun. The feel of steel and plastic sent a wave of relief through me. There was no movement outside my truck. *Thursday morning,* I remembered. *So much for two full nights of rest, I spent the first one in the backseat.* Still, I was safe and alone. The 4,000-pound elephant, which I had come to recognize as fear, lifted its oppressive hulk from my being.

Apart from the ringing in my ears, cemetery silence engulfed me. Rusting cars and trucks surrounded me. Stripped of their most valuable parts, the skeletons awaited the final step of *from dust to dust. They'll need a millennium more,* I thought, amazed by the condition of a 1934 Ford sedan riddled with bullet holes.

Twice, the night before, I nodded off while driving. Both times, I awoke to find myself careening across the highway's shoulder headed for the ditch. Uncompromising, I refused to stop until Barstow. Too exhausted to look for a bed when I arrived, I hid in the junkyard on the outskirts of town.

My lips hurt. I traced the raw cracked skin with my index finger and ran my thickened tongue around the inside of my parched mouth. My last water bottle lay empty in the front seat amid torn candy wrappers. It was worse than a hangover. My body smelled as my mouth tasted.

A sharp metallic clang shattered the silence. I froze. My elephant of fear straddled my chest. I dropped to the floorboard, slid the Benelli's safety off, and pushed the barrel out the partially open window. A boney black cat emerged from the smashed windshield of a rusty yellow school bus with a rat squirming in its mouth. *Yuck.* My skin crawled. I reset the gun's safety and bellied over the seatback like a beaver over its dam.

Too much of the first bottle of water from the gas station spilled down my shirt. The remainder made it to my throat giving me a brain freeze. I forced myself to slow down and drank every drop from the second bottle. Lip balm relieved some of my discomfort. I masked the rancid taste in my mouth with peppermint gum.

An old-before-its-time bronze face with fading blue eyes looked back at me from the smudged gas station mirror. I wiped my underarms with moistened brown paper towels. My disheveled hair no longer looked like an Amelia cut. There was no seat on the toilet. I wiggled my jeans down to my ankles, grimaced, and held myself above the filth.

If Leon Berger had seen me like this when we were married, he would have made an embarrassing joke of the whole thing and repeated it a thousand times. It might seem like no big deal to most. To me, even the most unimportant of my secrets have significance.

Leon was the product of an abused childhood and a lack of purpose as an adult. I tried to help him. I once thought I could save him. Finally, I realized there was nothing left to save. My only hope was to save myself.

With the gas station attendant's directions, I easily found the secluded bed and breakfast on the east side of Barstow.

A middle-aged man answered the door in paint speckled bib overalls and tennis shoes. A clump of mostly black hair on the crown of his head looked like a ball of sage balanced on a mile of forehead. Bent silver-framed glasses clung catawampus to the bridge of his nose. One errant eye set out on its own while the other focused on me.

"Sure do." He smiled when he answered my question about a vacancy, ending each word with a soft tenor hum. "Got a cancellation this mornin'." He joined me on the farmhouse style veranda. "You're lucky. It bein' a holiday weekend 'n' all. We've been booked for weeks. Will you stay three days?"

"No, just till midday tomorrow. I want to be on the coast by dark."

"Hmm." He tilted his head and gave me a concerned look. "Don't know what the missus'll say 'bout that. She has a three-night minimum."

"I'll pay for three nights." I removed my sunglasses so he could see I was sincere. "Just need one night of peace and quiet."

"Reckon she can't complain 'bout that. She'll save on food, and I'll save on cleanin'," he sighed. "Come on in and register." He started toward the screen door.

"One more thing," I touched his arm, "I'd really like to get my truck inside. Do you have room in your barn?" I pointed toward a red building with a hip roof. "I don't mind payin' extra."

"No charge." He smiled. The wild eye gave me a delayed wink as if it had just picked up on the end of the conversation. "It'll be between us."

Antique furniture crowded the immaculate room. The fainting couch was too hard for sitting. I wondered why anyone would faint there. *I guess if you're fainting, you don't get to pick the spot.*

I settled into a wooden office chair and spun around

twice in front of the matching roll top desk. The perfectly restored finish smelled of oily furniture polish. I spread open a magazine and made a place to lay my journal. *This may be my last chance*, I thought. *Bette, make this good— just in case.*

Barstow, California, Thursday Morning, April 20, 2000

"NOW I LAY ME DOWN TO SLEEP, I pray the Lord my soul to keep. If I should die before I wake, I pray the Lord my soul to take." My mother knelt in silence by each of our beds every night, tucked us in, and held our hands as we prayed our bedtime prayer of salvation.

If you are reading this, it means I did not survive. If you are not my parents, I beg you to return this journal to them.

Mom and Dad, if you have chosen to read this far, I must warn you. This is my attempt to cleanse my soul of all that has happened and all I have done. If you do not wish to know these things, please stop here and know I love you. I will be waiting for you, although not in this life, most certainly in the next.

I am guilty of arrogance. I have sinned against God. I brought the wrath of my enemies down upon my friends, loved ones, and myself. I neglected that which is important, disregarded the most wonderful days of my life, and wasted precious years.

I am guilty of trusting others too much. When I did something wrong, inappropriate, or just embarrassing, I tried to lighten my emotional load by sharing my feelings. I expected others to be sympathetic to my predicament. It almost never worked. Everyone has his or her own agenda. More often than not, others' agendas did not include protecting my confidence. I was devastated every time it happened.

Leon Berger was my greatest failure. He worked his

way into my life at a time when I thought I was happy being alone. He read me like an open book, said things that appealed to me, and convinced me we were meant to be together. After we married, I discovered his true nature. It was too late. I was trapped.

I have said I lived with my mistake because I thought I could make it better. I said I believed marriage was something wonderful and to turn away was wrong. The truth is I was weak. For years, I wished Leon was dead, or gone, or whatever it would take to get him out of my life. All the while, I suffered in silence. I told no one what really happened. The memories haunt me still.

Finally, I must bring my most terrifying secret into the light of day. I have always been too ashamed to tell anyone. However, I think of it often. In the last few weeks, it has all bubbled to the surface. If these are to be my last words, it must be included. I must cleanse my soul of this burden.

If you wish to understand better what happened, ask Mabel Reed. Her story is shockingly similar to mine.

Everyone knows Leon Berger beat me. What you don't know is he held a loaded revolver to my head and randomly snapped the hammer against empty chambers. Although I survived, for as long as I live, I will never be the same.

Ted saved me. He came back into my life at a time when my wounds were still open. I had lost faith in humankind. He taught me there are people who I can trust, with whom I can share my secrets, and not suffer at the cruel hand of betrayal. He was the only one who knew about the games of Russian roulette and the trauma they brought to my life.

When Ted died, the equilibrium he had helped me achieve died with him. The memories of all I have suffered are again fresh in my mind. The reality of my past has resumed.

I don't know why God chose to take Ted from me. I believe in God. I believe in His wonder and His goodness, but I don't understand His actions. If He has a greater plan for me, I would like to know what it is. Ted used to say there's a plan for each of us. His belief made him happy. I'm not sure he would have been so pleased if he would have known God's plan for him involved the taking of his life. Certainly, it did not please me.

If God has a plan for me, good or bad, I will know tomorrow.

I love you both, forever and always.
E.E.M

I ADDRESSED one of the three extra overnight delivery envelopes, which I had picked up at the post office in Kingman, to my parents. I fanned the pages of my journal. Words shaped incongruent images, which played out in succession, like a not-so-funny animation of my life. I wound the leather strap tightly around the nickel button. With one finger, I traced the cover's mystical image for the last time.

The envelope bulged with the small book inside. I fondled my birthday watch. I started and stopped the timer and unbuckled the strap. Finally, I wormed my great-grandfather's Claddagh ring off my finger and put it with my watch in the envelope next to my journal.

I ripped the paper strip from the self-adhesive, closed my eyes, and sealed the flap. "It's done," I said to the empty room. "First my airplane, then my history, and finally my last secret, one at a time I give up everything of importance."

"Jed," he replied. The seemingly disinterested eye swept past me. "My friends call me Jed, 'though it ain't even close to my real name.

"Yeah, sure, I'll be happy to he'p ya. I wanna get this right." He pulled out a scrap of paper and a pen and began to write. "You want me ta mail it Monday if'n I don't hear from ya before, right?"

"Exactly," I answered deliberately. "If I'm detained, I want you to put this in Monday's mail." I handed him the fat envelope along with a fifty-dollar bill. "The overnight 'ill be less than twenty bucks. The rest is for your trouble."

"Happy ta help." He smiled. Crooked glasses rode uneven facial movements like a surfer in a storm. "What else can I do fer ya?"

I liked Jed from the moment we met. I warned myself about my propensity to trust too soon. As always, I ignored the warnings. In contrast, I had a bad feeling about the mysterious missus. Occasionally, I heard her moving about the house, although I never caught so much as a glimpse of her actual person. In the span of a breath, I decided I was safe with Jed. "Well, if you don't mind, I'd like to try out my new shotgun."

"Shi-it girl, you kin shoot." He grinned. A couple of teeth were missing near the front of his mouth. Using a handheld thrower, he spun a fourth clay bird high into the desert air. For the fourth consecutive time, I turned it into a cloud of dust. My shoulder throbbed from the pounding of the magnum shells.

"That's somethin'. Hell, I know guys who can't shoot that good, and they use bird shot. Double-aught buck's gotta be 10 times harder!"

"You wanna shoot 'er?" I held the shotgun at arm's length.

"Hell, yeah." He handed over the thrower and took the gun. "I've heard these Benelli's are sweet. Where'd you learn to shoot anyway?"

"My dad and grandpa." I smiled. "My dad gave me my first twenty-two for Christmas when I was four and my first four-ten two years later. We mostly hunted squirrel and rabbits. My Grandma McKenna made wild game and dumplin's to die for," I gushed. "Grandpa held the family record for skinnin' squirrels. He could go from fresh killed to skillet-ready in less than a minute."

Jed pursed his lips and let out a long, low whistle through the gap in his teeth. "Ain't that somethin'." He shook his head.

I protested, but Jed insisted he clean my shotgun. In the back of the barn, he led me through a door concealed behind a haystack into his private sanctuary. On the south wall, two mounted ducks faced a shoulder-mounted, broad-antlered mule deer and spread their wings against weathered barn wood. An overstuffed red leather chair sat alone in the exact center of the room. A small antique end table was next to the chair's right side. Neatly arranged on its top was a cigar cutter, a box of strike-anywhere matches, and a hefty hand-blown glass ashtray.

"Missus don't let me smoke my cigars in the yard or the house," he commented with a whipped expression.

"Eight-shot extenders ain't legal, are they?" he asked as he meticulously swabbed the barrel with an oily cloth threaded through the end of a long metal rod.

"It's okay for huntin' ducks in Mexico." I countered, remembering what the man in the gun store had said about the previous owner.

"This gun might be okay for huntin' ducks in Old Mexico, but three and a half inch Double-aught magnum shells, now that's a horse of a different color." His mouth pulled up in a nervous twitch. "Hell, you shoot a duck with this rig, and there won't be nothin' left to mount—maybe even nothin' to retrieve." He nodded toward the Mallard on the wall. "There's huntin' and then there's killin'."

"I know." I lowered my eyes to the concrete floor. "I'm after bigger game this trip." I thought about the comments he had made about the missus and hoped he would understand.

"You know what you're doin'?" he whispered. "You understand the consequences?"

"I do." I looked straight at him. "Moreover, I understand the danger of doin' nothin'."

He glanced in the direction of the house. "I better get this gun plenty clean and check the mechanism one more time." He made a final swipe down the barrel with a dry rag and loaded eight shells into the tube. "Be careful." He held the shotgun up to the light, wiped away our remaining fingerprints, and wrapped it in a pillowcase.

Alone on the deserted veranda, I massaged my bruised shoulder and thought about Jed's words of caution. He had told me the weekend guests wouldn't begin arriving until Friday afternoon. The house creaked beneath human movement. I wished for Jed's company, but was sure he had been ordered to leave me alone.

At precisely six o'clock, I found my hot dinner beneath a stainless steel plate cover at the head of the dining room table exactly as the elegant pink note in my room instructed. Padded footfalls climbed the backstairs as I entered. Only a hint of the missus' perfume remained.

On the porch after dinner, I rocked at varying speeds, paced its full length, and studied the night sky. Finally, unable to find relief from my own mind, I retreated. At the top of the stairs, I turned the doorknob to my room. There was a rustling somewhere below. Magically, the entire house fell dark.

My spotless room with its antique furniture looked and smelled as a mausoleum. I wondered how much air I had left.

David, David, David, my disquieted voice called after the silhouette against the distant horizon. Everything was black and white. My frightened words were the only sound in the deathly quiet. Each subsequent syllable intensified and echoed recklessly through my mind.

Half awake, I rolled over for the umpteenth time looking for a comfortable position between the feather mattress' lumps. The headboard groaned. A yellow glow from the security light outside filled my room. In the shadows, the windup clock beside my bed looked like Mickey Mouse with large round bells for ears. Tick—tick—tick, agonizingly long minutes taunted me. It was nearly three o'clock in the morning. Lying on my side, I pulled my knees to my chest. Unable to recall a single untortured wink, I surrendered to my thoughts.

David's always been my friend. Why would he do anything to hurt me? Dawg's car was definitely at his house. David needs money. His ex-girlfriend works at the bank. She could have told him about the insurance money and the safe deposit box. Now he's MIA. No, I tried to reject my own rationale. *No, I can't accept that David is involved. There has to be something else.*

I arose, switched on two lamps, and tiptoed over to the desk. The floor creaked beneath every step. The chair squeaked when I sat down.

From my suitcase, I took three of the yellow envelopes and the last two overnight envelopes. On each of the envelopes with cash inside, I wrote a short note.

Jed,
You have shown me great kindness and understanding. We are kindred spirits. Please accept this gift of freedom. Use it however you wish.
Elizabeth

Mabel,
You gave me the strength to tell my story. You showed me I am not alone in my suffering. I hope you will use this gift to help others like us.
Bette

Pastor Steve,
Please accept this gift for Grace Church in honor of my parents and in memory of my grandparents. In

your sanctuary, throughout my childhood, the
foundation for my life was laid.
Elizabeth E. McKenna

I licked the flap and sealed Jed's envelope. I addressed one of the overnight envelopes to Mabel Reed in Ft. Myers and the other to Pastor Steve at my mother's home church in Stanville. On my way out of Barstow, I planned to buy cashier's checks for the church and Mabel and mail them from the Post Office.

Before breakfast, I would slip into Jed's haven inside the barn and leave his envelope inside the humidor, where I was sure the missus would never look.

TWENTY-ONE

J ED CARRIED MY SUITCASE across a tiny patch
of freshly cut grass, down a long pergola covered
with flowered vines, to the barn. I followed one-step
behind. Through dark glasses, the harsh morning light
stung my sleep-deprived eyes. *It's going to be a long day*,
I thought, wishing I had slept when I had the chance.

He leaned my suitcase against the outside wall and
heaved the wooden doors open. Rollers cried out against
metal slides. Just inside, my pickup waited in the shadows.

"It's Good Friday," I commented, trying to make
conversation. "Today we celebrate the ultimate sacrifice."

Jed nodded. "Never had much use for church, but the
holidays is good for business." He leaned against the front
of my truck and kicked the sand. A tiny cloud drifted away
and disappeared. "If what they say's true, Jesus was quite
a guy. Let 'em nail 'im to the cross so'ins it'd be good for
us. Shi—it, can't imagine."

"Maybe, Jed," I began, a little punch drunk from sleep
deprivation, "maybe we aren't meant to understand. They
say we should have blind faith. We're supposed to put

ourselves in His hands. He will provide. There are plenty of people who'll swear to it. This weekend they'll pack the churches, even if they haven't darkened the door all year. They'll bow their heads and swear to it again. They're probably daydreamin' about somethin' else the whole time. I guess the deal is people say they're Christians because they don't want to get caught in the last second of life without bein' saved. I suppose most folks don't want to take the chance the Bible is true."

"Heard all that too, 'cept He ain't never give me anythin'. Don't see how it all applies. I worked hard all my life without complainin'. Still, the missus kicks my ass cause it ain't never 'nough."

For the first time since we met, Jed pushed his glasses up his nose until they were nearly straight. His top knot looked exactly as it had the day before. He looked at me with focused eyes. "If Jesus was tired a gettin' his ass kicked, then I guess we've got somethin' in common."

"Amen," was all I could think to say. How could I argue with perfect logic?

With both hands clamped on the base of the open driver's window, Jed slowly snapped the truck door shut. He stepped back and leaned against the inside barn wall near the entrance. I turned the key. The starter engaged the flywheel. He tilted his head slightly to one side and nodded approval. He looked straight into my eyes. His glasses had slid back down his nose. His wild eye was still focused. He smiled. "Good luck," he mouthed.

My cheeks tingled. I swallowed the lump in my throat, pulled the gearshift lever into drive, and eased out of the barn into a brilliant cloudless sky. Jed held out an open hand as I passed. I pressed my palm against his. He glanced nervously toward the house and dropped his eyes.

I knew she was watching. She would play it all back to him in a verbal tirade after I was gone. I knew it because I have been in his shoes.

Two hours and seventeen minutes had passed since I watched Jed in my rearview mirror. He closed the barn doors and walked slowly back to the house. The bank and post office had been easy stops. I left town quickly.

The sun-scorched roadway linking Barstow to Los Angeles was a high-speed, bumper-to-bumper labyrinth in both directions. I stuck to the Interstates and kept pace with the traffic.

Sweltering air blasted me through my open window. Cleansing sweat seeped from my pores. I caught a second wind and began to envision the chess moves that would soon decide my destiny. Indistinct at first, like a mildewed rag in a confined space, ocean air filled my nose.

After a series of turns, the *American Diner* appeared in the last block of Santa Monica Boulevard. It was three o'clock in the afternoon. Inside the diner, I stared at the neon wall clock and picked at a hamburger. *In the Year 2525* by Zager & Evans played on the jukebox. "If man is still alive..."

It was hours until dusk. *I want this over,* I thought. *Surely, Dawg heard my message. He's listened to every other word I've said.*

I walked around until I found a quiet side street upon which to leave my pickup. I stuffed my suitcase and purse in the back floorboard and covered them with a monogrammed towel I stole from the missus. I triple checked the door locks, hid the keys inside the fuel cap door, slung the fishing rod case over my shoulder, and headed for the pier.

I must have been a sight in my cowgirl garb carrying fishing gear, but no one gave me a second look. *California,* I figured. I covered the last few blocks quickly. The closer I came, the stronger the salt air and the louder the carnival noises.

At the end of the crowded pier, I relaxed. I was no different from a dozen other fishermen who lined the rails.

I studied each face. A cacophony of voices hung in the air. Increased by stress, the ringing in my ears dulled my senses.

No familiar faces or movements and too many bystanders for a confrontation up here, I told myself. I hadn't envisioned so many people. *I don't want anyone else to get hurt.*

Halfway between the pier's end and the shore, I stood at the railing and studied the beach. Far below, waves gently lapped the sand. The beach was much less crowded than the pier and the south side particularly so. Although I could not see directly under the pier, not many people came and went.

Behind me on the pier, a man in a gray fedora strolled past and glanced my way. I froze and then breathed a sigh of relief. They were not Dawg's eyes.

Perspiration soaked my long-sleeved shirt. My straw hat shaded me from the sun, but the leather band felt like a circular vice around my skull.

I could strip down to bra and panties, dive in, and never come up. I daydreamed. *I'd disappear without a fuss. No one would be the wiser. Accidental Drowning would be the headline below the fold on page six—an inexperienced Missouri girl lost in the ocean. Murdered by Ex-husband would be front-page news. I'd rather just go quietly. Everyone says suicide is a coward's way out, a permanent solution for a temporary problem.*

The crowd on the pier interacted like a tightly woven mass of disjointed organic parts. Making my way through the jumble was like threading a moving needle. I left the pier and trudged through the deep sand toward the water's edge.

The underbelly of the pier reeked of decomposition and filth. I found it appealing because it repelled an audience. Without my watch, I was unsure of the time. The sun seemed frozen in the sky. I leaned against a smellycreosoted support post and wished I was anywhere but here.

I studied every face and traced the meandering water's edge for as far as I could see. *What are you doing?* I questioned my motives. *Can you really go through with this?*

I dropped the tubular case in the sand at my feet and buried my face in my hands. Remorse swept over me. I fell to my knees and emptied my stomach in the waves.

Everything in my life was uncertain. Most of all, I wondered if Ted would approve of what I was doing. In some way, I think he would have wanted me to forgive. It wasn't that simple. Leon Berger had painted me into a corner. Of one thing I was certain, had Ted been with me now he would have given his life to protect me.

The air around me filled with magic and calm. The people disappeared. I was alone on the beach. The pier overhead was quiet. The ringing in my ears was gone. My thoughts of Ted slipped away and something much more real took their place. An image appeared in the sand. It was unquestionably outside my mind, something apart from me. Amid softening shadows, with a broad smile on his lips and his hands on his hips, it was Ted. He was too real to be a hallucination, too vibrant to be an apparition, dressed exactly as he had been that Saturday evening in Florida when we boarded our Cessna for the last time.

His sweet voice was as I remembered, unwavering words crystal clear. "Bette, you've come a long way. I know it's been tough. I'm sure I can't convince you to not go through with this, so I won't try. All I ask is you be careful. I see you're ready for a fight, but don't start one. No matter what happens today, or in the days and years to come, don't blame yourself. You're an incredible woman. I'm proud to have loved you.

"We all make mistakes. Someday, when you join me, you'll understand the reasons for everything. What happened to me in the crash is unimportant. My destiny came early, nothing more. Everyone has a time. Don't be in a rush to get here. Enjoy what you have. Forgive yourself first, and then forgive those who have hurt you."

I tried to speak. The words wouldn't come. His mesmerizing eyes seemed to know my thoughts. He smiled and nodded. A sense of fulfillment surged through my veins.

"I hope you won't forget me," he continued. "Remember what we had, but don't let the memories stop you from living. The world needs you. It needs what you have to give. Bette, you make a difference in every life you touch. You always have." The manifestation grew more translucent with each word and began to flicker. "If you withdraw from life, it will feel safe in the moment, but in time, the loneliness will devour your happiness.

"Sweetie, I won't be able to come like this again. You're on your own. Share your life with those you care about, with those who care for you. Be selfless, as you always were with me.

"Elizabeth EraStella McKenna, your mother was right when she named you. You are truly a bright star of your own time. Don't forget, share your secrets... " His words faded away. I stood alone beneath the Santa Monica Pier.

The natural movement of the ocean and the sounds of people everywhere returned crisp and clear. I heard laughter, talking, and children playing. Even though they were distant, I understood every word. After more than six tortuous months of the debilitating roar in my head, what the doctors had said was incurable was inexplicably gone.

The sun freed itself and seemed to race toward the base of its arc. Far out to sea, it dove toward the horizon. My thoughts were distinct, my reasoning sound, I was filled with resolve.

A dozen feet from the water's edge, I dropped to my knees. Using only my hands, I dug a hole in the moist sand like a frantic hound. When I finished, it was 24 inches deep on the ocean side of one of the pier's support posts.

As though driving a fence post barehanded, I plunged the tubular fishing rod case straight down into the hole with all my strength. When it hit bottom, I twisted it hard like a corkscrew and added a few extra inches of depth. I mounded the excess sand around the two feet of case protruding from the surface. From a few feet away, looking like a sandcastle's spire, it was barely noticeable against the post. I released the lid's catch and touched the butt of the Benelli.

My weapon well hidden, I cautiously ventured back into the open. I slid my sunglasses down my nose, tilted my head back, and studied the crowd on the pier overhead. Near the ocean end, I recognized David threading his way through the crowd obviously headed for shore. I spread my legs, dug my boots in the sand, and watched in amazement. He continuously appeared then disappeared as a mouse lost in a maze. He was still a long way off. There was a lot of pier between him and the shore. With frantic head movements, he seemed to search the beach behind me. He paused, waved his arms wildly, and then grabbed the railing with both hands. For a moment, I thought he would jump. Instead, he pulled back and continued inland.

Paralyzed by fear, I closed my eyes and ordered my body to move. *Run to him, ask why, and forgive him!* My mind screamed. My body refused. Unable to force myself forward, I inched backward stiffly dragging my heels. Every few steps, David looked in my direction, never at me.

Incredulously, I watched as he passed directly overhead. Yet, he gave no indication he recognized me.

A young couple, with two small children between them, sauntered past. Here and there, a few individuals dotted my peripheral. Nothing seemed out of place.

A hundred steps away, a homeless man with a trash bag

full of aluminum cans slung over his shoulder walked toward me. Wearing a tattered straw hat, sunglasses, and a billowing red Hawaiian shirt, he shuffled along like a dirty Santa on holiday. He scoured the beach for cans and appeared oblivious to everyone around him.

Fifteen feet on my inland side, he passed me headed toward the pier. At the same time, I caught a glimpse of David still pushing his way through the mass of people. The bum stopped, dropped his bag, rolled his head around his shoulders, and touched his scraggly beard with both hands. I watched with amazement as he interlaced his fingers and cracked his knuckles. I froze.

The family of four gave him wide berth, quickened their steps, and passed between us. He studied the woman and then looked past her directly at me. After an almost indiscernible pause, he continued his visual sweep of the sand. He stopped for a count of five, and then slowly turned back to me. Leon Berger pulled his glasses down his nose, looked out over the frames, and smiled a sinister smile.

I couldn't look away nor could I move. He cocked his head, ripped his glasses off, grabbed his bag, and ran straight for me.

In the first of three bounding steps, he threw the bag open. In the second, he plunged his free hand down through the soda cans. In his final step, with one powerful swinging motion, he flung the plastic bag away scattering aluminum cans across the sand. In its place, he held a stainless steel revolver.

He caught my arm and stepped behind me. With the pistol in my back, he wrapped his free arm around my throat. My hat and sunglasses fell to the ground. He repositioned his hold and raised the pistol to my head. A brass tipped cartridge was visible in every chamber. He laughed and pressed the familiar Colt 45 hard against my temple. I winced and held my breath. This was not the same game as before. This time there was no way I could win.

My body rubber, terrified and helpless, I dangled from his arm and sank toward the sand.

Dawg scowled. "You ain't gettin' off so easy this time, bitch." He tightened his hold, a fleshy hangman's noose, around my neck. I choked.

Adrenalin coursed through my body. He redoubled the pressure. I could not breathe.

"Been waitin' a hell of a long time for this. You ain't passin out on me now." He relaxed his grip. I gasped. "I'm gonna enjoy it."

Air flooded my lungs. My vision cleared. I kicked his shin, and drove my elbow into his side. He groaned and squeezed my throat hard. I stopped fighting. He eased the pressure.

I steeled my nerves. *Think,* I told myself. *He's not playin'. He wants me conscious. He's gonna kill me, but he needs somethin' first.*

With the gun barrel buried deep into my temple, he dragged me toward the pier. As we moved, he shifted his weight and twisted my body to the right in an attempt to conceal the pistol from a small group of beachcombers. His forearm wedged under my chin forced my face up. Out of the corner of my eye, I saw David running. I prayed he was coming to help me and not Dawg.

Apparently satisfied that the people had not seen the gun, he pulled me further under the pier and closer to the water's edge. Reaching a piling, he slipped around to face me without removing his arm from my throat or the gun from my head. He pinned me against the shore side of the rough timber.

I reached down with my right arm, but felt nothing. *This has to be the one*, I told myself. Careful not to make any threatening movements, I stretched my arm. My fingertip grazed the top of my rod case. *YES*, my mind screamed.

Relax, I thought. *Don't struggle. Play along, distract him.* I intentionally sighed as though relieved and gently touched his arm.

"Leon, please." I mustered an adoring voice. I hoped he would remember it from before we were married. "Tell me what you want. It doesn't have to be like this. We had some great years."

Forgive me, Ted, I thought. "I'm single again," I cooed. The words burned my lips.

Dawg leaned in. His nose touched mine. His breath reeked of stomach acid. He increased the pressure on my throat. "Bitch, you don't fool me with your shit." Slobber dotted my bare neck. "Even if you wanted me, it's too late. You're used goods. If you had as many dicks stickin' out of you as you've had stuck in ya, ya'd look like a fuckin' porcupine. Look at your hair and fingernails, you even look like a whore."

I dropped my eyes. He forced my chin back up. His shirt was unbuttoned three down. A half-moon stain of sweat marked his chest like a filthy necklace. Just below the grime, Firewalker's talisman hung from a leather cord. "Whatever you want, Leon, just ask." I pretended to sob. "Don't hurt me, please."

"Hurt ya? Bitch please; you weren't worried about hurtin' me when you laughed at me and called me a dog. Is that what you think I am your lap dog? You need to learn, dogs bite."

"I'm sorry, Leon. I didn't mean to hu—"

"Save it, bitch. I want what you owe me." His spittle stung my cheek. "I want the fucking insurance money—all of it."

"What insurance?"

"Don't play dumb with me," he said disgustedly. "You know what I'm talkin' about, your boyfriend's payout."

"I don't have much money. You can have it all."

He laughed. "Bullshit, I know what you have, and you're gonna give it to me. I want the two million." He pulled the trigger.

In the millisecond, during which I felt the pressure of the barrel increase and saw his hand move, my life flashed before my eyes. The hammer snapped against what had to be the only empty chamber. Crimson flooded my mind. My knees buckled. *NO!* I ordered adrenalin to flow through my body. *YOU WILL NOT PASS OUT*, my mind screamed.

"Okay, okay, I'll give you whatever you want." I searched for exactly the right words. I reached for my shotgun. The increased pressure of his arm beneath my chin had forced me higher up the piling. It was out of reach. "I'll get you the money. How'd you know? Is David in this with you?"

"That fag, shit." His words dripped with disgust. "I wouldn't take that son-of-a-bitch to a dogfight, but he *was* good help." He laughed. "I bugged his phone and stashed a recorder in the vacant house next door. Almost never even had to go there. The radio guy from work showed me how to rig it so I could access the whole thing from anywhere."

Leon drew his head back and grinned. "Hell, I tapped your folk's phone too. Hid the device in your dad's precious fuckin' shop. Sounds like good ole Davey's after the money on his own. Maybe you shouldn't 've told him about it."

"I didn't tell anyone." I stalled. *If they aren't partners, maybe David's here for me.* I hoped. *Either way, David's the lesser of two evils.*

Dawg guffawed. Saliva sprayed my face. I closed my eyes against the blast. "Stupid cunt, there ain't nothin' I don't know. I knew 'bout the insurance the day after he bought it!" he bragged. "I've got a key to your house. Hell, I've practically lived there since you threw me out."

His words plunged a dagger into my heart. "You killed

Ted for the insurance money?" I bit my lower lip and braced for the pistol blast.

"Yeah, ain't that the shits?" he gloated, relaxing the pressure of the barrel against my temple and loosening his grip on my throat.

I slid down the post. With two fingers, I felt the case, flipped it open, and touched the butt of my gun.

"I had ta fuck with your plane twice 'fore I got it right. Figured I'd teach your boyfriend and your ole man a lesson and give 'em the ride of their lives." He locked my eyes in a reptilian glare. "But my fuckin' fuel line patch let me down." He snickered. "The engine explodin', now that was a thing of beauty. I caught a ride to Florida on one of our company planes. Right there on the tarmac in Tampa, with plenty of traffic all night long, I dropped the pan and loosened a rod bolt. I even told some old rent-a-cop I worked for you and showed him my ID. Sure enjoyed listenin' to your boyfriend on the radio while you were goin' down. Sounded like he was scared shitless. Hope ya heard my little contribution. Wanted ya to know I was with ya." He laughed. "Bitch."

His grip on my throat loosened further. "Looks like that God of yours is on my side."

I relaxed my knees and closed my eyes as though I had fainted. It caught him off guard. He nearly let me go. Slumped against the piling, I grabbed my shotgun. With all my strength, I jerked.

Bewildered by my sudden movements, Dawg dropped to one knee. I tried to step away. He caught my leg. I fell to the beach.

From nowhere, David appeared. With a wild scream, he leaped toward Dawg with both arms fully outstretched. They collided and rolled like battling wildcats toward the water's edge.

The pistol was nowhere in sight when a muffled blast roared from its barrel. Simultaneously, the sand between the water and me erupted and rained down upon the ocean. With arms and legs intertwined, they thrashed violently across the sand. The pistol appeared clasped in Dawg's hand.

I stumbled to my feet and threw the shotgun to my shoulder. Before I could take aim, Dawg landed a blow to the side of David's face with the pistol and then pointed it at me. I dived for the ocean. A muzzle blast followed. As I hit the water, a bullet tore through a piling. Chunks of wood and splinters rained down. Salt stung my eyes. Two feet beneath the surface, it was deathly quiet.

Another bullet exploded against the water. Shockwaves vibrated through me. My lungs empty, I groped for the hard sandy bottom in the waist deep ocean. In one seamless motion, I bent my knees, planted my feet, and catapulted to the surface with the Benelli locked against my shoulder and the safety off.

Fully expecting to meet a bullet, I gritted my teeth. Instead, I saw Dawg shake David off, rise to his knees, and fire from the waist. From a few inches away, the bullet blasted through David's side. A million micro-droplets of blood spewed into the air.

"DAVID," I screamed, took aim, and fired. Double-aught buckshot erupted with a ball of fire from the shotgun's barrel and flew through 20-odd feet of air in a tight pattern. Dawg's right hand, its finger still in the Colt's trigger guard, tore from his arm, arced skyward, and plowed into the sand.

I dropped my gun and raced to David. On my knees, I scooped him up. "CALL 9-1-1," I screamed at the gathering crowd. "SOMEONE CALL AN AMBULANCE!"

David's right eye was swollen shut; the other open, but lifeless. I touched his throat and felt a weakening pulse. With each beat of his heart, blood spurted from the gaping hole in his right side. "David, you will not die on me!" I leaned in. "If you needed money," I whispered, "all you had to do was ask."

His eye rolled back in his head. "I'd neve... I wanted ta help. I love..."

"An ambulance is on the way," a woman called from the crowd.

"But the two million—your girlfriend—why else would you come?"

David wheezed. Blood streamed from the corner of his mouth and soaked my jeans. He took my arm and pulled me closer.

"What money?"

TWENTY-TWO

Stanville, Missouri, Friday Morning, April 20, 2001

"*T*HERE but by the Grace of God go I."
It's been one year and one day since my last journal entry. I feel like a Catholic girl overdue for confession.

I think of Ted every single day. I don't mourn him so much as miss him. At least he lives on through all I do in his memory.

I have willed myself never to think of Dawg again. This will be my last reference. My final wish is—may he rot in his tiny prison cell and be reminded of what he did to Ted and I every time he looks at the stub where his hand once was. When they finally put the needle in his arm, I want his last thought to be of the hell that awaits him.

Ted's life insurance helped me open 'Phenix House for Abused Spouses' in Missouri and a second facility in Fort Myers, which Mabel Reed manages. I'm proud of the work we do with battered women. I know if Ted could see what we've done, he would indeed be honored.

Perhaps there'll never be another man in my life, although I'm not closed to the possibility. I just don't see it happening. It doesn't matter. I have my family, my friends, and my work. For the first time, I'm truly content. Too bad, I had to give up the love of my life to get here.

I always called my innermost thoughts, "my secrets." Now I just call them common knowledge. I say what I want, when I want, and never worry about the consequences. If people like me for who and what I am, then I'm pleased. If they don't, who cares? I am me. Good or bad, happy or sad, this is my life.

I'll never again live in fear of what others think or say...

"DAVID, you're gonna have to leave one of those bags." My voice sounded sterner than I intended. I laughed and tried to make a joke of it. "The Champ's not even used to two passengers. She won't tolerate too many bags. It's a long way to Santa Monica. One small bag each, okay?"

"Whatever." He smiled and dumped the contents of both his duffels on the hangar floor and began sorting. "Although," he gestured toward my gear, which lay next to the Aeronca's tire, "looks like you're packin' some unneeded weight too."

"I'd rather leave my clothes than this." With the toe of my boot, I slid a sealed plastic bag across the floor for emphasis. Inside was a lump of ragged, torch-cut stainless steel. "I'm gonna drop what's left of his pistol in the Pacific if it's the last thing I do."

David laughed nervously. "I guess it's a good thing they wouldn't let you keep what was left of the hand."

"Yeah, that sucks." I laughed. "Watching it burn was all I got for paying the bill at the crematorium."

BY THE TIME the EMTs arrived on Santa Monica beach,

I thought David was dead. He was unconscious. His breathing was too faint to detect.

The police arrested me and kept me in a holding cell for 24 hours while they checked my story. Fortunately, the detective in charge was a woman. She seemed to understand. They dropped the weapons charge and closed the file as self-defense. They released me. I went straight to the hospital.

I never left David's bedside. We had plenty of time, so I told him every detail of my cross-country debacle. When he was well enough to travel, we flew home on a commercial flight.

Easter Sunday afternoon, I called Jed and asked him to mail the package home anyway. He had found the yellow envelope in his humidor earlier that morning while all the houseguests were in church and the missus was busy with lunch.

"You've made me think there might be somethin' to this God thing," he said after thanking me for the money at least a dozen times.

I gave him the 10-minute version of the events on the beach. "Things happen for a reason, Jed," I said when I finished telling him David was resting comfortably in critical care. "It can't have been an accident that I stumbled into your B & B. You were there for me without askin' a bunch of questions or expectin' somethin' in return. You were a better friend than a lot of people I've known my whole life."

"Whatta ya reckon I oughta do with the money?" he asked.

"I reckon," I giggled, "I reckon you can do anything you want Jed. It's clear you feel trapped. Use it for your business or make your personal life better. The choice is yours. Do what *you* want, not what someone else tells you."

Within a week, my mom and dad caught a flight to

Arizona and flew home in the Champ. They detoured to Waxahachie, Texas and visited the place where the crop duster airfield used to be. A bean field replaced the hangars and dirt runway. My dad remembered exactly where everything had been and gave my mom a tour, including the spot where in 1949 he and the original Kitten posed for my favorite photograph. They later told me those were two of the best days of their lives. They finally understood what I found so special about crossing the country in the Champ. When I arrived home from California with David, they couldn't wait to show me what they had hand-lettered on the Aeronca's fuselage. It was four words in three lines precisely like in my dad's photograph, *Kitten, Pilot, Bette McKenna.*

My mom's church used the money I sent for new Sunday school furniture. They wanted to make a big deal out of a dedication ceremony and make it about me. I refused. In a private conversation with Pastor Steve, I asked that they put a small plaque under one of the new tables. "Make it in honor of Grandma Damon." I insisted. "She wouldn't have wanted the limelight either."

Pastor Fid tracked me down at the hospital in Los Angeles. He spent 20 minutes on the phone telling me about the new church kitchen they could finally afford. Then he told me what Brother Elmer did with his cow pasture.

"Brother Elmer showed up with a hand carved cedar sign the day after you left. He named the field where you landed, *HOPE FIELD.* It's plum elegant in my book." His voice quivered. "But that's not the miraculous thing. Along with the sign, he brought the deed. Elizabeth, he gave the field to the church and committed to whatever improvements are necessary to make it a park and playground for the kids. He told me he did it 'cause you droppin' out of the sky reminded him; it's not what we do for ourselves that matters. It's what we do for others."

Although I haven't seen Firewalker or Augie, I talk to one or the other nearly every week. Violet recently turned seven. Firewalker surprised them with a house he built next door to his.

"I saw the house in a vision when I read your note," he explained. "I did the work myself. With a little additional from my savings, the money you gave me was enough. It's what Ted's money was always intended for."

David manages the halfway house. He tells everyone he works for me. However, I insist we're partners. His work is exceptional, and he's always available when I need a copilot. Sometimes, I think *Phenix House* is David's therapy right along with the residents. He doesn't speak often about what it was like to be shot. Occasionally, he adds some detail to the ongoing story. I never ask.

In spite of his insistence to the contrary, I feel responsible for the whole thing. I wish everyone could have the kind of friend I have in David. With Ted, I knew unconditional love. In David, I feel the true meaning of unconditional friendship.

Prosecutors from Florida, California, Arizona, and Missouri made a gentleman's agreement. They extradited Leon Berger back to Missouri where he was convicted of premeditated murder in the death of Ted Wilson, two counts of attempted murder, two counts of sabotage, two counts of assault, and one count of arson. *Too bad misogyny isn't illegal,* I thought when I heard the verdicts. They sentenced him to death by lethal injection. He sits on death row.

During the trial, I had plenty of time to read and think. I dug out the neuroscience book I found after Leon moved out of my house and studied the sections he marked. I wanted to understand how I could have been so wrong. When I read the section on dopamine, I knew.

The way he showered me with attention and

compliments before we were married caused a chemical reaction in my brain. I felt fulfilled. The more he did for me, the more I wanted him. Like a drug addict, when we were apart, I went through something like withdrawal. I felt as though I couldn't live without him.

After we were married, and he began a pattern of physical and emotional abuse, I again felt a chemical reaction. The similarity to my earlier fixes caused me to crave the abuse because, in the moment, it also fulfilled me. I rationalized my feelings. *He loves me enough to pay attention to me. He only wants me to do better. It's my fault.*

Even though in many ways I was naïve, I accept responsibility for everything that happened in my relationships. I have only been intimate with three men in my life. The first time was a onetime thing with a long lead up followed by disappointment. After the fact, I realized it was a mistake. The second time, I was sucked in, discovered I was trapped, and allowed it to go on far too long. The last time, with Ted, was the real thing. Only he made me feel whole. He and I felt the same about each other. We were truly connected, a feeling I will never forget.

I have never told these things to anyone. How embarrassing to admit to others you can be manipulated. I have had my share of secrets, some insignificant and some monumental. After all, how could I ever explain to another person how a pistol barrel pressed against my face in a game of Russian roulette could give me an emotional high?

Leon Berger's trial drew national attention. As a result, so much money poured in for *Phenix House* my money was unnecessary. It's probably the only worthwhile thing Leon Berger has ever done in his life. I guess I should have known he would make a good sideshow. No one I know has ever been to visit him in prison, not even his sister.

Agents keep calling me about a book deal. They may be right; too strange to be true really does sell.

"YOU'RE HAULIN'" a lot more than just that hunk of pistol." David pointed at my shotgun propped against the inside of the airplane's open door.

"It's for Jed. I wanna give it to him personally." I touched the scrap of pillowcase wrapped around the Benelli. "I want something to remind him of the strength he gave me to finish."

I smiled at the memory of Jed standing in front of his barn door. *I'd like to track down the missus, give her a little girl-on-girl slap, and scold her for abusing such a good man.*

I turned to face David. "I called Jed last month to tell him we were comin'. He sounded pleased. The money I left helped him to finally do somethin' he's been thinkin' about for years. He's divorced and runnin' the B & B alone. Said he's never felt better."

"Sounds like a friggin' milk run," David teased.

"Whatever," I remarked, dosing him with his own style of disdain. "Every stop's important to me." I squeezed the Talisman, which had hung from my neck, on Ted's gold chain next to his peso, for the past year. "First big stop's Holbrook. We'll stay two days or so. I'll finally get to meet Violet. Next trip we'll visit the Reed's and Pastor Fid and Libby."

"I can't believe it's already been a year." David shook his head and touched his side. "I'm glad you asked me to go. I wanna meet the people who mean so much to ya. They were there for you when I wasn't."

I turned away. "'Nough talk, David. Get in—we're burnin' daylight."

EPILOGUE

MAC McKENNA shook the last of the dry fertilizer from the burlap bag into the hopper of the modified crop duster and tossed the empty sack into the bed of the farmer's brand new 1949 pickup.

"Field's clear," the farmer shouted over the idling aircraft. One hand hanging by its thumb hooked on the gaff of his faded overalls. He made a sweeping gesture with other. "Get 'er ever' inch!" he ordered. "I'm payin' good money fer this dustin'."

Mac nodded and slid his goggles down over his eyes covering the only part of his face that wasn't already caked with grime. He wedged the stem of his freshly packed corncob pipe between his teeth, threw his leg into the cockpit, and patted the hand-lettered *Kitten* as he pulled himself in.

Home to Missouri and my bride tomorrow, he thought of his upcoming wedding. He threw the throttle full open, lifted the tail wheel off the rough two-track, and hauled the overloaded airplane clear of the ruts just as the road took a 90-degree left.

Twelve feet and level above fresh furrows, Mac opened the hopper slightly. A white fog billowed out and settled on the field below. At the tree line, he turned and followed the field's doglegged border dividing his attention between the airplane and the fertilizer.

A miniscule adjustment of the hopper door matched product flow to airspeed. Mac lifted his eyes from the handle. A low-hanging power line was less than 50 feet straight ahead.

He dumped the fertilizer, slammed the throttle forward, and dove to within inches of the ground. The aircraft's tail passed beneath the wires; he horsed the stick all the way back. The fabric airplane stuck its nose almost straight up, and dragged its tail through the branches.

Clear of the treetops, his first thought was of Maggie. "Our children will be ready for anything!" he shouted to the wind. The farmer's duplicitous *"field's clear"* echoed through his mind.

I AM A PRODUCT of heredity and upbringing. Long ago, my family fled Ireland. After a generational roundabout, they settled first in North Carolina and later in the Ozarks of Missouri.

Ireland was their home. The hills and hollows of the Midwest are mine. I have never thought of fleeing, but I often dream of shedding my inherited paranoia.

With every flying lesson, my dad harped about being ready for anything. "You never know what's on the other side of the dogleg," he constantly repeated. In my heart, I know it was Mac McKenna and God who saved me the night Ted lost his life.

I am third generation born in Missouri, descendent of resolute Irish immigrants, heir to hundreds of years of suffering, and the daughter of loving, protective parents.

I am Elizabeth EraStella McKenna. I am a survivor.

12064997R00147

Made in the USA
Charleston, SC
09 April 2012